Death Before War

Brent Filson

Huge Jam Publishing, 2023

Copyright © 2023 by Brent Filson

Published by Huge Jam Publishing
1 The Glebe, Gravenhurst, UK
www.hugejam.com

All rights reserved.

No part of this publication may be reproduced, distributed, or transmitted in any form or by any means, including photocopying, recording, or other electronic or mechanical methods, without the prior written permission of the publisher, except as permitted by English and U.S. copyright law. For permission requests, contact the author.

The story, all names, characters, and incidents portrayed in this production are fictitious. No identification with actual persons (living or deceased), places, buildings, and products is intended or should be inferred.

Book Design by www.hugejam.com

ISBN: 978-1-911249-29-0

For my dream lover, the last for which the first was made.

*T*his was the second dead man U.S. Marine Lieutenant Colm McCabe had ever seen. This one was sprawled in weeds beside aluminum piss tubes just outside camp. He remembered what his boss, Lieutenant Colonel Ajax, had said when the battalion first landed on this Philippine Island. "This isn't the Spanish American War, lieutenant. Doubleyou. Doubleyou. Two. But mark my words: even though it's twenty years later and a peace time exercise, we're at war with these people. Keep focused on that or there will be hell to pay."

"For this poor bastard," McCabe said aloud into the tropical night, redolent with the stench of blood, "hell has been paid."

1

McCabe finds what he isn't looking for.

McCabe stepped on something soft in the night that wrapped around the shaft of his combat boot. The boot's blousing band stopped it from slithering up his leg. He jumped off the trail into creepers that tumbled over him like a hundred clutching fingers. He stamped hard. The thing let loose and scurried away, ground cover rattling.

His carbine sling slipped off his shoulder. The weapon plunged into thick vegetation. Jungle-blackness pressing against his eyeballs, he pulled the weapon out, leaves and stalks catching on the starlight scope. He poked with his bamboo club, trying to find the empty space in the vegetation that indicated the trail. Where the hell was the trail? He had jumped only a couple of feet. How could he lose the trail? Worse than being lost for him was being *found*. Showing the whole battalion he had let down Lieutenant Colonel Ajax.

He remembered Ajax saying, "What you learn about war, you can't unlearn. In combat, shit shines. So, when fear freezes you, McCabe, make fear a lesson in courage learned. Slow down, connect with your spirit. It'll be there. You don't have to look for it. It will look for you. Then focus on taking a single, physical action. Even if that action is only lighting a fucking fag."

Never having been in combat, McCabe willed himself to follow his hero's advice. A main course in a mosquito feast, he remained motionless. *I'll come through for you, sir.* Minutes passed. Something crawled under his cuff and up his forearm, introducing itself with latch-on teeth. He smashed it with his thumb. The creature's splattered-out protoplasm mixed with his sweat and blood. Obeying Ajax finally paid off: a breeze jostling foliage revealed speckles of light, light he was sure came from lanterns in the fuck-huts. *To hell with the trail: target eyeballed.*

Carefully lifting and setting down his feet in that special recon way Ajax taught him, McCabe moved toward those lights. Ajax had taught him a lot about recon stealth: in tall grass raising feet low; in short grass raising feet high; going downhill, planting the heel first; going uphill, planting toes first; walking in shadows; avoiding sudden starts or stops on gravelly ground or a descending slope. Moving, McCabe imagined Ajax standing right beside him scribbling his characteristic thunderbolt evaluations in his commander's notebook. *I won't let you down, sir!*

Corporal Phord had set up the nipa huts as good offices for horny troops. There, Marine, Army and international troops fucked island girls and Manila hookers. It was a simple but effective operation involving four huts at a road junction twenty-minute walk from camp. McCabe heard that Phord had used his salesman talents that'll get him a stack in civilian life once he gets out, bad conduct discharge or no, to set up a sex-crazed round-robin. He heard there was one open-air hut. He heard the troops sat around on the floor or on the bamboo benches lashed to the supporting posts in the light of Coleman lanterns. He heard that under the roof-thatch, populated with little, green lizards, they drank slings (local fruit-and-alcohol hooch) dispensed from a coffee urn out of canteen cups and selected girls who paraded past them. They took those girls into the fuck huts, each divided inside by rattan mats strung on wires and replete with Sealy mattresses. He heard that when finished, they stood on duck boards, washed themselves scooping rainwater with a tin ladle from a 55-gallon drum before returning to camp. He heard all this from Gunny Lawler, his senior, guard NCO, who was master at reading the beating pulse of the troops.

A creature flapped past his face, U-turned, and came back at him. In the dark, he had no idea what it was. He swung his bamboo club, knocking it into foliage where it buzzed about before getting airborne again and flying away.

He raised the carbine stock to his shoulder, pointed the muzzle toward the huts and peered through the night-scope aperture. The wonders of the new night-vision technology revealed the foliage as dark green phosphorescent splashes crowding the lighter green rattan-sided huts. The lights in the windows spilled out liquid and bright. McCabe would use Ajax's cover and concealment techniques to move unnoticed to the huts. There, he would jump Phord and cuff him before he knew what was happening.

At the edge of a stream, he removed his leather boots, stuffed his socks inside, tied the laces together and hung the boots from his neck. Leaving the Philippines shortly to go where the troops were issued M-1945 Tropical Combat Boots, with their mud-pushing, angled, rubber lugs and water-flushing cotton-canvas-duck uppers, this was the first and last time in his life he would cross a stream barefooted.

Holding the carbine and battery pack over his head with one hand and with the other probing with his bamboo pole, he lowered one foot into water and wiggled his toes in mud. He pulled up his foot, heel first, to avoid make a sucking noise: Ajax's way.

The current rose to his chin. It smelled like a latrine and clawed like an attack by the Creature from the Black Lagoon. Buoyant boots crisscrossed in the water flow drawing the laces across his Adam's apple. His soaked utilities hanging heavy, McCabe clambered up the bank and connected with his spirit by pulling three leeches off his neck.

He stalked toward the huts, confident Ajax would be writing good things about him in his notebook.

He froze. A dog, standing in the undergrowth between the stream and the huts, was watching him. He trained the starlight scope on it.

It was typical of the mongrels in the countries his battalion visited during the eight months spent in the Far East: tan, sheep-sized, curled tail, black muzzle and paws. The dog whimpered, flattened its ears and dropped its tail in a let's-be-friends body language. McCabe petted its head.

The dog chomped the pole. Vibrations went up his arm. He wrenched the club free of the dog's teeth and, battery pack flapping, ran after it as it loped, barking, toward the huts. He swung the pole but missed. The lights in the hut went out. There was crashing inside the hut then crashing in the foliage behind the hut. The crashing went off into the jungle in several directions. He ripped mosquito netting aside, unclipped his gooseneck from the suspension ring and shined light on what looked like a ransacked, Goodwill store: clothes, papers, crockery, glasses, food scattered all around.

Beads hanging over a back doorway were swinging and clicking. "Halt!" He burst through the beads and mosquito netting. Outside, he stepped into a hole. Sprawling, his head snapping back as it hit the ground, glowing concussion blobs floating before his eyes, he heard the crashing in the foliage growing distant. Encumbered by battery pack and carbine, he heaved to his feet and stumbled back inside.

By the door was a naked girl pressing a dress against her breasts. Her eyes were liquid and welcoming in the light beam, a true beauty. Where did Phord find her? "No hurt, Marine."

"I won't hurt you."

"Your eyes," she said.

He shined the light on his face. "What's wrong with my eyes?"

"They're angry eyes. We're all angry. I fix your anger."

Her knees clumped on the split-bamboo floor. Her fingers undid the top button of his fly.

"Don't, sweet. Not in your mouth."

Her head snapped back. With her thumb and finger, she squeezed her nostrils. "Phew! You stink, Marine."

"I was in bad water, my love." He hooked his finger under her chin. He raised her to her feet. She pressed against him. He kissed her forehead.

"Make love, not war, Marine. Stink okay." She cupped his cheeks in her long, perfumed fingers and pressed her lips against his. She took his hand and lay down on a mattress, black hair spilled across her breasts. Her fingers beckoned, and she spread her legs.

"My angry one," she said.

His erection pushed against his Marine utilities, the fly buttons pinching his foreskin. Focusing on being the best leader he could since coming to the Far East, he had kept away from the fleshpots the troops frequented. Sexless during the months the battalion was abroad, he had horniness baked into his tissues. He placed his hands on the mattress athwart her shoulders and leaned close to her face. Within her jasmine perfume there was a slight sour dough odor, probably the natural odor of her body.

"I'm sorry." He rose and backed up a step.

She frowned and licked her lips.

He said, "Look, I'm supposed to be breaking up the parade not joining it. My commander has this thing about *integrity*. Understand integrity? I know that's the stuff fed to the troops, but it's what I believe."

The corners of her mouth drooped. Water filled her eyes. She leapt to her feet and clenched her fists.

He snatched all the MPC from his soaked wallet, pried open her fingers, and pressed the money into her hand. "Maybe twenty-bucks. Take it all."

She pushed the heel of her hand that clutched the money against his chin, rocking his head back. "Blow it out your ass, Jar Head."

A half-hour later, sopping utilities sticking to his skin, wet boots squeaking, McCabe double-timed to the sentry at the camp entrance.

"Good morning, sir," the sentry said. Tropical rain rattled on his nylon-twill poncho. He unslung his M-14 and launched into a precise port-arms, slapping the stock. McCabe knew that righteous port arms and sharp slap on the wooden stock was gunnery sergeant Lawler's handiwork. Lawler's fierceness reached as a packet of pure energy through the drizzly dawn into the tissues of this single Marine on an outpost, having him act as if he was in formation on the parade deck in front of packed reviewing stands.

Heart racing, saliva tacky, McCabe said: "Troops. Running on this road back to camp. I've been chasing them. They had to have passed your post." McCabe pointed his pole at the three rows of duck tents. The tents were lit by 1000-watt, spread-beam floodlights attached to commandeered telephone poles. Two weeks before, combat engineers laid down those tents along with showers, latrines, and kitchens on the tarmac of what had been an airfield abandoned after the Americans in bloody, bitter fighting captured the island in 1945. Often, carrying out his duties as camp guard commander now in 1965, McCabe felt haunted by the ghosts of the dead American and Japanese soldiers.

Peering out from his M1 helmet-liner, dripping with rainwater, the sentry looked where McCabe pointed then looked back at the lieutenant. "No troops passed my post, sir. No disrespect, sir, but you smell like shit."

"Bullshit."

"Sir?"

"You saw no troops? Sonofabitch, are you on corporal Phord's pay roll?"

"Don't understand, sir."

"I'll deal with you later."

McCabe double-timed up one row of tents. The flaps were up, rolled inboard. Troops lay on their cots in the floodlight shadows under mosquito nets. He ran down another row of tents. He went to the guard tent located on a dirt road bisecting the leading edge of the weed-choked, tarmac airstrip from which Mustangs and Hellcats once bombed and strafed the Japanese.

Gunnery sergeant Lawler was inside the guard tent with its supernumerary, sergeant of the guard, and corporal of the guard cots, the field phone with the comm wires spidering to the sentry posts, the PRC 9 radio, the acetate-overlaid map, 1: 25,000, on a tripod. Lawler was sitting on a camp chair, back straight, dozing. When McCabe's boot plunked on the duck boards, the Gunny stood up, wide awake. Years of infantry life honed his ability to transition instantly from deep sleep to full-throttle consciousness.

"I'm being bullshitted, Gunny."

"Who's the bullshitter or the bullshitee, lieutenant?"

"The sentry on post four says nobody came into camp. Bullshit. I chased at least a half dozen troops out of the fuck huts and back into camp. To get back into camp, they had to go past that sentry."

Wearing salty utilities, pushing his thumb against the prosthetic dental plate on the roof of his mouth, Lawler rolled his shoulders forward. McCabe knew that Lawler shoulder-roll. There was an unwritten rule in the battalion: don't fuck with Gunny Lawler's troops, especially if you're a lieutenant. That shoulder-roll was a warning, like a silverback's chest whomping.

"No corporal Phord, sir?"

"I just about had him, but a dog showed up and started barking, and everybody cleared out."

Lawler said sadly, "FUBAR"

"What?"

"FUBAR, sir. Fucked Up Beyond All Recognition. If lieutenant colonel Ajax told you to get on the other side of a stone wall, you'd do it without looking for a door. Take this for what it's worth, lay off my sentries. Also: no offense, sir, you're a hard charger, but it's your ideas

FUBAR fits."

"Oh?"

"*A capella* don't cut it. I told you a couple of squads would have unfucked your cluster fuck."

"*That* would've been fucked up. I wanted silence. I wanted cunning. I gotta do this right. No slip ups!"

"Running around in the dark in the jungle with a goddam bamboo pole and a carbine and starlight scope … what did that get you? Whew! You stink. Take it from me, you ain't god's gift to fire and maneuver like most lieutenants think they are."

Lawler's words woke up the supernumerary and sergeant of the guard who were lying on cots under the corkboard with bulletins of the day. Not wanting to miss the spectacle of Lawler chewing out a lieutenant, they rubbed their faces and looked over the camp table on which was a Willy Peter bag filled with sandwiches beside a 55-cup stainless steel coffee urn.

The gunnery sergeant said, "Like I told you before you went on this snipe hunt, there are other ways of getting Phord and his whores. You know he's the old man's driver. The old man has his back. Word is that unless it's murder one, don't fuck with Corporal Phord."

"Come with me and talk to the sentry." Anger strangled McCabe's voice.

Lawler sat slowly on the camp stool and cracked a much cracked and swollen knuckle of his middle finger by prying the finger backward and giving it a little jerk. This outright disobedience made the Marines on the other side of the coffee urn grin.

Lawler was McCabe's NCO in charge of guarding the camp. He was short with shoulders built big from years of carrying tons of infantry gear on long humps. His blond hair, crosshatched with bloodlike streaks, was cropped so short his head looked like a skull.

"Lieutenant, your quick temper makes you stupid. To speed up, slow the fuck down. I told you, one squad the anvil, the other squad the hammer, and it's hi diddle diddle."

His face squeezed into a deeply disgusted look. Two decades ago on Tarawa, he fell into a pillbox full of dead Japanese, goulashed in the tropical heat, and emitting odors he still smelled all these years later. When angry, his inward disgusted look at the stench coming back in his memory, turned outwardly murderous.

"Goddamnit, Gunny, wake up. You know what SEATO means." Lawler was suddenly flying across the tent and landing on wiry, bowed legs that could walk Marines half his age into the ground, in front of some poor lance corporal. He chewed the lance corporal out in his inimitable Lawler way, skull-head to one side, barking out of the side of his mouth, the lance corporal at attention and blinking furiously.

Then Lawler was back in front of McCabe. He said, "Five minutes late for sentry post. Gotta put more screws to these troops. Slack is what they won't get. About SEATO, lieutenant. That's what this exercise having grunts run around shooting blanks is all about. The rest is too complicated for me. You're a college grad, not me. You tell me."

Knowing that once he got Phord locked up aboard a Navy ship with à la carte bread and water, he'd relieve the Gunny, McCabe said, "South fucking East fucking Asian fucking Treaty fucking Organization. Seventy-five ships and twenty thousand soldiers and sailors from eight countries on this exercise. I don't have to tell you Ajax has his head up at the turkey shoot. If the press finds out his troops are making whoopee in the bush, he can kiss his star goodbye. And since I'm the Guard commander ..."

"So, you're guard commander? What a surprise."

Kill-you-motherfucker!

Outside the tent, two Marines laughed, reminding him of the laughter in the fuck huts. Were Phord's shenanigans a moveable feast? Was the party moving into tent town? *What would the Americans who shed blood retaking this island from the Japanese think of the chicken shit*

I'm involved in?

He shouted into the dark, "What's going on out there?"

Lawler said, "Sir, before you open up on those troops, read this. From guess who."

McCabe turned his hand over and opened his fingers. Lawler placed the canary-yellow paper in McCabe's palm, reminding McCabe of when he played football at Wake Forest and would come away from shaking hands with an alumnus with a hundred-dollar bill in his hand.

SEE ME NOW
IN MY TENT!
–A

"Better wait, sir. The old man may be hugging his rubber bitch."

"Don't matter, Gunny. Ajax sleeps like a whale, with only half his brain. When he wakes up, he's never really been asleep."

No time to shower, he hurried toward Ajax's tent. Passing the laughing Marines, McCabe said, "I hope doc's got some super penicillin for the righteous clap you picked up in the fuck huts."

"We've been to no fuck huts, lieutenant. We're cooks, sir, heading for the kitchens. Look at that snuffy over there tossing his cookies. Too much fire water last night."

"Going for distance or volume?" laughed the other cook.

In the dark near the piss tubes, aluminum cones attached to tubes stuck in the ground, a Marine had his hands on his knees, his back lifting and falling. McCabe grabbed the Marine's arm and pulled him to a standing position. "Drinking Corporal Phord's slings will always get you barfing your insides out. What's your name?"

Liquid jetted from the Marine's mouth. McCabe skipped backwards out of splash-range. The Marine pointed at a pile on the ground.

McCabe snapped on the gooseneck revealing the pile was a Marine in sateen utilities.

"Great. Another card-carrying member of the passed-out club."

"No sir. Not passed out."

"He's doing a good job of pretending."

"The blood, sir. Smell all that blood. That's what's sickening. Too dark to see what killed him. An artery ripped open."

"Bug out, Marine. I'll take care of this."

McCabe trained the gooseneck's beam on the face on the ground. The eyes were wide open. A bug was crossing an eyeball. The tongue, pulled through the slashed-open neck, lay athwart the breast of the field jacket. It was a "Spanish Necktie" mutilation that McCabe had been told was a favorite technique of the Japanese insurgents to terrorize the Americans re-taking the island.

McCabe snapped off the gooseneck. In the dark, there was gurgling and bubbling in the dead Marine's gouged throat. He started for the guard tent but stopped because Ajax should be the first to learn of the Marine's death.

Making an identification before reporting to Ajax, McCabe went back to the corpse and switched on the light.

Because the face was a frozen mask of death and horror, McCabe had not recognized it when he first shined the light on it. Looking at that face again, he felt a hammer-like shock in his chest. The poor bastard festooned by a Spanish necktie was U. S. Marine Corps, lieutenant colonel, Alfred Ajax.

2

Why Corporal Phord steals Ajax's whore.

Several hours after McCabe found Ajax's body, Corporal Phord secured his spit-shined belt buckle then flung himself out the door of the nipa hut and down the lashed-bamboo ladder. Field jacket in one hand, he gripped a rung awkwardly with the other. His unlaced boot slipped, and his jaw came down on a rung. His teeth snapped on his tongue. Tasting blood, Phord jumped off the ladder and onto sand. He threw on his jacket, tied his boots, then hurried, untucked jacket flapping, through the sea village toward his vehicle.

He ran along the packed-dirt, rain-wet road between thatched huts, their roofs shaped like Homburg hats. The palm-leaf window-coverings were propped up with bamboo poles. Bamboo drying racks flanked the huts.

Arms wrapped around his leg. It was an old woman. She was holding his leg. She wore a red bandanna and a long, many-colored skirt. Her blouse was pulled down off her shoulders, her clavicle sticking up like a towel rack in her skin.

Phord gently swung his leg. Though her limbs were like kindling, she nonetheless held on, implacable as a coiling python. He dragged her for a couple of meters until he reached the Mighty Mite. Not wanting to hurt her, he lifted her to her feet. She came up as if spring-loaded. The Tagalog spewing from out of her betel nut blackened mouth was a wonder. The language sounded to Phord like the sucking of liquid down a drain.

A shake down, he figured. All these Filipinos wanted money. So what? They needed it. He would give it to them – except his mother was first in line. He spun out of her clutches and slapped a back pocket. The pocket was empty. His wallet was gone.

The hatred coming out of her mouth in that glub-glub language was out of proportion to whatever wrong he had might have committed in her eyes. He shouted. "Makisig! Makisig!" It's the only word in Tagalog he knew.

"Makisig?" she said. The scaffolding of rage stiffening her brown face collapsed. "Ah, Makisig! Makisig!" She flung her arms wide, reminding Phord of a vulture braking its dive above a carcass. Her black lips, cracked like a dry lakebed, puckered. Old, dry arms hugged his neck. It was like being embraced by an erector set robot. He peeled her arms away then ran for the Marine vehicle, wiping betel nut juice off his cheek.

Pulling the key from his trousers' pocket, he climbed behind the steering wheel. "Don't give me any problems, you piece of shit," Phord said to the pile of aluminum called a Mighty Mite. The Mite was a jeep-like vehicle built light enough to be lifted by a Chickasaw chopper and thus conform to the "vertical envelopment" tactical requirements in the 1965 Marines. Phord needed to get back to camp without the ultralight Mite breaking down, which it did a lot. He turned the key. The air-cooled, aluminum engine came through for him – at least for now.

As he was pulling away, the old woman grabbed the windshield frame and lifted her leg to get into the passenger's side.

"No, you don't honey!"

He tromped the gas pedal. The momentum of the Mite spun her to the ground. As he saw her sprawled figure getting smaller in the rear-view mirror, she shot her fist above her head. "Makisig!" she shouted.

Phord steered the vehicle on a dirt road between wattle fences and rattan-sided, pole-supported huts. The road broke into jungle, leaving the huts, their Filipino smells, and fences behind. Now that he was on the way toward camp and away from the Filipinos, his thoughts stopped racing. His Marine mindset started a comeback. Like: situation awareness. *Where exactly is camp? And what about my wallet?* He was foolish to go back to camp without it. It wasn't the money. He didn't care about the money. It had his military green card. Some Filipino could steal his identity. He hit the brakes. The Mighty Mite pitched into a waterfilled pothole, liquid mud splashing his face, the right ball joint making a sickening cracking noise. Rubbing chin-stubble (better shave before reporting back to Ajax), he stared at the road/jungle intersection that in his sleep grogginess looked fake; a pastoral painted on a stage canvas. He spun the vehicle around and drove back to the hut. Motor left running, he scrambled up, spat a little blood over his shoulder into the sea-breath, then hurried inside.

Standing naked by the bare mattress combing her waist-length black hair, her head rocking with the downward slash of the comb, Mariko said, "What're you doing here? Get out." Her voice was harsh. He had spent hours with her last night as they poured their hearts out to each other, yet she had never spoken harshly to him.

"Don't worry. I'm leaving."

"No, you're not. You're standing there. Go!"

"How the hell do I get back to camp?"

"Take the road north. Sea on your left. Five miles you'll come to a flying horse gas pump. Turn right. That's the camp road. Now go."

"My wallet's gone."

"Makisig will be here soon. He's on the way. I think I hear his jeep in the distance. You don't want to be here when he shows up. Your wallet's over there. Get it and go." She jabbed her comb at a simple chair that resembled Van Gogh's chair in the asylum cell. The black chiffon gown lay over the chair's back. She wore that gown last night under the many-colored lanterns at the international social held on the gun platform of the abandoned Spanish fortress overlooking the sea. Back then, he watched her incredible beauty, her strange, sloe eyes, the Filipino grace of her features, seeing her not simply through his eyes but from the lusting eyes of the SEATO dignitaries. Holding the arm of the Aussie medical officer, unmindful the dignitaries were undressing her with their stares, she moved with poise both chaste and sexual.

Phord reached beneath the gown under the chair and grabbed his wallet off a split-bamboo floorboard.

"Count it." She turned around and faced him fully naked and stunning and unashamed.

Blushing, Phord averted his eyes. "I trust you, Mariko."

"Why should you? I wouldn't."

Somebody shouted from below the window. Mariko, pressing the gown to her breasts, leaned out, the long muscles of her long legs flexing. She spoke in Tagalog to a young woman in a black, widow's dress standing beneath the window. Mariko kissed her fingers and turned those fingers affectionately toward the woman. Unlike Phord, she was not a stranger here.

Mariko said, "The landlady says Makisig rented the house for the night. She wants her money."

"No problem. How much?" His thumb raked the thick sheaf of green, red and blue MPC notes stuffing the wallet. "And you too, Mariko. How much?"

"No fuck, Marine, no sale."

As she lifted her hands to gather her hair at the nape of her neck (last night it was layered in an Audrey Hepburn bouffant), there was the sound of a jeep approaching. It parked beneath the ladder.

"Bloody hell," she said.

"What's the matter?"

"You'll find out soon enough."

"What?"

"It's Makisig."

"So what? What will he do?"

"Nothing much. Just kill you."

She dropped her hands, the ebony, crocodile-print hair claw clip snapped open. Her released hair sprayed down her back. Stepping into the gown and pulling the roach up over her breasts, she was transformed into last night's wild, dark, bare-shouldered beauty in black chiffon. "Zip me, please." As he zipped up the back of her dress, he felt her sexual vibes flow into his fingers.

Clutch purse in hand, she went to the doorway. The spring in her step indicated to Phord her anxiousness to go with Makisig.

Makisig bounded up the ladder and into the hut. Despite being crippled, he moved quickly.

"What is this? Phord, what're you doing here? Where's Ajax?"

"You know each other?" said Mariko.

"Sort of," said Phord.

Wearing a leather vest, over a naked torso, chest caved in from childhood rickets, he pulled a curtain to one side. He peered into the small room behind the curtain, the dim light making his facial scars particularly appalling. "Ajax isn't here." He limped up to Phord with such fierceness that the Marine put his hands up and took a backward step. "This is not good, My Sweet. Not good at all. Ajax wanted her."

"How do you know?"

"He told me last night."

"You were at the social on the fortress?"

"Of course. I saw you, but you didn't see me. That's the way it's supposed to be. Ajax told me he told you to get rid of that Aussie and take her to his fuck shack."

"I did the first. The Aussie couldn't take a punch. But I didn't do the second."

"You stole her from him?"

"*Stole* is the wrong word, Makisig."

He looked Phord up and down as a hangman might scrutinize the hooded head and bound arms of the victim to make sure all was in order before pulling the trapdoor lever. "I hope you didn't use the missionary position. This island has too many missionaries fucking locals."

"I didn't touch her."

"I'm hard of hearing." He cupped his hand behind what was left of his ear. He fought the Japanese in the jungles for a year and a half before being captured and having his body parts rearranged by torturers. After the war, surgeons in Manila left much to be desired trying to put him back together. "What is that you just said?"

"You heard me."

"Hearing doesn't mean believing."

Phord opened the wallet. "For you. Take it all. I'm outta here."

"What're you doing?" Mariko said. She had the same inflection in her voice that when they shared their life stories on the beach last night. The harshness was gone. But only for a moment. It was back when she said, "Last night, you told me that money's for your mother."

"My mother's already gotten more than I ever expected. Makisig and I made a killing with the troops. Giving the rest to him will make a clean break."

Makisig's three-fingered hand stuffed the big roll of bills into his shirt pocket. Phord noticed the Filipino always had a predatory way of taking money he gave him.

He said, "I don't have to count it. I know what it is. It's one hundred percent. You're giving me one hundred percent of the money you collected from the troops. That's breaking our contract. Remember our contract? We shook on it. Fifty-fifty. You get the troops and the money, I get the girls. But one hundred percent for me now that I have come for Mariko comes up way short, My Sweet."

He clasped her bare arm. Mariko's lower lip curled under her teeth.

"Don't touch her, Makisig."

"Get out," Mariko said to Phord.

"Mariko, how can you stand there and let him grab you like this? After what you told me last night your mother did to you?"

Makisig released her arm and grabbed the back of her neck. Her knees flexed. Holding Mariko, he gave Phord a strange, new look. His eyes resembled black agates smashed by a hammer and scraped together in two tiny piles.

"Stop!" said Phord. He clutched Makisig's arm, all bone, little muscle. It was like grabbing a fungo bat. He spun Makisig in a circle then hurled him toward the door. He kicked the Filipino's ass. Makisig tumbled down the ladder and sprawled on the sand. He picked up the aviator glasses that had popped out of his shirt pocket and wiggled the pad plates on the Frankenstein flap of skin that covered the bridge of his nose. With his good hand, he brushed sand off the sleeve of his crippled arm and off the knees of his jeans. He was rather fastidious about grooming his grisly appearance. Brushing sand out of his hair, he looked up at Phord, the green glasses hiding his eyes, making his gaze look, strangely, more penetrating. He laughed. "Top of the world! Keep her, My Sweet. Make your pretty goodbyes in private. Now I'm driving off. That's what you want. You want me to drive off and forget her. I'm driving off, but I'm not forgetting. In the end, I'll be keeping her, so there's no forgetting."

He paid off the young, widowed landlady who was amused by the Makisig's falling-down-the-ladder burlesque. She grinned widely with betel nut blackened gums and her remaining few teeth.

Makisig drove off between cement block pig stalls, his thick, black knots of hair swinging against the back of a white barong. Passing the outskirts of the village, his jeep scattered spotted whistling ducks that flapped over a scum-rimmed pond where a green-and-black snake was emerging from a hole.

Phord shook his head from side to side.

"What's so funny?" Mariko said.

"Me."

"You? Funny? Don't you understand what's going to happen to you?"

"I gave up understanding what's going to happen to me when I raised my hand to join the Marines."

"Marines have rules. Makisig doesn't have rules. He'll rip out your throat and laugh about it. Stop grinning. You don't know."

"Something I remembered."

"Stop remembering and start leaving."

"Me spinning Makisig around. The same thing happened years ago. When my father came back unannounced from the Korean War. I was fifteen. He was wounded. Dishonorably discharged. Drunk. Raging. He spun me and my mother around and slammed us against a wall. Then he left. Never saw him for years afterwards."

Pointing out the window, Mariko said, "I told you to go. You didn't listen. Now look."

Phord looked. The Mighty Mite was moving. The old woman was behind the wheel jerkily steering. He hurried down the ladder and sprinted. He grabbed the rear spare tire. She gunned it. He lost his grip and sprawled in mud. Mud spewed from the rear tires against his face as the Mighty Mite fishtailed then straightened out. The Mighty Mite went up the same road Makisig took a few minutes before. Watching her go, he stood up and spat bloody saliva that glittered momentarily in the dawn rays before it fell into the sand at his feet.

The sun was up above the jungle and the village structures were sharpening in the thinning mist. He licked sea mist off his upper lip then began walking. He walked up the road Mariko had told him led to base camp.

A young man in loose cotton work clothes passed him. He had a long, scrawny neck and long hands with small wrists and wiry forearms. A bolo in a leather scabbard with a brass throat was roped to his G. I. web belt.

Phord pointed toward the pig enclosures around which Makisig drove his jeep. He said, "Taxi? Cab?"

The young man looked where Phord pointed then looked back at Phord. The whites of those eyes were yellow, maybe the result of liver worms. He raked his thumb across his neck. He gestured into his mouth with two fingers. He licked his lips. Phord remembered reading that many natives on these islands had once practiced cannibalism, preferring Chinese cooked in rice to the "tough, salty" taste of a white man's flesh. Though the Spanish halted the practice, Phord figured it lived in the undercurrents of the village's culture, hence the young man's gestures.

The bolo glinted in the sunlight as the youth raised the weapon.

"What the hell?" said Phord. He stepped back.

The young man stepped forward on rubber shower shoes. Phord jumped to the side as the bolo went past his head. As the youth raised the weapon to strike again, Phord hit him on the point of the jaw with his fist. The youth dropped to the ground, out cold. Phord flipped him on his side, lifted his chin, and pulled the tongue away from his epiglottis with a hooked finger. The eyes fluttered open. He rolled over into a four-point stance and tried to stand up, but his knees buckled, and he fell over. Another young man, scowling at Phord, pulled the youth to his feet. He slipped his shoulder under the limp armpit and staggering under the weight and glancing angrily now and then back at Phord helped the young man along a path that curved through a garden behind a hut.

Phord heard a grinding in the trees. A Mighty Mite was approaching. He knew it was a Mighty Mite because of the signature metallic coughing of its air-cooled engine. He figured it was the old woman coming back from her joy ride.

As the Mite lurched into view from around pig stalls, Phord saw not the old woman behind the wheel but a Marine in utilities. "Oh, my lord," said Phord. He called to the driver, "Corporal fucking Byrne."

Byrne stopped the vehicle beside Phord. The old woman still had his Mite. This was another Mite. Byrne laughed, "The Marines have landed, Shooter, and the situation is totally out of control."

"I can hide from you, Byrne, but I can't run." He rubbed the aching knuckles of his punch-hand.

"Get in. I'm taking you back to camp. We're living the Chinese curse."

"*You* live in *your* interesting times. Leave me out."

"The trouble is, the times just got more interesting. When I tell you, you'll need to change your skivvies."

A corporal in the battalion's mortar platoon, Byrne was short, skinny, with a blocky-jawed Errol Flynn face, an Errol Flynn in his later-years dissolution. "What the hell you doing in this pig heaven of a village?"

"It's the magic kingdom, Byrne."

"Sure, if cunt's mixed up in it. A cunt is pixie dust. I've come to get you. Let's go."

"How did you find me?"

"The camp's turned into a goat rodeo."

"What's happening?"

"Get in. I'll fill you in on the back. Like I said, you'll shit."

Phord jumped in, ready as always to follow Byrne who himself followed unquestioningly the dictates of a goat-horned spirit dancing continually inside him. Harmful was joyful to Byrne. "Woh-who-ey! who-ey! who-ey!" Phord yelped the rebel yell they often exchanged during their alcohol-fueled, liberty exploits – though both having great, great fathers who fought for the Union, they had no sympathy for the Lost Cause.

"You louse, it's great to see you! And great to get the hell out of here!" Phord squeezed the ball of the shoulder of his bar-hopping buddy. "Wait, Byrne. I forgot something. Stop!"

"Wait hell! I'll stop at camp."

"Go back."

"What?"

"Go back!"

"Go back hell!"

Phord grabbed the wheel and jerked it hard. The Mite plunged off the road. Byrne jammed on the brakes to avoid crashing into a kamagong tree. He hit the brakes in that hateful way he had of operating a Mite. Byrne's hatred for these light, easily broken machines spilled over into the way he operated them, stomping the brakes, grinding the gears, cursing the workings.

Phord was out of the Mite and jogging toward the village. Byrne got the Mite back on the road and pulled up to Phord.

"Okay. Get in. You want to go over Niagara Falls in a barrel? Sign me up too, Shooter. If it's bad, I'm good. I love living the unexamined life with you."

Jogging, Phord said over his shoulder, "Mariko. I have to say goodbye." Why did he say that? He already told her goodbye. But he kept jogging anyway.

"What? Say what to who?"

"To Mariko."

"Who the hell is Mariko?"

"My fairy godmother."

"*Now* is the order of the day!"

"Be just a minute."

"Your minute expired last night."

"Tell it to Ajax."

Byrne swung the Mite off the road through a wattle fence, the tires smashing melons, their liquids spilling across red dirt, then back onto the road. He pulled up beside Phord. Phord had reached the ladder. Byrne leaped out and grabbed his shoulders.

"You don't get it, Shooter. This is the interesting times we're living! Ajax is gone."

"Whaddaya mean gone?"

"Kaput."

"Kaput meaning …"

"Kaput. Kaput is kaput in my book."

"Explain."

"Dead."

"Dead? What?"

"You got it."

"Ajax?"

"Murdered." Byrne grabbed Phord's shoulders and shook them back and forth.

"Mur – what?" Phord laughed, slapping Byrne's hands away. Occasionally, Byrne got too physically personal with Phord for Phord's liking. "Never! The Japs couldn't kill him. The North Koreans couldn't kill him. Ditto the Chinese. Antibiotic-resistant syphilis is the only thing that might do the trick."

"A knife did the trick."

"Knife?"

"Murder. They found his body beside the latrines this morning. The Marine part of the exercise has been called off. The troops are being called back to camp. It's raining investigators. I stole this aluminum wreck to run you to earth. Get in, and let's get back before they know it's missing, and we become cell mates in a Navy brig."

"Be right with you, Byrne." Phord felt he was engaged in an out of body experience, watching himself climb back into the hut. A place he didn't have to go back to. A place he knew he shouldn't go back to.

Mariko wasn't there. Good. *It's back to camp. But where is she?*

His legs took him out the back door and down a ladder to a plywood-sided, metal-roofed outhouse on stilts over a creek emptying into the sea. She and he had taken turns tight-roping several times during the night across a plank leading to the outhouse where they pulled the rotting burlap aside and went into the rollicking stench to relieve themselves.

Now, spreading his arms, Phord made his way over the plank. He yanked the wet burlap. In the dark was the circular opening cut with a coping saw in a slab of rotting plywood over the quicklime-sprinkled creek pit. On the floor and coming out of the opening scurried the largest cockroaches Phord had ever seen. Mariko wasn't there. He went back over the plank, cupped his hands to his mouth and shouted, "Mariko!"

Villagers stared at him. An old fisherman, who had one end of rope between his empty gums while he curled the other end around a dock cleat beside which was a long, blue-painted boat rigged with two outboard motors, gestured with his grizzled chin toward a path in the jungle.

Phord ran down that path. Mariko was up ahead, trying to run, stumbling because her tight dress impeding her knee flexion. He grabbed her arm then remembered Maksig doing the same thing and dropped his hand. "Mariko, please stop." She stopped but did not turn to face him.

"What are you doing? Where are you going?"

"Where do you think? New York, of course. I'm Holly Golightly." She turned around. Her upper lip and forehead were sweating. "Hands off. We said goodbye."

"Did we?"

"I did. I said, *hands off.*"

"Let's think about this."

"Think? There's no thinking. Just doing. You can do, can't you? One foot in front of the other and *do*. That's what goodbye is."

"I won't forget last night."

"Try."

"I told you things about me I never told anyone."

"How romantic. The moon. The sea. Two lonely people sharing their heartaches. Excuse me if I barf. Look, I'm sorry for you. I'm sorry for your childhood. The pre … pre … What's the word?"

"Preemptive."

"Whatever it means."

"The preemptive beatings."

"You told me. I still don't know what the word means. But I can guess."

"After my biological father ran out on us, I had two stepfathers. One of them used to wake me in the middle of the night and beat me. He called it a 'wakeup call'—just in case I screwed up in the future."

"Lovely fathers you Americans have. We all have our heartaches. What a laugh. But so what? What does it mean? It means nothing now. It means goodbye."

"What's going to happen to you?"

"Me? My life'll get a whole lot better with you out of it."

Byrne pulled up, pushing the Mite through the narrow path. Keeping the motor idling, he looked at Mariko then at Phord. A beautiful girl by the sea combined with an AWOL Phord was the disaster-in-the-making he loved. "Let's roll, Shooter. Didn't you hear me about Ajax?"

"I heard you. I'm trying to digest it. Who did it?"

"God knows. That's what's being investigated."

"Ajax … well, goddamn." Phord pressed his tongue against the roof of his mouth and gnashed his teeth. He'd be damned if he'd let Byrne see him blubber. Over the months he had run point for Ajax in civilian haunts, he had come to feel distressing sympathy for his boss. He saw the appetites that delighted Ajax also caused the hard-charging battalion commander anguish. For the few seconds he ejaculated in some girl's orifice, he paid a terrible price in terms of expended energy and career risks. This paragon of rectitude and prowess, this Marine legend, was in truth brittle. Now that he was dead, Phord's heart broke for the man.

"Now it's sinking into that mud for brains." Speaking to Phord, Byrne was looking at Mariko. He bit and sucked his lower lip. He was always attracted to girls who were interested in Phord.

Phord said, "Wait a minute. Let me think."

Mariko started to walk away. Phord grabbed her hand, gently. "Mariko, please …"

Byrne looked at Mariko. He looked at Phord. He said, "Marines don't leave Marines."

"With my boss dead, maybe I have other obligations."

"What obligations?"

"My feelings."

"Did the Marines issue you feelings? Then you don't need them. Tell me, where'd you find this one?" Byrne called the girls he and Phord interacted with by impersonal designations – "This one." "That one." – negating their human dimensions to define them as merely seasonings for the delightful stews of their adventures.

"She was Ajax's girl."

"Hot dog! Ajax should be alive to take this in. His girl taken by his driver! Poetic justice on stilts for that asshole!" He crossed himself. "May he rest in peace." Raised by a single, Irish mother in Chicago's southside, he was a seriously practicing Catholic, despite his flagrant ways. "Remember our motto, 'never let reality get the upper hand.' Now let's roll." Byrne looked at Mariko again. There was a different look on his face. His face was freckled with reddish skin that burned instead of tanned, causing that skin to be in a constant state of peeling, and the blue eyes that occasionally took on a crazed look, especially when he was drinking, that startled onlookers. Several times, when Phord and Byrne were on the town, bouncers seeing that look would refuse to let Byrne into their establishments. The bouncers were right. Phord knew, when that look came into Byrne's eyes, bars had better be up to date on their insurance. Byrne had not been drinking (he was a stickler for never drinking on duty), but the look was there.

Knowing there would be hell to pay both with Byrne and the Marines if he didn't get in and get out of there, he nonetheless did not move. Then another out of body experience: He took Mariko's hand. Her palm sweat was hot against his fingers. That she did not pull away startled him.

"Don't take this wrong, Byrne. You know we're brothers in pain and suffering, but …"

Byrne held up his hand, palm out. "Don't say what you're going to say."

"What am I going to say?"

"I don't know. But I know you. You're the consummate salesman. You can sell snow to Innuits. Many times, you convinced me black is white. Now, don't say nothing. Cause I'm not in the mood. Just get in."

Mariko made a vicious gesture with her chin indicating for Phord to clear out. He sensed there was some black current inside her. He discovered that last night when he asked why she kept her Japanese name in a community that hated the Japanese, and she said, *to have the last laugh.*

"Okay, Byrne. I'm trying to see what's right." He let go of Mariko's hand and threw his around Byrne's shoulders and walked him out of earshot of Mariko. "Let me explain."

Byrne peeled Phord's arm off his shoulder. "Don't get touchy, Shooter. And don't talk me into whatever you want when I don't want it."

"This started last night at the VIP social. The old man saw Mariko and told me to get her away from the Aussie doctor she was with and take her to his special hut where he scratches his itch. The doctor wasn't a problem. When he had taken her outside the fortress headed for fornication, I closed the sale. I told him I was CIA, and she was a security risk. He was skeptical but my right cross made him a believer. The problem was her. Or maybe me. I got her in the Mite and looked in her eyes and saw … I don't know what. A better way to say it is, I *felt*. I felt I couldn't let Ajax do her like he had done to the other girls I got for him. I took her to this place she said Makisig had rented."

"And fucked her eyes out, Shooter. Right?"

"No. I didn't. I couldn't. I wanted to. Look at her. But I didn't touch her."

That Mariko stood at the edge of the trail watching them was a curiosity for Phord – simply because she wasn't leaving.

"Agreed. She's a knockout. But in the end, she's just a vagina."

"I figured if I wasn't going to let Ajax touch her, I couldn't either."

"That's your trouble, Shooter – you're a moral shape-charge. Like you're broke most of the time sending your mother all the money you make. Your mother gets money, but I end up paying for drinks." He shouted to Mariko, "This dope ought to be a staff sergeant. But he lost stripes disobeying orders that he felt went against his brainless principles."

"Listen. We talked all night. I never talked like that with anyone. She understood me. Maybe she's the answer."

"To what?"

"Don't ask me. And now with Ajax dead …"

"Shooter, look!" Mariko was gone. A big, orange flower on a long stalk was swaying in the space she had been in. "Now what're you going to do?"

Running, Phord shouted over his shoulder, "Go fuck yourself, Byrne."

"It's another service I offer," Byrne shouted back.

"Woh-who-ey! who-ey! who-ey!"

Before turning around to keep going after Mariko, he saw Byrne wink – the same us-against-the-world wink that two months later he gave in Phord's arms, shot in the chest by a sniper, on a I Corps upland trail, just before he died.

3

McCabe meets Father Baum and finds out Ajax's murder is connected to the devil in the mountains.

"Mister Marine ... helps me."

The girl was sitting in a dark room on the stone floor in the fortress ammunition room against the masonry wall wearing a yellow Barong Talog with a shear wrap-around embroidered with flowers. She was still a child. There was the odor of jasmine perfume. And another odor. He took her trembling, outstretched hand in his. Her hand was clammy.

"What's the matter?"

"Helps me ..."

Sixteen hours after Ajax's corpse had been found by McCabe and forty yards from the spot at which McCabe found it, Father Baum told the lieutenant, "You sink a man killed your battalion commander? I tell you, no man did it. It's a *Geist*."

"A what?" said McCabe. The Father had interrupted his thoughts, unkind thoughts it was a pleasure to think.

"*Geist*. Spirit," said Father Baum. "A spirit killed him."

"That's my man talking, Colm," Father O'Toole said. "I risked a lot bringing him to camp to meet with you. Listen to him."

McCabe was sitting with the two Catholic priests at one of a dozen A-frame tables in the O Club tent in tent-town on the abandoned World War II airfield. At the end of the tent was a yakal mahogany board laid across two sawhorses. Behind the board, a black-haired, blue-eyed Marine sergeant in utility trousers and jungle jacket was lifting dripping bottles of San Miguel out of a ripped-lengthwise, ice-filled 50-gallon steel drum and snapping off the caps with the butt of his K-Bar on the edge of the board.

Every night during the two weeks the SEATO exercise had been staged, this tent was crowded with officers of many nations getting hammered. But tonight, Ajax's murder had put the kibosh on international cheer. Few officers were in the place.

"Spirit, schmeer-it, "replied McCabe.

"Mocked," said Father Baum. He turned to Father O'Toole. "I'm mocked." Squat and barrel-chested with a bull's neck that pushed against his priest's collar showing in the open-necked, short-sleeved shirt, Father Baum used his whole body when he turned. He reminded McCabe of a massive tree, the chain-sawed undercut finished, beginning to twist and fall. "I'm telling you who killed Ajax, and he mocks me. Don't you see?"

"I never see what I look at," said Father O'Toole. "It's an acquired skill."

McCabe raised a San Miguel to his lips but did not drink. Instead, he wondered what sin it would be to slam his fist into Father Baum's florid face with its green-ice eyes. He also wondered what might have happened if he hit that ONI investigator in the face.

The colonel's murder had thrown the machinery of the SEATO exercise into reverse. The Marines who were supposed to be the bad-guy "aggressors" against the good-guy U.S. Army were ordered to secure and return to base camp where a half dozen ONI investigators were digging into the crime. The investigator who interviewed McCabe was a tall, skeleton of a man in tan trousers and navy-blue cotton shirt with the sleeves rolled up above the elbows. He had the same speech impairment as Tweety the canary in the cartoon with Sylvester the cat (*"I tawt I taw a puddytat"*). Going at McCabe for an hour and a half in a special tent set up for the investigation, he treated the lieutenant with leery distain as if he were somehow involved in the murder. He said, "If you won't talk, I'll tape you to a polygraph and let the needle do the talking." During the interview, McCabe thought many times, *your face badly needs a fist.*

Now with the two priests, McCabe stopped wondering about doing bad things that made him feel good, and drank. The liquid broke through the chips of ice jammed in the glass neck. He chugged. Coming to this island, McCabe found that drinking ice-chip-laden San Miguels in this tropical heat was veritable enchantment. Except now the iced beer tasted like bitter herbs.

McCabe set the bottle with a click on the tabletop made of toe-nailed duckboards and stared out from under the up-rolled tent flaps to the newly installed, upgraded spotlights shining in the night through the post-rain mists. In those mists, he imagined again Ajax's pulled-out tongue across his chest, the silver oak leaf on the collar, the P-41, herringbone twill jacket with "Ajax" sewn above the stenciled USMC and eagle/globe/anchor, black blood soaking the jacket. McCabe saw O'Toole was watching him. He said, "Worried for my soul, Padre?"

"Not your soul, McCabe, I'm worried about," said O'Toole. His raspy voice resembled that of a pro wrestler who has been clotheslined too many times in the throat.

Baum said: "I tell you the man who killed Ajax isn't just a Japanese soldier who's been running loose on this island for nineteen years, not knowing the War has ended. Of course, Lieutenant Shimada, the man, killed Ajax. No doubt about that. But that man is also a spirit. The islanders call him the devil in the mountains. That devil's killed many islanders over the years. But if we're going to track him down, you have to understand the spirit in the man."

McCabe lifted the bottle to eye level, trying to ignore O'Toole's stare—the priest's gray-blue eyes black in the dim electric light from the bulb hanging off BX wiring—a stare brimming with compassion McCabe thought was lunacy. "Dead soldier," McCabe said. Checking an urge to fling the bottle at Baum, he underhanded it toward a fifty-gallon drum. It broke inside upon empties from the previous night, the night of the murder. "Swish," McCabe said. "Three in a row." He stood up, quickly withdrawing his steadying hand from the table to show he needed no help to get to his feet. He'd show this German peasant how New York pros drank beer. He started drinking on the streets in the East Village around age 11, but never let it get out of control. Having seen what street thugs did to homeless winos motivated him to develop the skill of keeping a corner of clarity in his consciousness. "Gentlemen, duty calls. Though I'll refrain from saying *Auf Wiedersehen*."

"*Bis bald* is more appropriate," said Baum.

"Fuck you, my love," McCabe said.

The Marine sergeant, popping a bottle cap with his K-bar on the edge of the plank, checked the slapping action of his hand to look over. O'Toole moved around the table and grabbed McCabe's arm. McCabe was over six feet but had to look up at O'Toole. The priest was not only tall but wide. Playing tackle for Notre Dame before he got his knee destroyed by a crack-back block in the Army game, he had been called by his teammates, "Beast." McCabe tried but failed to wrest his arm from Beast's grip.

Baum stood, keeping a stiff-necked Prussian bearing. "Wait. Don't go, my young friend. Here's a fact for you." He clapped his hand – dirty knuckle-cracks, Baum helping poor people in the fields and on the roads – on McCabe's shoulder. For a moment, McCabe was priest-afflicted, gripped on the arm by one and on the shoulder by the other.

McCabe turned his head slowly and stared at Baum's hand. Baum's grin dismissed McCabe's theatrical show of displeasure. Still, he removed his hand. O'Toole held on. McCabe's arm tingled as the priest's big fingers pressed deeply into his muscle against the radial nerve. Baum said, "I was the best cotton-picker in Texas in 1943-45. Here're the secrets: bend the knees to take the pressure off the back and use leather gloves against the bristles. Feel that." Baum tapped his shoulder beside his white, cardboard collar with a thick finger, the nail of which was chewed, confirming in McCabe's mind there was something neurotic about this man. McCabe did not move. "*Betasten*," ordered Baum. "Feel it! Feel it!" McCabe reluctantly touched where Baum tapped. Through the cotton, he felt a knob of flesh. "That's a scar," said Baum. "From the strap of the twenty-foot sack I dragged around. Look at it."

"The twenty-foot sack?" McCabe said.

Baum said to O'Toole. "See, my young friend's mocking continues." He said to McCabe. "No, I mean the scar. Look at the scar." Baum unbuttoned the first button of his shirt. McCabe noticed the buttons were metal each imprinted with the German black eagle. O'Toole released McCabe's arm and stopped Baum from unbuttoning the next button. "Before I was captured in the Libyan desert and sent to Texas, I was a tank platoon commander," Baum said re-buttoning his shirt. "A lieutenant. My young friend, that makes us brothers. Sure, we have our differences – I, in Fallschirmjäger-Brigade Ramcke with the Desert Fox in 1942: 'Heia safari!' And you're a Marine infantry officer today in 1965. But those differences are minor compared to what bonds us. We're brothers in the lieutenant corps. Here's to the lieutenants of this world. May we all listen to our noncoms. And may Shimada be captured, and justice prevail." On his feet, Baum drank, head back, a drop of sweat running down his throat into his collar. Baum lowered the bottle, wiped his mouth the German-peasant style with heel of his hand and sat down. He said: "Tonight we will begin to run Shimada to earth and justice will roll down like waters. Please sit. Let me tell you about Shimada."

McCabe did not move. He said, "Let me tell you where I'm coming from. My father saw enough death in the Pacific to make him a proselytizing atheist. Every Sunday, he sat down with me for an hour to go through the Bible, pointing out wrongs. I remember the finger he pointed with was gnarled by years of firing a machine gun. So, my German friend, feed me no flimflam. Though I am open to what you have to say about Shimada."

Baum laughed. "I say 'sit' and my young friend stands. Disobeying an *un*lawful order."

"You're a real jokester, Father Baum. But don't you know the biggest joke of all? That you're asking me to believe I can live forever if I eat flesh and drink blood."

"I really enjoy your insights, my young friend. We should talk sometime, heart-to-heart as you Americans say. Be careful. Your sarcasm makes you easy prey to be converted. But let's get to the subject at hand. Your boss was murdered. Don't you want to get the murderer?"

"Go on," said McCabe.

"Shimada won't give up. Hiding out for twenty years. Japanese officials have been coming to the island to convince Shimada in the mountains that the war is over. Even Shimada's own brothers showed up a few years ago. They sent up balloons with signs. They trekked into the mountains with electric megaphones."

"But Shimada goes on," said O'Toole, watching McCabe. "Listen to him."

"That's why Ajax is dead, my young friend."

"Okay, tell me more."

"Are you listening just to make fun of me?"

"Here's what's fun, a rib-woman talking to a snake and eating a magic apple. Let's laugh over that."

Shades of the Beast clearing a hole with a drive block for a Fighting Irish, O'Toole abruptly pushed McCabe out the tent into the sweet/rotten jungle air. Their boots sucked in the tarry, former-airstrip glop, softened by recent rains and vehicle and foot traffic.

"Lay off, Padre. What did I do?"

"Can your attitude. Then I'll let you go back."

"I want to hear more about Shimada."

"You gripped that table with bad intent. I wasn't saving the Father. I was saving *you*."

"Maybe he deserves a table getting flipped in his face."

"If Ajax were alive, Colm, he'd be giving you a royal chewing out."

"For what?"

"For falling on your sword."

"He was murdered on my watch. How else do I react?"

"Why are you angry at the Father? The Father didn't murder him. Baum is gruff, but he's done incredible work on this island."

"What work?"

"Tending to the poor. People say he's doing a saint's work. They say he'll be canonized. The islanders love him."

"Just what I need for my screwed-up life, a goddam saint."

"You don't need Father Baum. Maybe he needs you."

"Wrong. If he can lead me to the old man's killer, I need him."

"Oh, my," Father O'Toole said, deep sadness giving a special flavor to his gravelly voice.

"Padre, you remind me of my favorite movies. Remember? It came out ten years ago when Ike was President. Robert Mitchum played the preacher in "Night of The Hunter." He had LOVE tattooed on the fingers of one hand and HATE on the other. Okay, maybe MISERY is more appropriate for the way you see things than HATE. But with MISERY, you'd run out of fingers."

They both laughed. McCabe couldn't stay angry for long with O'Toole. He loved this sorrowful man. Despite carrying out his usual chaplain's duties of organizing religious events, bible studies, pre-marital classes, counseling, and drafting and filing correspondence, he was constantly with the troops: in their vehicles, in their holes, on their hikes, in their tents. He ate their food, shared their misery in the field, and cried with them when the inevitable "Dear John ..." letters showed up at mail call. The troops affectionately called him "Father Tool." He was Navy; he was a chaplain; but they considered him one of their own; and they would die for him. Though he spread cheer wherever he went, he was the saddest person McCabe ever knew.

"You're a sad case, Colm."

McCabe put his hand on O'Toole's shoulder. "Taking lessons from the expert, Father."

"I deal with the Black Dog by praying for the likes of you. Compassion gives meaning to depression."

"It's coming out your ears. Neurosis is your style. Ever since we've known each other, you've been looking for me. But you can't find me. Look, I've got things to do. I'm checking the lines."

"Okay, I said my say, Colm. But I'm not through with you."

McCabe walked into the CP tent. The gunny was on his feet that must have humped half a million miles in his career, staring at the acetate-overlay of a map of the area, mumbling to himself. Ajax's murder had affected the troops in different ways: Sergeant Major Crow's taut, healthy, sun-browned face was now a little jaw-bloated and sallow as the throat-pelt of a mouse; Major Gord, the old war-mustang who had been to hell in back in Korea and never cracked a smile—even in the O Club when Ajax, surrounded by his admiring officers, was throwing out one-liners – now went around with the corners of his mouth pulled back a little, maybe not a smile, maybe a half-crazed grimace; Captain Northcross, one of Ajax's company commanders, never having been in combat now had the eyes of somebody who's seen lots of it. Gunny Lawler reacted to Ajax's murder by mumbling.

Hearing McCabe's step behind him, Lawler turned around. When he faced McCabe, his eyes opened, and he came awake, those eyes lying he was fresh and ready to go.

"Nothing up on your Policy Paper, lieutenant." Mention of this "Policy Paper" sent blood rushing to McCabe's face. *Kill you motherfucker!* He'd had it with Lawler. The time for relieving him was now. He was sure Ajax would have agreed.

The "Policy Paper" was what Lawler derisively called McCabe's camp guard system, part of which focused on catching Phord. Phord had incidents involving troops on the loose around the camp located with colored pins on the map correlating color-coded write-ups in the logbook. This was supported by orders he wrote detailing the radio, telephone, voice communications, the call signs, and counter signs, along with rotations of troops throughout the guard. There was nothing overtly derisive in Lawler saying, "Policy Paper," but his tone betrayed his contempt for McCabe's efforts.

"No mims." Lawler pronounced "pins" "mims." There was one more thing that made this moment particularly explosive: Lawler's teeth – or lack thereof. All his teeth had been pulled in Okinawa; and the battalion shipped out for exercises in Taiwan before the dentures arrived and then shipped out again for the Philippines when the teeth finally caught up with him here on this Filipino island. But they were the wrong size—too big for his face. And the sight of those monstrous teeth in his face in the field shaving-mirror and the pain in his empty sockets and the frustration of having those teeth chase his ass all over half of the western pacific had made his ordinary, Tarawa-stench raving almost benign compared to what he was capable of now.

He removed his choppers from his trousers' pocket and filled his mouth. "No pins up there. No logbook entries. Nada."

"Nada will get nada, Gunny. Compliments of corporal Phord."

Lawler blinked his bloodshot running lights trying to hide that the brain behind them was running on empty.

"Phord?" Lawler concentrated on the name, seeming to look at different aspects of it, in the slow-moving, ponderous way a deep-sea diver in brass helmet, air lines, and lead boots gets around a sunken ship.

"The reason why troops are not running out to the bush is they lost their organization man. He's either dead ..."

"... or he killed, Ajax, sir."

"No, I killed Ajax, Gunny."

"Or he knows who did. Why else would he disappear? The connection's there."

Trying to make his "connections", Lawler's face had the same look – Manny remembered – as Rollie's face when the poor bastard was trying to assemble an M-60 machine gun in boot camp. Burly, black-eyed Rollie racked up the highest intelligence and physical conditioning scores of any candidate in Manny's boot platoon. But he was a total screw up. Not that he lacked motivation. He was motivated. He tried as hard an any of the candidates. But he just kept screwing up: showing up at boot camp right off the train with a set of golf clubs, falling out for a night march with tennis shoes instead of boots, calling off the wrong number in the count-off! sequence. Whenever he'd realized he'd screwed up, he'd smack his forehead with the palm of his hand and say, "Rats!" His crowning screw-up was his amazing inability to assemble and disassemble weapons. And when such assembly and disassembly really counted, when the platoon would be given their first 48-hour liberty once every member did the honors with an M-60 machine gun, Rollie lay in the grass on the yard in front of the wooden barracks beside the railroad tracks in Quantico, Virginia in the October gloaming, looking at the M-60 parts spread out before him as if they had dropped from Mars, his fellow boots, the delights of their first liberty going a glimmering, screaming, "FIT THE GODDAM COCKING HANDLE ASSEMBLY INTO THE RECEIVING ASSEMBLY!"

"This is the way I see it, sir. The Old Man's murder has come down to a lack of discipline in this man's Marine Corps."

"Ajax's death ... lack of discipline, Gunny?"

"Yes, sir. Don't you see it? Well, I see it. Because I saw it. The discipline is gone. And it's gone because the discipline with the drill instructors is gone. You can see it in the private and lance corporals. You can see it in the corporals. You can see it in boot camp now. They have the instructor centered on the marching platoon. Can you believe that, sir?"

Manny shifted his feet. He nodded.

"The discipline all starts in boot camp and now in boot camp they're telling the drill instructors to be centered on the marching platoon. Now you can't observe from that close. If you're centered on a platoon, you can't tell what's going on in the first squad behind you. Understand, sir?"

Manny nodded. He was interested. There were a lot of pieces about this murder needing to be stitched together. Maybe this maniac possessed some kind of needle and thread.

"There's a lot of eyeballing, moving, scratching, which certainly wasn't done when I was a DI. The discipline in the recruits is not there because the discipline with the drill instructors is not there. It's not their fault. They're just not to be as good as they used to be. The degree of excellence in the DIs in the forties and fifties is gone forever. It's gotta start somewhere. It's gone. I don't think it'll ever come back."

"Where's the connection with Ajax's murder?"

"It's clear and simple, lieutenant. Look, the object of recruit training is to break down the boots. Take away their individuality. Make them feel totally useless. Then slowly build them back up, over a nine or ten-week period. It works. Basically, it works. And the best way to break them down is to scare hell out of them. And here's the connection to the murder. One way to scare hell out of them is to grab them. I grabbed. It was accepted that a DI could grab. Grabbing's not accepted now. And grabbing's important. Only way to get a recruit's attention is to grab. But today, things have changed to the point now where I don't think we're doing in boot camp what we need to be doing. Everybody's scared. I talked with officers at Parris Island. They're scared. When I was a DI, it wasn't that I wasn't scared. There's a lot of pressure on the street. It scares any DI. It's just that I knew what my job was. I knew what I could do and what I couldn't do. What I couldn't do – thumping for instance – I didn't do. I can't say I never did it. I may have done it unintentionally. One time, I was correcting a recruit's position with an M!4, and I had done it about four or five times in a row, and I finally got disgusted, and I slammed the rifle hard, to bring it up to the position it was supposed to be in. It hit him in the head, caught him over the eyes, and he bled a little. I didn't do it intentionally, but it was done. And I could've gotten in trouble for it. And then we played a lot of games you really weren't supposed to play. Like when I was a DI staff sergeant, and during hygiene inspection, I stripped naked except for my hat and belt and walked down the center of the squad bay in shower shoes while the platoon of recruits stood at attention, naked themselves except for skivvy drawers. You should've seen the looks on their faces. I put the fear of God in them. 'What's WRONG with this guy?' The only trouble was that the company commander came into the squad bay when I was doing it, roared, "Get into my office!" and told me never to do that again or he'd hang me for it. Hell, my other DIs and me would eat onions and drip shaving cream down the corners of our mouths and come onto the recruits like evil-smelling mad dogs, one DI roaring in one ear, the other DI roaring in the other ear, one in his face, the other directly behind him. That's what we called stereo. You see, the worst part of combat is the noise. It's not the bullets. It's not troops getting wounded and killed. It's the noise that's scary. I've often felt somebody totally deaf would do well in combat, because he couldn't hear it. So the louder it is in boot camp, the screaming and hollering, the better you scare them. Now, I'm coming to the point, lieutenant ... the point about Ajax and what happened to him. On one Sunday, the recruits were slow to respond to my commands. I sat down at a long table we had at the center of the squad bay. I told them, 'I understand you girls are a little loose this morning, right?' 'No, sir!' They were real quiet, you know. No noise. No motivation. 'Oh, is that right? Well, I'll tell you what. You're not going to waste my time. I'm going to waste yours. Get online.' They got online, and I made them stand there all day long. I took a stick and hit the table about every minute or so. And I did that right up until the time to take them to chow. I took them, and they came back, and I did it again. By the end of the day, I had almost driven myself crazy. Every time I hit the table with that stick, those recruits would almost come unglued. You could see it. It was really wearing on their nerves. I probably did it for about seven hours. And it took a lot of discipline on my part to sit there and do it. But I'll tell you what. That was one tight-assed platoon when I got done with them. And they never sloughed off on me again. Never. And I didn't want them to, cause I didn't want to sit there and hit that stupid table anymore. I mean I was sitting at the table, totally exhausted, my legs aching, feet swelling, and I'd see some turd down there reach up and scratch, and I wanted to ignore it. I said to myself, "Ignore it, you're too tired." But no matter how tired I was, I'd flip that table over, and it made a hellacious noise when it hit that cement deck, and I'd scream, run down there and grab him, drag him up to the PT corner and PT him for five minutes hard. I could be horrible. Not thumping horrible but crazy horrible. And here's the point ... there were times I'd put on a chrome dome, war belt and walk out into the squad bay after lights-out, holding a lighted cigarette. Recruits, thinking I was a fellow private walking fire watch, would whisper for a drag. I'd lean my face close to the recruit as he sucked the butt and the blooming light would light up my face and the recruit, seeing it was me, would shout in fright and pitch off his bunk. But that wasn't all. There were times when just before lights out, I'd have the recruits see me climb into a wall locker, in full uniform, cross my arms and close my eyes as if I was going to sleep. I'd have an aide let me out later when the recruits were asleep and then I'd get back in just before reveille, and after they woke up, I'd come out and they'd think I slept the whole night standing up in that wall locker and it scared hell out of them wondering what kind of animal I was. Of course, you have the ten percent who are too damn smart to fall for stuff like that. But the one thing that always worked was what we called 'Daddy is gone.' We'd purposely fail them during the first phase drill competition and then I'd say, 'Well, that's really good, girls. I take you out there and you make a darn fool of me. All this training that I've been giving you, coming in on my days off to teach you how to drill, and you go and blow it right out of your butt. You will pay the price for making me look like a damn fool.' Then before the final drill competition, I'd quit. I would come in on the Sunday before the final drill day and drill them and no matter how well they did, I'd find something wrong and pretend enormous disgust. I'd try a drill movement one more time. 'They'd screw it up, and I'd say, 'That's it. I've had it!' I would skim my hat across the grinder, tear off my belt, slap it onto my assistant's hand and say, 'Find yourself a new drill instructor, girls!' I'd stomp off the grinder and not come back till Tuesday about an hour and a half before final drill competition. Wearing loafers, civilian slacks and a polo short, I'd walk past the platoon as they were coming out of chow. My assistant would say, 'There's your old drill instructor, girls. Do you want him back?' They'd shouted, 'YES, SIR!' By God, you could hear that YES, SIR! All over the island. Then my assistant would shout that they should run over there to say they're sorry, say they wanted me back. Did you ever have seventy recruits coming toward you at about ninety miles an hour? They'd beg and beg and beg for me to come back. Half of them would be crying. I'd say, 'Okay, this is your last chance. You blow this one, I'm leaving.' We'd go upstairs, and I'd get dressed and take them outside and say, 'Right face!' and you could hear their heels come together, BOOM! I won the drill competition, almost every time! But the year I left the drill field, I saw the changes coming: an extra officer assigned to each series, the elimination of the punishment platoon; our DI games were cut down. I didn't know how bad things were getting until I was on pit duty during rifle qualifying before leaving Parris Island. I poured myself a cup of coffee from a thermos and began unwrapping sandwiches. A lieutenant came up to me and said, 'What are you doing, Gunny?' 'Getting a cup of coffee, sir,' I said. 'You can't do that.' 'What do you mean I can't do that?' 'You can't eat in front of the recruits.' 'Well, Jesus H. Christ!' 'You can't do that either, Gunny.' 'Can't do what?' 'Swear. You can't swear in front of the recruits either. That's a fifty-dollar fine.' 'All right. Fine, sir. No problem.' I stuffed the sandwiches and thermos under the bench and lit a cigarette. 'You can't do that either, Gunny. You can't smoke in front of the recruits.' 'Well, sir. I'm not a recruit. I'm not in goddam boot camp. Sir, you'd better get me the hell out of here. I might wind up in jail today!' The Gunny shakes his head. 'Couldn't swear. Couldn't smoke. Couldn't drink. Couldn't eat. What the hell! But that's the way it is today. I just stay the hell away from it. I don't want anything to do with it. And I think they're going to find out, the next battle, or the next war, that I'm right, and they're wrong. And you know what, lieutenant, now that I look back on it, I realize that that was the only time in my entire career that I felt like I accomplished something. That's my opinion. But who the hell am I? I'm only a gunny. Now here's the point, lieutenant .... "

On the far side of the tent, there was the commotion. It was a fire team returning to the CP. The team was one of the roving patrols acting battalion commander Major Gord instituted as extra security after the murder. Lawler looked at the team members grabbing coffee and sandwiches. Then he looked back at McCabe. He said, "Wait one, sir." Lawler flew across the tent. Spotting this onrushing terror, the members quickly dropped their snacks and assembled outside at port-arms, panicky swallowing. Lawler went from man to man conducting an inspection. His inspections of the troops had a unique intensity that strangely seem to encompass in thoroughness the entire electromagnetic spectrum. Those inspections left individual Marines believing they were better Marines than they ever thought they could possibly be.

After chewing out a Marine who had some discrepancy of uniform or equipment that Lawler spotted far away in the dark, he dismissed the patrol then returned McCabe. As the gunny approached him, the lieutenant saw the man's bloodshot running lights revealed that the brain behind them was running on empty.

"Here's the point, lieutenant ... the point I'm getting at. Your *Policy Paper* is fucked up. And that's one reason why Colonel Ajax is dead."

The worst thing about McCabe's violent temper was its gentleness, gentleness that wasn't apart from the violence but was the violence. In the throes of anger, he would be aware of a gentle admonishment. Like right now when he said, "I love you too, Gunny," and reached under his collars and removed the retaining clips to his first lieutenant's bars. He knew he shouldn't have said that. He knew he should not be doing this. But the gentle *Stop. Shut up.* in his mind actually egged him on. He inserted the clips into the bars' spikes then shoved the bars into his trousers' pocket. He said in a thick voice, "Let's settle this Policy Papers outside the tent."

Lawler raised his eyebrows. He grinned. He spit out his choppers. "Okay, sir, after you."

The temporarily de-commissioned lieutenant led the way into the dark so the troops in the tent couldn't see what transpired. As McCabe turned around, Lawler's fist came hurtling toward him. What McCabe understood in that moment he would never forget.

This battle-hardened Marine, the terror of the battalion, threw a klutzy punch, a right lead exposing his jaw. It might have served him in bar fights over the years; but from McCabe's perspective, it was pantywaist. But that punch wasn't what would stay with McCabe. What stayed with McCabe was this: he dropped his hands and let Lawler's goofy punch come at him.

Dropping his hands was Dimitri's handiwork.

Dimitri was a Ukrainian baker in McCabe's East Village neighborhood who taught the teenager McCabe Combat Sambo, a Russian military martial arts technique, that uses throws, kicks, punches, head butts and groin kicks. McCabe became a walking, lethal weapon on those mean streets. Few hooligans messed with him, and those who did regretted it in the forms of broken bones and hammered testicles.

Now, as Lawler punched, McCabe knew he could use the gunny's momentum to flip him on his back then with the heel of his hand, ram the gunny's nasal bone into his sinus cavity—courtesy of Combat Sambo.

But instead, McCabe dropped his hands. He didn't have the heart to take the gunny apart no matter how much he disliked him. He couldn't do that to anyone who didn't deserve it. The gunny's fist bounced off McCabe's shoulder.

"Okay, Gunny, I give up. You win." Giving up, McCabe felt a burning in his chest. The mean-street-educated McCabe – who cultivated a *killyoumotherfucker* look on his face when on those streets – felt that giving up was a violent repudiation of that street life. From his *kill you motherfucker!* perspective, it was wrong, but from both a moral perspective and the practical perspective of good-order-and-discipline, it was right. "Shake on it, Gunny." The gunny nodded, his expression saying, *mission accomplished against this goofball lieutenant.*

They shook hands. "Let's go back to work. We got a camp to guard. A murderer to catch."

"Aye, aye, sir."

"Call me *sir* after I get my bars back on." Despite his animus,

McCabe basically liked this man, who was your typical Marine madman noncom who could have the troops do extraordinary things. Though he knew that with Combat Sambo out of the question, he was going to have to do the old-fashioned thing and somehow, somewhere, relieve the bastard.

The mists McCabe walked through were shot through with light from the dozen internal-ballast, stud-mounted, 24-volt flood lights bolted to pine pitch-soaked wooden poles sunk into the tarmac around the perimeter of the camp. Right after Ajax's corpse was discovered, panicky Major Gord (the acting battalion commander) ordered extra safety measures, like equipping the sentries with bayonets and extra magazines of live rounds and having engineers install new, high-powered lights. Rubbing his shoulder where Lawler's fist had struck him, he came up to a sentry.

"Halt!"

"Lieutenant McCabe here." He was suspicious of the feeling of having bars back on his collar. He had spent his youth on the streets despising authority; and the payback was he became, as a Marine officer, an authority.

"Rabbit."

"Hole."

"Advance, lieutenant."

"Seen any troops?"

"No, sir. Just a ghost."

McCabe looked at the sentry in the steam-bath, flood-light glowing air, at his steel pot with the Marine camouflage cover (sentries were now ordered to wear brain buckets), his locked and load rifle at port.

"Where's this ghost?"

The sentry pointed. He turned his whole body in one motion to point. "Out there, sir. Twenty meters forward and three clicks port."

"What did he look like?"

"Like a ghost, sir. What else?"

"Walking these lines will I see him?"

"Most definitely, sir."

"Should I be careful?"

"Can't say. But he's not happy. I know that."

"Carry on, then."

"Aye, aye, sir."

He liked this lad. For that matter, he liked all the enlisted troops, except for Phord – though he probably liked even Phord, if only because he was enlisted – especially the ones below E-5. Even with his bars on, he felt he was one of them. He liked them as much as he disliked his fellow officers. And when this lad was killed a few months later in Viet Nam, cut in two after stepping on a Bouncing Betty (USA-made, our chickens coming home to roost, as McCabe thought Ajax would have said), McCabe, in his deep distress, thought of the boy and his ghost.

After checking on the sentries and the jumpy Marines on a roving patrol, McCabe returned to the guard tent. Lawler was not there. In the logbook was the yellow message paper Gunny Lawler had handed him right after he came back from his fuck-hut debacle.

SEE ME ASAP
IN MY TENT!
–A

McCabe remembered Lawler putting that message in his hand just before he found Ajax's corpse. The message prompted McCabe to head right away for Ajax's tent. He guessed Ajax had just written it. However, McCabe did not look at the time it was written, 21:47. Now McCabe understood the mix up. Ajax wrote the message at that time and gave it to a runner to deliver to the CP. The runner brought the message into the tent when Lawler and McCabe just happened to be out checking the lines. When McCabe didn't show up, Ajax went to the fortress to be a part of the social taking place there. Several hours after Ajax wrote that message, 2300, some five or six hours before he was murdered, the colonel still participating in the social sent a radio message to the CP for McCabe to meet him at there. McCabe was in the CP at that time. He got that message and drove to the fortress. When he met up with Ajax in the crowd of looped and horny dignitaries, his boss said, "Where the hell were you? I sent a message for you to come to my tent. Didn't you get it?" McCabe didn't know what he was talking about—until he got back from the fuck huts at dawn and Lawler handed him the message that had been lying on their shared desk all those hours. That "see me in my tent" message to McCabe was long out of date. FUBAR was alive and well.

McCabe crushed the message paper in his fist and tossed the paper into a 155-shell casing that acted as a trash can. He thumbed through the entries in the logbook, a dried coffee-spill forming a Rorschach ink blot on the facing leaves. McCabe took the test. He saw a bat. The bat changed into an image in his mind of Ajax's death face. That image changed into another death face, showing what a 230-grain APC round can do when a forty-five muzzle is placed against the temple and the trigger pulled. Another change: he was walking in mists toward another nightmare. The nightmare was forming into some horror he could not yet identify. He opened his eyes and shook his head. He slapped his cheeks. With mists boiling in his vision, he went down a walkway of side-by-side boards, sinking into mud-slop, to the piss tubes behind a canvas screen. He stood at the edge of the duckboards and emptied his bladder into the aluminum cone. Rising from the very ground just a few feet away from where he found Ajax's corpse 15 hours before, mists sprinkled his face.

Walking around the cook tent was a figure, singing. *"Wir sind das deutsche Afrikakorps,"* He spotted McCabe and said, "Ah, there you are, my young friend. I thought I had lost you. Father O'Toole said you were checking the lines. I wondered if you were coming back to hear about Shimada. You forgot your beer. You ordered a beer and didn't drink it. I have that beer and another beer for you and two for me. Father O'Toole has two too. We have a moveable Octoberfest. Doesn't matter. Father O'Toole, where are we moving to?"

Through the mist McCabe saw his friend trailing behind Baum, limping slightly, the old football grievance, his foot turned inboard, giving the appearance he was going left though he kept going straight. O'Toole said, "Back to the O club tent. We have found our fish. We will sink the hook and land him."

"But it's closed," Baum said. "We closed it."

"What's closed can also be opened, "O'Toole said. "What's lost can be found."

"Versalzen dem Tommy die Suppe," sang Baum softly.

"Oversalt the Tommy's soup," said O'Toole. "I've heard it before."

"We sang it on the retreat after El Alamein when the *khamsin* was blowing and our wounds were on fire because we had run out of morphine. Here's to the marching songs, and the troops who march to them. Here's to morphine, may it never run out." Handing two beers to McCabe with one hand and lifting one beer of the two beers he held in his other hand to his mouth, Baum drank deeply. His Adam's apple pushed against the priest's collar. McCabe saw in Baum's eyes that squinted and blinked fiercely when he drank that the man liked alcohol not wisely but too well. "We will now look at who killed Ajax through the reverse telescope of Shimada. And you must do what I say, my young friend, to track down Shimada."

"Who said anything about tracking down Shimada?" said O'Toole. "Colm, did I say anything about tracking down Shimada?"

McCabe looking at Baum said nothing.

"Maybe you don't want to track down Shimada," said Baum.

"Of course, we don't want to track down Shimada," said O'Toole. "We're leaving this island."

"Let him talk," said McCabe to O'Toole.

Baum said, "Look, you don't know me. You don't like me. I'm not sure I like you. But whether we like each other or not is beside the point."

"What's the point?" said McCabe. "Schopenhauer?"

"Blind, metaphysical will isn't the point. Need is the point. But even if you don't want to track Shimada down, you might need to track him down. Because Shimada is the answer to the murder."

McCabe was trying hard to convince himself this man was a spiritual force inspiring the island's people.

"The only thing we need now," said O'Toole, "is to get you out of here before Major Gord comes back to camp. Major Gord has been made acting battalion commander, and he's scared as hell he'll fail the job. He's panicked and ordered no outside personnel allowed in camp. I snuck the Father in to talk with you about why Ajax was killed."

"So, let him talk," said McCabe. "Rains, heat, mosquitoes, murder, ONI, and now this Kraut multiplies the delights." He said to Baum, "What do you want?"

"He doesn't want anything. I brought him here just to tell you about Shimada. I figured once you know about Shimada you'll see that Ajax's murder had nothing to do with you. Like your father's death had nothing to do with you. By the way, we need to pray for Shimada too."

"Your forgiveness depresses the hell out of me."

"I depress the hell out of me too, McCabe."

McCabe said, "Father Baum, what do you pray for? The return of the Third Reich?"

Baum looked at McCabe, his mouth straight.

"You miss the point, Colm," said O'Toole.

"Oh, it's the point again. The point is let's let him talk."

"Who doesn't piss you off since Ajax's murder? I'm afraid of what you're going to do in this pissed-off state."

McCabe said, "Tell me, my old friend, so what if you deep fry yourself in German guilt? So what if you become a priest and spend the last few years living in these jungles trying to get the locals to believe in some cosmic Jewish zombie? Is that an excuse to expiate your own sin of being in the wrong army at the wrong time?"

"Is being in the wrong a sin, my young friend?"

O'Toole said, "If he's right about Shimada, you're off the hook, Colm. There's nothing you or your guards could have done to prevent the murder."

"Talk," said McCabe.

"Get in my jeep, my young friend. Our finding Shimada will do my talking."

"I didn't bring him here to camp for you to go AWOL, Colm," said O'Toole. "He can do all his talking here."

"I can't talk here, my young friend. My talking means *showing*."

McCabe said nothing. He didn't move.

The German said, "Colm, do you just want to know about Shimada? Do you want to do something about him?"

"How long are we gonna be gone?"

O'Toole said, "Are you crazy, Colm? If Major Gord finds out …"

"I'll get you back for you to continue your camp commander duties. I know about duty, my young friend."

McCabe looked at Baum then at O'Toole. He looked at Baum again.

O'Toole gave McCabe the drive-block push again, pushing him toward the CP, except this push, though insistent, was gentle. McCabe pushed back against this gentle giant with his own football technique, an arm-flipper. O'Toole stopped pushing. Getting into a shoving match with a lieutenant wasn't in the battalion chaplain's job description.

"Maybe later," McCabe said.

"There's no later, my young friend."

"What're you saying? That you're going to take me directly to Shimada?"

"He can't do that," said O'Toole.

"Suit yourselves." Baum got in his jeep, beat-up WWII vintage. He started the engine and shifted into gear. The gear had a solid sound. McCabe noted they made things well back in WWII.

As Baum was letting up on the clutch, McCabe said, "Stop. Okay, but make sure we get back within the hour."

"Good move, my young friend. You won't regret it. Are you coming, Father O'Toole?"

"Don't do this, McCabe!"

McCabe started to get into the jeep. "Bring a weapon, my young friend."

"This is getting worse!" said O'Toole.

McCabe went into the guard tent. Lawler was standing at the overlay, maybe asleep, maybe awake, probably both.

"Looking for fuckups, Gunny?"

Lawler watched McCabe take the carbine off the hook on the test post beside his desk and sling a bandoleer of ammo over his shoulder. That look McCabe knew so well came into his eyes.

"I'm going to get the murderer."

"Good thinking again, sir."

"By the way, you can tell your grandchildren how you beat the shit out of a lieutenant."

Lawler was about to say something, but McCabe walked out before he did.

At Baum's jeep, O'Toole grabbed McCabe's arm.

"Are you nuts?" said O'Toole. "You have two choices, face reality or be disappointed."

McCabe gently pried O'Toole's fingers off his arm. He got into the passenger's side. He motioned with the barrel of the carbine for Baum to take off. Baum released the clutch. The jeep started to move.

"Wait!" came O'Toole voice from behind him.

Baum braked. O'Toole came running up, limping, the tropical moisture playing havoc with the arthritis in his knee. He got in the back, a San Miguel bottle he held clinking on an aluminum flange, and said, "Back in an hour. Understand, Father Baum?"

No answer from Baum.

"You're taking us to Shimada, right?" said McCabe.

"I'm taking you to where you must go," Baum said

As they drove, the one headlight that worked on Baum's jeep illuminated first jungle, then a cattle pasture, and then a village, kerosene lamps burning in windows behind mosquito mesh. Now and then, McCabe heard sea waves against a beach. He felt Shimada hiding out there in the night.

Baum laughed, "We're going to hell and back, O'Toole. Let's pray!"

"Watch it!" said O'Toole from the back.

Baum turned around and looked at O'Toole. "What?"

"Watch out!" shouted O'Toole. "Eyes on the road!"

"Shimada here we come!" shouted Baum.

"Stop!" shouted O'Toole. Sudden speed made McCabe's head snap back. McCabe turned around and saw O'Toole wasn't there.

"Stop!" said McCabe.

Baum kept going. McCabe swung his legs out then pushed with his hands against the seat. His feet hit the ground hard. Baum was going faster than he thought. He rolled over in tall brush. The headlight was going off in the dark. "O'Toole!" he called. *"O'Toole!"*

There was a crashing in the brush in the dark. The crashing approached McCabe. There was heavy breathing. O'Toole's beer-breath breathing. "That you, McCabe?"

"What the hell, Padre? Why did you jump out? You could've killed yourself."

Ahead, the jeep's red taillights and headlight froze. Then the light stabbed different parts of the underbrush as Baum turned around.

O'Toole said, "The only way I could get you to come back to camp. Come on, we're walking back."

"What about your colleague in magical thinking?"

"Forget Shimada."

"I'm talking about Father Baum."

"Colm, don't you see what you're doing?"

"Tell me."

"Going after Shimada is your private pay back."

"What're you talking about?"

"Your father."

"My *what?*"

"Your father's death and Ajax's death and coming out here with Baum … it's all connected. It's all bound up with the constant rage you're carrying around. When are you going to finally accept what is right in front of your nose? You didn't shoot your father."

"Padre, we're in the Philippines. We're in the boonies. We're after a Jap soldier. What the hell?"

"He shot himself."

"So what? That happened eight years ago. In another world. It's over and done with."

Baum pulled up. "My young friends, what's all this jumping out about? I'm not awarding paratroopers' wings."

McCabe hopped in the front seat. "Get in, Padre. We won't be gone long. Don't go bailing on us again. And shut up about shit you know nothing about."

O'Toole started walking. McCabe exited the jeep and got in front of him. "Do this for me. Do this for us. For our friendship. I just want to see what Baum wants to show us. Then we'll go back to camp. I promise. No obsession."

O'Toole was silent. Then he said, "Okay. But back to camp right away."

"Right away, Padre."

The jeep bounced down what was more footpath than road in the beam of the headlight then punched into a wall of vegetation, which crashed upon them like breaking waves. Masses of insects erupted in the headlight. Foliage-entangled, the jeep stopped, throwing O'Toole against McCabe. Baum stomped the pedal, the spinning wheels showered mud and vegetation.

Baum laughed. He switched off the engine.

McCabe rubbed his eyes and said: "Holy shit."

O'Toole said, "I knew I shouldn't have come. Start her up!"

Baum said, *"Heilige nacht."*

"Start her up. Let's split!"

"I grew up on a farm in Bavaria. The darkest night there was never as dark as the brightest night here. These stars are like the North African stars. This black night in the jungle will give you the shits, the holy shits, my young friend."

"Start her to hell up!" O'Toole said.

Baum said, "You too? You getting the shits too? Didn't you tell me, Father, you're great at not seeing what you're looking at?"

Baum switched on the headlight. There were leaves and shadows. He switched it off, and there was blackness. He laughed. "What about you, my young friend? What do you feel in this night?"

"Shimada! Shimada!" said McCabe.

"For twenty years nobody's been able to actually touch Shimada. I'll show you where he's recently been. I'm taking you to the bridge where he shot the girl."

O'Toole said, "What'd I tell you, Colm? He's not taking us to Shimada."

"Turn around!" said McCabe. "Go back!"

"My young friend is scratching an itch. *Ein jucken kratzen.* I know how he feels. I've had many itches I've had to scratch. Right now, I feel Shimada more than any other time. I can smell the stink of his spirit. Poor bastard. You know what that spirit is – that spirit that won't allow him to surrender, that spirit that's been killing the islanders and that killed Ajax? It's the spirit of *integrity*. In German: *Ehre*."

"You're a crazy coot, Baum," McCabe said. "Turn around."

"Drinking radiator water to stay alive in the desert will make anybody permanently crazy."

"Go back!" said O'Toole. He said something in German to Baum. Baum replied. Baum stopped and got out. He slammed his hand against the hood. The sudden noise made McCabe jump. "No going back!" Baum raged. "We've come too far!"

Baum got back in and started the engine, the headlight came on, and McCabe saw the dark pits of Baum's eye sockets in the headlight back-splash.

"I didn't know you spoke German, Padre," McCabe said.

"A smattering from a football player crip course."

The headlight illuminated a concave curtain of foliage that looked to be an overgrown trail. Baum pushed the jeep through the foliage then braked. He got out and unhooked a rat rod spotlight connected to a battery pack and said, "Follow me."

Baum's spotlight picked out another trail that angled off into the darkness beneath enormous, overhanging pink leaves that looked like the tongues of giraffes. Having had unfortunate experiences rubbing up on this island against innocent looking greenery that turned out to be mean-spirited, McCabe pushed the leaves away from his face with an arm protected by his buttoned P57 sateen sleeve.

Baum stopped. "Look," he ordered.

The light from the spotlight aimed by Baum broke up like broken glass against the wall of foliage tumbling in a breeze. There was an opening in the foliage, framed by sharp-edge rocks. It was big enough, if one stooped, to walk into. A jeep or maybe two could fit in the cave.

"Shimada's hideout?" said McCabe. He looked inside. He jumped back against O'Toole, knocking the remaining San Miguel out of the priest's hand.

O'Toole said, "Mother!"

McCabe said, "What the hell is *that in there?*"

"The living dead, my young friend."

"What's this have to do with Shimada?"

"Everything. It's why he killed your boss. You see, the Mangyans don't believe in death."

"Who are the Mangyans?" said McCabe.

"Natives on the island. The original people here. There're about forty thousand of them today. Go about in loin cloths. They hunt and slash and burn. They used to live on the coasts, but the Spanish and later the locals drove them into the mountains. Most of them reject Christianity. Don't believe in death. When a member of their tribe dies, they dig him up a year or so after the burial, clean and cover the bones with padding so he looks like a living human. They call the thing they create a *'sinakot'*. They welcome the sinakot back into the village with gongs and traditional dancing. Keep him in their house for a year or so then place him in an open coffin in a cave. There're caves like this all around the island. That's what they've been doing since when they first came to this island thousands of years ago. But the locals have robbed many of these caves. You saw what's left in this cave."

"Skeletons with knees drawn up to their chins," said McCabe. "Doing cannon balls except there's no water. But what about Shimada? The bridge?"

"This is all about Shimada. What's in the cave is the living soul of the people. To the Mangyans there are no dead, there are only living ancestors. The mountain forests they live in belong to their ancestors. Without these forests …"

"But Shimada …" said McCabe.

Pain radiated through the ball of McCabe's shoulder.

"Shhhh," said Baum. Baum was squeezing his shoulder. The power of that grip came as a revelation to McCabe. Baum was short. He was wide. And he was damned strong. "Listen," Baum said. He turned off the spotlight.

In the dark, there was the ticking of the cooling engine block. Something plopped in the leaves, a dropping fruit or nut, a ripping through leaves then plopping on the ground.

"Hear that?" Baum said.

"Jungle nuts," said McCabe. "Back to camp."

"No, *that*."

McCabe, rubbing his shoulder, said: "I hear nothing."

"Listen," Baum said. "You haven't spent half your youth inside the cockpit of a Panzer *Kampfwagen* with the musical strains of a V-12 Maybach in your ears. How come your hearing is worse than mine?"

McCabe listened to a faint, whooshing pulse, tinnitus triggered when his father, drunk on ethyl alcohol shortly after they left his mother in Cleveland and moved to New York, boxed him on the ear. (The only time he raised his fist to McCabe, let alone hit him.) Now on the air came a barely audible metallic sliding sound.

"*Listen!*" Baum switched on the motor. He stood up, his palm a visor, and squinted in the headlight beam, reminding McCabe of the photos of Rommel standing in his open Mercedes in the desert, goggles clamped to his *Schirmmutzen*, binoculars hanging.

He sat down, hammered the gear shift into reverse then forward and took off, leaves, branches, vines raining down. McCabe flailed the foliage and insects off his head and shoulders.

The jeep broke out into open pasture, jungle-rot odors giving way to cattle smells, cattle grazing in the moonlight. On the far side of the pasture, light flickered in trees. A vehicle was moving. McCabe heard the faint, metallic slithering, the sound of a motor, a truck motor. Out of the trees two headlights appeared. The truck was coming right for them, headlights jerking as it bounced over rough road.

Baum tramped the pedal. His jeep headed straight for the approaching truck. McCabe laughed. "What's this, Baum? Playing chicken?" McCabe and O'Toole trampolined in the bouncing jeep.

McCabe's teeth clicked. "Steer clear!"

The oncoming truck was almost on them, its headlights turning McCabe's world in the jeep to bright day. "You crazy! Turn! Turn!" O'Toole shouted. Both McCabe and O'Toole grabbed the steering wheel at once and jerked it hard to the right. The truck's driver was blasting its air horn. *I'm going to die on this godforsaken island,* McCabe thought. He clipped the truck's bumper. The jeep and the truck went off opposite sides of the road. Baum hit the brakes and half-tipped over. The truck splashed to a halt in a bog. McCabe saw large logs on the truck's carriage. The smell of fresh-cut wood and chainsaw oil was in the air.

O'Toole said, "Colm, I told you to stay in camp."

Having jumped out when the jeep nearly overturned, McCabe and O'Toole stood beside it watching Baum run to the truck and open the cab door. He pulled the driver out and swung his arm – again and again. There was a wet, cracking sound as one of his wild punches apparently connected with the driver's flesh.

The driver, hands covering his head, ran off, abandoning his truck.

Baum came back, breathing hard, illuminated by the headlights, his eyes jumping about in a crazy way.

"Help me right this jeep," Baum said.

Baum gripped the running board, crouched in a weight-lifter's squat, and heaved. The vehicle came upright, mud dripping and splattering in its wheel wells. Baum leaped in and started it again. "That truck is loaded with rose wood. The syndicate cut that wood on the Mangyans' land. That's their ancestor's wood. The syndicate has no right to it. They're stealing it from the Mangyans. That driver is complicit. He deserves a worse beating. And if he didn't run away, I'd give it to him. Get in! Are you with me or against me?"

"Against you," said O'Toole. "Colm, you got us way the hell out in the boondocks."

"We're fucked," said McCabe sadly. A curious aspect of his temper was that it often underwent a phase-change into great sadness. "Walking back is out now."

O'Toole and McCabe climbed in, O'Toole this time riding shot gun. Steering round the bend where jungle creepers spilled across the road, bulbous seed-scabbards growing from the creepers crackling under the tires, Baum said: "Look! Look!" A hundred meters upstream, a Mitsubishi 8X4, loaded with sawed-lengths of old-growth timber, was about to cross a truss bridge. "More rosewood," Baum said. "They're stealing more rosewood! *Ungeziefer!*"

"Where's Shimada?"

"I told you, my young friend." His breathing was asthmatic. "Didn't you hear me? Deaf lieutenants quickly become dead lieutenants. I told you I'm not taking you directly to Shimada. If I could take you directly to him, he wouldn't be Shimada. He wouldn't be the Japanese who's outwitted everyone on and off this island since the War. I'm taking you to where he was last seen; and from there …"

"You tricked us, Baum," said McCabe.

"If I really tricked you, you wouldn't know it. I learned how to trick from the best teacher, Rommel. He'd trick the Tommies so thoroughly that they didn't know it until it was too late. The trouble is, the trick was on him when he ran out of gas. And he knew it. We all knew it."

Baum looked hatefully at the bridge. He switched off the motor and walked to the bridge, bandy-legged, tanker's walk. Even his walk exuded hatred. The truck pulled up to the far edge of the bridge. Baum got in front of it and crisscrossed his hands above his head. The truck halted. Gas and sap odors got stronger. The driver got out. Three men, who had been standing at the end of the bridge, one with an M-1 slung over their shoulders, gathered around the priest. The silver in Baum's black hair, illuminated by the headlights, looked like flecks of foam. One man pounded his fist several times into the palm of his hand. The other men shouted into Baum's face. Baum threw himself down. The men shouted at him. They grabbed his arms and a leg and heaved.

Baum kicked and twisted and got free and stood up and walked back to the truck and lay down on the ground under its front tires. The men conferred with the driver, the three standing in a circle, their heads bobbing, arms waving. The driver broke off from the group and climbed back in the cab. One of the men waved the truck forward. The truck rolled slowly. The driver gunned the motor theatrically. On his back, Baum didn't move. He raised his head and looked at the wheels approaching him. He spit at the wheels. The men grabbed Baum's arms and legs and, leaning backwards, their boot heels digging, began dragging him to the rail.

O'Toole took off down the bridge. His bad knee made him move slowly and jerkily whereas decades ago, before his injury on the gridiron, he was fast and agile and hazardous to the health of opposing players.

McCabe ran. He reached O'Toole just as the American priest flung himself upon the three men who were trying to throw Baum over the bridge rails.

McCabe landed a haymaker on the ear of one of the men. O'Toole, raising over his head a stunned man whom he hit with his own haymaker, accomplished a helicopter spin. Then he tossed the man over the rail and into the water.

McCabe and O'Toole waited outside the office tent of acting battalion commander, Major Gord. O'Toole's arm hung limply at his side. The right side of his face was bloated and purple, and the eye that gazed out of the slit made by the folded-up flesh was not O'Toole's eye, not the eye of the philosopher/priest. It was a mad man's eye. Yet the eye on the other side of his face was inexorably O'Toole's: sad and compassionate. McCabe thought these two smashed-together looks were laughable, he who had nothing to laugh at since Ajax's murder.

McCabe was unmarked. His freshly shaved upper lip was raised a bit as he took in the faint offal odor emitted by his newly cleaned and pressed utilities.

Upon first arriving at the air strip, the battalion had secured the laundry services of a local family who, as it turned out, washed the Americans clothes in soiled water. The "washed" clothes all smelled faintly of feces. S-1 had switched laundry people, but McCabe had not gotten his utilities washed by the new group, hence that familiar odor.

There was another, different odor that was not on his utilities but in his nostrils. That was the odor of the local jail he and O'Toole were locked in last night. It was worse than any odor McCabe had ever smelled of; and it stayed with him even after he washed and shaved and changed utilities.

Sergeant Major Crow appeared at the entrance of the tent. He had broad, affable features, with permanent swelling of unknown origins on the side of his face. Though he went through heavy combat in Korea, he came back home unscathed except for an ear being half-shot away. "The major will see you now," he said. He winked at McCabe as if they were members of a secret society. McCabe had no idea what the society was about, but he let the man carry on with his knowing winks and nods. McCabe knew that having the battalion sergeant major on your side is always good. McCabe smiled and nodded. The sergeant major's wink seemed to say: *you'll get chewed out, but so what? You and I know the secret of what's important.*

Major Gord was behind the camp desk in the dim light of the half-rolled down tent flaps. He said, "I've never seen a bad situation that McCabe you can't make worse. Okay, gimme the skinny."

Gord looked out of eyes from a brain recently knocked cockeyed by San Miguels. He was in his sweet spot: being a terror of a boss while simultaneously bushwhacking through a brutal hangover. Gord lived two lives during the battalion's Far East tour: raving drunk nights, bear-trap sober days. The two endeavors overlapped. He never drank on the job, though he carried the effects of last night's drinking around in a kind of mystical aura of debauchery. This only enhanced the daytime terror.

"It is what it ain't," said O'Toole. He smiled out of the good side of his face, his mad man's eye glinting merrily.

"What? WHAT?" said Gord. His bleary eyes flashed, not unlike the madness in O'Toole's eye. McCabe wondered if Gord knew about the necktie. The image of that mutilated corpse came to him again, the tongue pulled through, the "necktie" establishing a kind of murder-marketing, the message being *get scared, we're coming for you*. ONI got the message. It made such an impression on the investigators that the one who interviewed McCabe told him the butchery had been declared classified; and if he told anyone about it, he'd be charged.

"We're all losing it in peace time," said McCabe. "Maybe an old-fashioned war will be good for what ails us."

"Be careful what you wish for," said O'Toole.

"What? WHAT?" said Gord. He put his fists on the desk and stood up. He was short with a round, muscular body that would go to fat when he became a civilian—if he lived as a Marine infantry officer to become a civilian again. His round, red face glowed as if a neon light were behind the skin. "What'd you mean losing it? Who's losing it? Who's losing what? And you ... you, Father ... you're our battalion chaplain ... fighting ... fighting!" His eyes darted back and forth between O'Toole and McCabe. He started to grin but mashed his lips. "See what I mean?" Gord's ready-fire-aim way was superficially pressed upon a basically sensitive nature. His tyrannical outbursts were facsimiles of the leadership style of the Marine Corps icon Chesty Puller. His tirades were often sprinkled – un–Puller like – with an occasional apology.

"It's all in the report McCabe and I wrote," O'Toole said.

Gord wadded up the papers and threw the wad at McCabe. His hands at his sides, McCabe let the papers hit him in the chest and fall to the duckboards.

"That's what I think of your report."

"Then you know what it says," said McCabe. He added after a pause bordering on insubordination, "Sir." He had learned that pause from the insubordinate guru, Lawler.

"I don't know what it says. I don't give a damn what it says. I want you to say what it says. You tell me what it says." Gord had a master's degree in international relations but being dyslexic – a wonder how he got the degree – had scant faith in the written word. He demanded oral reports from his subordinates.

O'Toole said, "Father Baum's got this idea that there's a Japanese soldier running this island who doesn't know the war is over."

"Tell me something new, Padre. Father Baum has already bent my ear about Shimada terrorizing the islanders."

"Baum figures Shimada killed Ajax."

"Yeah, yeah, he told me, he told me. He wants the Marines to go after Shimada. He wants us to do his dirty work. Good luck with that." Gord went around the desk and looking at McCabe secretly sheepishly out of the corner of his eye picked up the wad and came back and sat down and spread the paper out flat with an exaggerated attention to getting the job done right. McCabe remembered that's the very same way the major would spread paper money out on a bar just before starting a round of drinking or out on the table of a brothel living room before paying for multiple girls. "What I can't figure, how come you got beat up doing his dirty work?"

O'Toole leaned forward and with his finger tapped the papers in Gord's hands.

"What'd I tell you about the report!" shouted Gord. Shouting was his daytime mode of interacting with juniors, though he and O'Toole were the same rank.

"I wrote in the report that Baum drove us off into the jungle to a bridge. That bridge is Baum's Gethsemane."

"Don't get theological on me," said Gord. He pronounced it *theoloccical*, his tongue thick from last night's bender.

O'Toole took a deep, turn-the-other-cheek breath—trying hard to like, no love, this man—and said: "After the War, Father Baum went back to Germany and became a priest and came to the island a few years ago and immediately began ministering to the Mangyans. They run around in G-strings and fuck like rabbits. Unlike the Moros in the southern islands or the head-hunting tribes in the northern islands, they're peaceful. If you pop off in front of them, they won't retaliate. They'll pity you, thinking something's wrong with your character. That's why they so easily got kicked off their lands. They'd rather starve on poor lands in the mountains than go against their gentle ways. Also, they'll give you anything you ask for, which is nothing to begin with. Baum told us that a year or so ago a logging syndicate paid off enough officials to make a killing clear cutting their forest. Baum went high and right and got all Martin Luther King and set up a non-violent blocking action at the single bridge that led to the forest. He got Mangyans, Filipino students, and some locals to have a sit-in so the trucks couldn't pass."

"Cut the bedtime stories," Gord interjected.

O'Toole's forced smile displaced his irritation. "This is what really happened. The action worked. The trucks were halted. Baum said his action got play in papers across the Philippines. The loggers were checkmated until Shimada showed up before dawn to steal supplies. The German had them stocked by the river. Against Baum's nonviolent rules, a protester had a pistol. There was a shootout in the dark. A little girl heading for the latrine was shot and killed. Shimada spooked everyone involved in the action. They all felt they were in danger of being killed by him at any time on and around the bridge. They quit. The bridge action collapsed. The trucks rolled again. About that time, we came to the island for the SEATO exercise. The trucks are rolling over the bridge now. The forest is being clear cut. Baum says he can't get his action back on track until Shimada is killed or captured. Baum's got Shimada on the brain like a ..."

He stopped. He came around the desk and in a kindly, priestly way placed his hand, with its Notre Dame class ring, on Gord's shoulder. "Major... Are you all right?" Half of Gord's face looked like melting wax. One corner of his mouth unhinged and seemed about to drip off his jaw. O'Toole barked, "Sergeant Major, get the doc."

Gord's hand had turned into a claw that dragged papers off his desk as the acting battalion commander fell backwards onto the duck boards. He lay motionless. O'Toole dropped to his knees and cleared the major's airway by tilting his head and lifting his chin. The sergeant major came into the office, saw his boss on the floor, and hurried out. McCabe heard the clattering rings of a field phone being cranked and then the sergeant major yapping orders.

"What the hell?" shouted Gord. Abruptly, he sat up and looked around, confused. One second, he was on the floor unconscious, the next, he's wide awake. Blinking *Where am I?* He could be coming to bed after a night's carousing for all he knew. The drooping side of his face flushed. The corner of his mouth returned to its normal line. He got to his feet, picked up the papers from the duckboards and sat down behind his desk. He looked back and forth from O'Toole to McCabe then said, "Hot damn! What're you guys doing here? Oh, now I know. Where were we?"

"Major, you've just had a mini stroke," said O'Toole.

"To hell you say, Padre." He opened and closed his hand then flapped it hard. "Tingles like hell."

"We got the doctor coming," said O'Toole.

"For who?"

"For you."

"Not for me. For you maybe. Or that piece of shit lieutenant."

"Stress spiked your blood pressure."

"Padre, I eat stress for breakfast. I know why you're here."

McCabe said, "You seem okay now, sir. But you gotta see the doc."

"I don't gotta do anything but listen to your song and dance. Talk to me, Padre. What were you talking about?"

"The bridge and Shimada."

"Okay, the bridge and Shimada. Keep talking."

O'Toole looked at Gord out of his beat-up face. He had played football in the days when flimsy helmets could almost be folded up and stuffed in a back pocket. That's when men who had their own front teeth never really played the game. O'Toole's bruiser's features were counterpoint to the tenderness in his good eye. "Let's talk about this later. Doc will be here soon."

"Soon is too late. Talk about it now."

"After the doctor comes."

"To hell with the doctor. Go on. Go on!"

O'Toole swallowed. He shrugged. "Okay. Last night Baum took us to the bridge."

"Of all the stupid things for you to do!"

O'Toole glanced at the perpetrator of the trip to the bridge. McCabe raised his hands, palms up, and raised his eyebrows. "Figures," said O'Toole to McCabe. He looked back at Gord and said, "Trucks, loaded with rare rosewood … Major, why go on? Let's wait for the doc. After he checks you out, I'll go on."

"O'Toole, were you taught by Daffy Duck at the seminary?"

"Okay. I'll finish. At the bridge, Baum lost it. He lay down in front of a loaded truck. Guards jumped him. We rescued him."

McCabe said: "You should've been there, Major. Our battalion chaplain used one thug as a helicopter rotor to knock another off the bridge." McCabe sang: "Rah! Rah! For old Notre Dame."

Frowning on the good side of his face, O'Toole interrupted McCabe and said, "Enough! No more!" He turned back to Gord. "Baum got hospitalized. McCabe and I jailed – as you know."

"You don't want to know about that place," McCabe said. "On the concrete floor was a black splotch where a guy stole a can of gas, doused himself, and lit it to get out of there. We got sprung by some diplomatic maneuver."

"Diplomatic maneuver, hell," Gord shouted. "*I* got you sprung! I get woken up last night by a runner with a radio transmission that says two of my Marines are in jail. I thought it was some lance corporals out on the town they shouldn't have been in." Gord rubbed the side of his face then flexed and unflexed the fingers of his hand. His brush with a stroke enraged him. "Then I find out it's my chaplain and my camp guard commander. What the hell is this battalion coming to? I sent a message by corporal in a Mite to the town's mayor to spring you jerks immediately."

"And here we are."

"Yeah! Get the hell out of here. And by the way lieutenant, you're relieved as camp guard commander. This isn't a war. This is a goddamn peacetime exercise between us and others in the SEATO nations. The only war around is in Viet Nam. And we're not there—for now. So, you're relieved and confined to quarters until we can get the hell off this hell hole and I can get you written up properly."

"What?" said McCabe, unconsciously, or maybe consciously, emulating Gord. *"What?"*

"Don't what-what me, lieutenant."

"Not fair, major, relieving him over a minor transgression."

"A minor transgression? Oh, I guess brawling and getting jailed is a minor transgression. Just like you're not passing the swimming qualification before we shipped out was a minor transgression?" Good's one clear, sober eye, the other eye playing catch-up from last night, glared at O'Toole.

"What's O'Toole's swimming have to do with the price of bread?" asked McCabe. McCabe had heard Gord complain many times about O'Toole failing the qualification. The major seemed to take it personally. The battalion going overseas with swimming qual failure did not look good on the pre-deployment, inspector's report.

"Lots, lieutenant. Of course, you don't see it. Typical of you to condone officers busting requirements. You who've busted your share."

Gord opened himself up for a great reply. McCabe wanted badly to make it but kept his mouth shut.

O'Toole said, "Father told us he could link us up with someone who might help get Shimada. After all, if he murdered the colonel …"

"Father, have you heard of ONI.? OfuckingNI?"

"Office of Naval Intelligence."

"A bunch of the bastards flew in here. Interviewing everybody and his sweet brother. Messing with my battalion." (McCabe thought: *It's not your battalion. It's still Ajax's battalion even if he's dead.*) "Did you bring this information to the ONI guys that are fucking with our lives?"

"No."

"Why not?"

O'Toole was silent, trying to transmute his annoyance into love, a water-into-wine trick he was continually struggling, not too successfully, to accomplish.

McCabe said, "My call, sir. My call as camp guard commander."

"Which you are no longer, if you've noticed."

Killyoumotherfucker! McCabe's eyes said. He said, "Baum said he could take us to somebody who might give us leads to go after Shimada." He forced himself to soften his voice. "Baum said he's been studying Shimada and his actions for years and he feels he can finally put a stop to him. But he needs our help."

"Why didn't you talk to those ONI, Sam Spade wannabes about Shimada? They're not hiding. I can reach up my ass any time and pull one out for you. Like that red-haired, red-faced bastard who thinks he's Mike fucking Hammer. He even carries a forty-five in a shoulder harness. If he calls her 'Betsy' I'm going to barf. Which I've been almost doing a lot these days anyway considering the crap we're eating on this island."

McCabe said, "I figured we didn't have time to burn. So we took off to see if we could do it ourselves. "

"Great initiative, lieutenant. Poor fucking execution."

"Can you smell it on us?" said McCabe. "I can smell it on me."

The question went over Good's head. He had never been in a Filipino, rural jail. He kept on, "Ajax murdered. Filipinos up in arms. State Department all over me like cancer on a chain-smoker's lungs. ONI contractors crawling into every nook and cranny of this camp. Troops picking up superbug clap in the boondocks. My goddam chaplain duking out with Filipinos while standing side-by-side with a lieutenant who should've been tossed out of this man's corps a second after he jumped off the flying bridge."

From his trousers, McCabe took out a book of matches he used to light Coleman lanterns. He lit a match and held it up before Good's face.

The back scatter of Good's carousing last night dissolved in his eyes. Those eyes cleared. The skin under them tightened. His lips parted the way a python's jaws unhinge to eat its prey.

Gord spoke in a barely audible, quivering voice, "Get to your tent! I'm running you up right here on this island."

"What're the charges?" asked McCabe. He blew out the match. "Sir."

Good's normal high-tension voice returned. The side of his face had an odd, flat look, resulting from the stroke's after-effects. "Who the fuck knows what charges. Get out. Both of you."

McCabe and O'Toole walked out, past the Sergeant Major who said, "Doc's on the way." Having heard Good's rant, he winked knowingly at the lieutenant. At the same time, with his thumb and finger, he rubbed his shrapnel-kissed ear, the crus and scapha twisted scar tissue. McCabe winked in return, taking the ear gesture as their secret society communiqué – whatever it was.

"Tell him to hurry," said O'Toole. "A stroke is no joke."

In the sunlight, O'Toole, squinting out of one eye while the bad eye seemed to look in a different direction, said, "That was scary. For a few seconds, I thought it was all over for Gord. He's got to let up a little. The stress is clobbering him."

"Marine officers are addicted to stress. Anger pressure-washed Good's arteries. That's why he shook off the stroke."

"McCabe, you ought to charge admission for people to see a Marine lieutenant trash his career." He spoke quietly to keep the troops passing them on the camp street from catching his words. Quietly but with a ferocity that came all too naturally to the priest.

"He got to me."

"Who doesn't get to you, McCabe, since Ajax's death? You get pissed at anyone who looks at you the wrong way. What the hell was that with the match?"

"Checking his breath for combustibility. He didn't get it."

"He got it, all right. Another crazy stunt of yours—like jumping off the flying bridge. I heard about you and that flying bridge."

"That's behind me. I've got other problems now."

"The way I see it it's the *same* problem. In Basic School, there were strict orders not to jump off the flying bridge during mess night. Your unit had a mess night."

"Just sprained my ankles. Nothing broken. The higher ups understood I might not make such a bad leader in the Fleet after all, so I wasn't charged. A righteous chewing out was all I got."

"You've become a minor legend in your own time. The trouble is for the wrong reasons. Forget for the moment about getting relieved. Let's look at the deeper things. Jumping off the flying bridge, lighting that match in front of Good's face, all the other crazy things you've done that I know about and I'm sure those I don't know about … put a circle around all of them and they get back to one thing: You've been living a lie since you were a teen. Stop living the lie and join the human race."

"I said last night, *let's shut up about it.*"

"You were an angry teen. You hated your father. What's new? What teenager doesn't at times hate their parents?"

"No excuses, sir. Except he was a broke, action painter. The only money came from his disability check. We lived in a shithole apartment in a shithole neighborhood."

"So once, the angry teenager, postpones bringing his father his morphine. But don't you see? He was worn down by years of pain. All those purple hearts were enough for any Marine. It was *his* choice. *His* finger, not yours, pulled the trigger. In his place, with his pain, I might make the same choice. You too."

"I thought about that."

"What'd you mean?"

McCabe did not answer.

"Now I'm *really* scared."

"Nothing scares you, Father. I found that out last night at the bridge. And in the jail, you laughed at our jailers. Have you seen your face lately?"

"I've seen it. It doesn't win me a door prize." The Black Dog stared out of O'Toole's messed up face. "McCabe, get to your tent and sit there and don't do anything till this blows over with Gord. Sure, he's a hot head. But he's mostly a thoughtful guy. And secretly compassionate. All you have to do now is get off his radar screen for a while."

"He took my job away."

"Screw your job, McCabe. You wouldn't take my advice last night. I told you not to go driving off with Baum. Take it now. "

"Did I miss something? Weren't you there with me? Your face answers that."

"Do you think I was going to let you go on that suicide mission alone? I agree with Major Gord, going off with Father Baum was a stupid idea. I told you it was stupid. Even you knew it was stupid. You knew it was stupid even before you left."

"Next time I'll take your advice."

"I'll believe that like I believe the Second Coming's tonight. Sit in your tent and twiddle your thumbs until the storm blows over. Later, go to Gord and tell him you screwed up and won't happen again."

McCabe thought of accomplishing his own de-classification and telling O'Toole about the Spanish necktie. That would shut him up. But he decided against it. He knew the poor, sad priest was just giving boilerplate guidance—nothing to take personally. "Humble pie is indigestible."

"He'll probably give you your job back and we can all live happily ever after—that is, if there is "happily" where we're going."

"Going where?"

"Scuttlebutt. Look, I got some chaplain's work to dig out from under that's piled up since what happened to Ajax. After a couple of hours, I might walk past your tent. I want to see you doing a great job of thumb twiddling."

"Thumb twiddling isn't my military occupational specialty."

O'Toole's big hands wrapped around his rather smallish head. "Now I *am* scared as hell." He dropped his hands. He looked at McCabe as if he was seeing something new in his features. "Oh, no, don't tell me. Now I understand. Colm, last night you didn't just go to the bridge to see where Shimada shot the girl. Before we drove off with Baum, you had made up your mind about something else. Don't do it."

"Don't do what?"

"Don't do what I think you're planning to do!"

Three enlisted Marines passing by and saluting the officers looked puzzled at their chaplain's outburst. McCabe waited for the Marines to walk away.

"Thumb twiddling won't get Ajax's murderer run to earth either. "

"Colm, listen, listen, listen."

"You told me we should listen to Baum. You brought Baum into my life."

"I said listen to Baum. I didn't say follow Baum."

"My choice."

"I took a helluva chance bringing Baum into camp last night. After Ajax's death, you know Major Gord ordered that no locals come into camp. Baum's a local. I brought him into camp last night when Gord was off on a ship about to have a stroke briefing general. If he knew what I did, I'd make history being the first Marine battalion chaplain to be relieved."

"Did they teach you in seminary about the unintended consequences of Christian love?"

"I just wanted him to tell you about Shimada. I thought once you knew about him, you would understand it wasn't your fault Ajax was murdered. I thought you'd come to your senses and stop trying to fight anybody who looked cross-eyed at you. I didn't know that information would pull a slip hook on your inner catapult. Colm, get this getting Shimada outa your head. Let the Navy experts do the work."

O'Toole's sad passion combined with his recently misshapen face made McCabe stifle a laugh. He said: "Fuck the experts, O'Toole. You might not realize it, but I'm the only expert around these parts—except you."

4

Phord challenges the local law.

Phord walked with Mariko down a jungle road. Hard rain fell abruptly as if a prank bucket of water rigged over a door emptied on them. He removed his jacket and held it over her head, but she pushed it away — and pushed it away a second time. Her dress, now drenched and frazzled, her hair, strips plastered to her head and shoulders, her bare feet plopping in the mud, she walked through the rain by his side.

She said, "Father Baum told me. I didn't listen to him."

"Told you what? Who is this Father Baum you keep talking about?"

"My Jimmy Cricket. He told me to stay away from you Marines when you came to the island. I should've taken his advice."

From behind came the *brrr-rap, brrr-rap-rap-rap* of a jeep's engine and the blaring of the Beatles, singing. She pulled up the drenched chiffon roach, the rubber strip that was meant to hold up the dress but that kept slipping down off her breasts. The jeepney came up behind them, bouncing from side to side, its tires throwing water from holes in the road, the Beatles singing from Sony speakers bolted to the dashboard and hooked up to a reel-to-reel tape recorder in the passenger's foot well. As it went by, Mariko shouted a few words in

Tagalog. The jeepney stopped and backed up. It was an improbable sight: its stamped, slotted grille with a yellow-painted, rolled-steel guard; the shiny body three times its normal jeep length, painted with stylized flames colored orange, green and blue; the whole contraption chockablock with fancy mirrors, disk-lights, and a half dozen whip-antennas; three chrome horses attached to the hood; strings of lights decorating the top cargo rack where the spare was bolted.

She opened the back door, twisted her arm out of Phord's helping grip, and said, "Don't think it hasn't been lovely." She lifted her skirt, revealing her thighs, and put her muddy, bare foot on the mud-slathered rubber mat covering the steel passenger-step. Bouncing slightly in that athletic smoothness that defined her movements, preparing to spring into the back of the jeepney, she said, "What're you going to do?"

"Do? Me? Nothing. I just want you to be safe."

She pulled herself in, turned around and held the flat of her hand gently against his face as he tried to follow her. "Where're you going?"

"With you. Where're *you* going?"

"Home. Go back to your Marines. That's your home. This jeepney is going another way. See that road into the forest over there. Stand there. A jeepney that can take you close to your camp will be by sometime in the next few hours."

"I won't leave you till I know you're safe."

"Me safe? You don't get it. I'm not the one in danger." The driver hit his horn.

He said, "To hell with the driver. We belong to a mutual protection club."

"You protecting me? What a laugh."

The driver hit the horn hard. He looked over his shoulder and shouted in Tagalog. She jumped out, walked around to the driver, holding the wet, elastic of the roach up with both hands. Standing in the rain, crossing her arms to keep the roach up and her hands free, she drew greenbacks out of her clutch purse. She handed them to the driver. His hand snapped back and forth dismissively. She snatched out more notes. She grabbed his hand and turned it up and slapped the notes against his palm. She closed his fingers violently on the currency. She came back around the back, got in, and said, "The driver's agreed to go out of his way. He'll take you to a road that leads to camp. Get in." She held out her hand.

Batting her hand away, he jumped in beside her. As the jeepney shot up the road, she sat on the red upholstered bench, anchored her elbows on her bare knees and dropped her face into her hands. Her roach started slipping off her breasts. She straightened up and pulled the roach up and looked at him with hatred he found enticing.

Two men, sitting across from them, watched her.

"You're not safe wearing this dress. I don't care what you can do with that knife." Last night outside the fortress when he knocked the Assie doctor down, she did a thing that got his attention. She pulled a butterfly knife from a secret place in her dress in the small of her back. She flipped it open with an expert flick of her wrist, her thumb hiding the full length of the blade, the knife pressing against her hip. When she saw he wasn't going to try to harm her, merely take her away in his vehicle, she reached behind her back – her hand coming back empty.

"How safe do you think you are wearing this foolish American uniform? You think people on this island adore Americans?"

He looked at the two men. Dressed in Levis and tank tops, they stared at Mariko, their eyes eating her up. Both carried machetes in canvas scabbards hanging off web belts. "Don't argue. I'm going with you."

"Obviously. You're sitting beside me. But you don't know where I'm going."

"Doesn't matter."

She clasped her hands prayerfully. "Father Baum, help me!"

"I don't like this, Mariko," he said into the booming Beatles. "We shouldn't have gotten in."

She snapped her thumb and finger closed in front of her mouth then pointed at him to do the same with his mouth. She spoke a string of Tagalog to the driver. As the jeepney barreled down the jungle road, the driver looked at her over his shoulder and grinned. He wore a yellow Polo shirt. His arms were skinny but muscular. The two men sitting on the bench opposite her laughed, what was left of their teeth showing dentists were in short supply in this area.

"What're you laughing at?" said Phord to the men. The driver was laughing too. "What's he laughing at?" he asked Mariko. She shrugged.

The driver leaned over the steering wheel to peer through the windshield, wipers slapping. Visibility was reduced to the chrome horse ornaments at the end of the hood. The bucket burst of rain made a racket against the windshield and roof. Headlights of an approaching vehicle showed in the wall of water. The jeepney sped up. The headlights swerved off the road and stopped, and the jeepney plowed on, bouncing from side to side, throwing Mariko and him against the front seat then practically into the laps of the two men. Mariko, putting a steadying hand on the front seat, let her dress momentarily drop off her breasts. The men watched. "What're you looking at?" shouted Phord over the music. The men looked away.

The rain stopped quickly as it started, and the driver pulled up beside a cement shed topped with galvanized metal. There were five gold stars painted on the whitewash and the handwritten letters ← HE SHE→ beside two doors above short steps. Phord sniffed the odor of human waste. A shaft of sudden sunlight lit the wet concrete, garnished with Tagalog graffiti. The men piled out, one surreptitiously brushing the back of his hand across Mariko's exposed thigh. They went inside.

Mariko said, "The driver's stopping for a few minutes."

"What're you grinning about, Mariko?"

She made an impresario's sweep of her arm as if introducing him to the scene: the public toilet, the concrete sari-sari store, the tin roof propped up stripped-bark posts, the two, ragged-clothed, bare-footed men sitting under the roof in front of the store, vapor rising off the tin, the muddy, steaming road curving out of sight into the jungle.

"Don't look. *See*." Mariko said.

Phord looked again, thinking maybe he had missed something: mud, heat, vapor, low-lifes staring at Mariko, the cacophony of now Filipino music pouring from the radio in the jeepney: Phord took it all in.

"It's heaven," Phord said. "With you." It was a joke, but saying it, he believed it. He cupped her face in his hands and, without thinking, kissed her lips. Their second kiss. She let him—which was strange because his being an American in Marine utilities kissing her in broad daylight, her strapless dress plastered to her glorious body, was a violent transgression of the locals' mores. And a transgression of the vow he made last night.

He had taken this fatuous vow of celibacy many times before when it came to the females he procured for Ajax. Many of them offered their bodies to him, but he refused, though he wanted to accommodate. The vow wasn't for Ajax's sake but for his, afflicted as he was by an unbending probity in his character.

"I'm going to go in the store and see if we can get clothes for you."

"Another bright idea. You don't run out of them."

"You can't be running around in this wet dress."

She started to speak, but he placed his fingers lightly against her lips. Her eyes said she did not like his touching her. "There's nothing to say, Mariko. I'll take care of everything."

She peeled his fingers from her lips—as one might remove foul dressings from a suppurating wound. "You taking care of things? I'll see it to believe it."

The sari-sari store adjacent to the public toilets the driver stopped beside was an outpost in the jungle. Two low-lifes were sitting outside under the galvanized steel overhang framed by the colorful placards on the concrete walls advertising for CocaCola, Extra Joss "Extra Energy" and a medical brew in Tagalog with a fighting cock trademark. In their twenties, they sat at a little, round, steel table their dirty fingers wrapped around coffee cups. They sported the boiler plate machetes. Unlike the men in the jeepney, their machetes were strapped to their backs with the web belts. One of them carried a forty-five in an Army surplus holster. Their eyes followed him as he went inside.

He said to the fat, old woman, with half a nose, the missing part a fleshy nodule, sitting on a high stool, "Dress."

The sari-sari was a little bigger than the back of a 3/4-ton truck. Thousands of items were crammed into it, taking up every square inch of space, even ceiling space, many individually wrapped in colorful, plastic packages, a micro-economy wonder, down to the cigarettes, cut in half and up for sale in a glass jar next to a tin cash box on a mahogany board. That board, in the States, would have fetched more than the store and its contents were worth.

The woman frowned and shook her head. "Dress," Phord said and ran his hands down his hips and shimmied. The woman buried her face in her hands and laughed.

A finger tapped his shoulder. He turned around. One of the young men had come inside, the one who packed the forty-five. "Out," he said. "Out." He pointed to a back door. Phord wondered if he should take this guy down here, half-wrecking the place, or get the job done outside, when he saw in the sunlight that the man's face had undergone a transformation. "Out the back, please!" Phord looked out the front door. A pink jeep with a candy-cane surrey top had pulled up outside the public toilet. The jeep had no doorjamb rods, normally found in front of the G.I. half top bows. The driver, a young Filipino man, was talking with Mariko who had just come out of the toilet.

Phord started outside. The man stepped in front of him. "No. No. Don't! Don't! Man in jeep. Bad man. Bad man. Very bad. Go out back. Don't let him see you."

Phord brushed him aside and went outside through the sunlit vapor to the jeep.

"What gives?" he asked Mariko.

"Great news. You're under arrest."

"By whom?"

"Him. Pulis."

"Where's his uniform?"

"His badge is his uniform."

The young man in the jeep wore U. S. Army fatigue trousers, a white shirt and a Marine officer's cover with "scrambled eggs" on the visor. The cover was pulled down at the sides as if he had been wearing a double-ear headset. A brass badge with a spread-winged eagle, its talons clutching a banner that said POLICE, was pinned to the cargo pocket of his shirt. He had a forty-five in a side holster. His face was pinched in around the nose as if the eyes and mouth were folding into his nasal cavities, and there was concave piece of skull above his ear the size of a golf ball. He motioned over his shoulder with his thumb.

"Get in the back," Mariko said.

"Who says?"

"He says."

"Who's he? Him?'

"You nearly murdered that local back in the village."

"Mariko, get in the jeepney."

The driver of the jeepney hit his horn. It sounded Mary Had a Little Lamb. With the usual aggression she showed Filipino men, Mariko barked in Tagalog. The driver shrugged and pulled around the jeep. Roy Orbison's *Pretty Woman* was the new, high decibel offering from the scratchy, pirated tape – fading as the jeepney went off down the jungle road.

McCabe said to Mariko who was in the back of the chief's jeep. "How could he do that? Why didn't he wait for us?"

"That's not your ride."

"What?"

"Here's your ride." She leaned forward, wet, black hair swinging off her cheek, which had become pale now under the brown, and patted the back of the front seat.

The chief behind the wheel looked at McCabe and grinned.

"To hell with that." McCabe made an ump's safe call with his hands. "No way."

The chief swung his legs out of the jeep and stood up, wincing and pressing his fingers into the small of his back. He walked around the front and came up to McCabe, reeking of cologne.

He raised his hand, an effeminate hand with long, manicured nails — though his fingers were dirty — and hooked his thumb on the holster's hammer strap. He was looking, not at Phord but the road into the jungle where the jeepney had disappeared. He avoided looking at Phord's eyes.

"I don't like this, Mariko. It doesn't jive. Pink jeep. Surrey top. He won't look at me. What the hell?"

"Get in. We have no choice."

"There're a lot of choices."

"Like what?"

"Like think."

She pointed with the finger of her hand that pinched the top of her dress tight. "Your thinking isn't on his radar. He wants you in jail so other people can think. You really hurt that young man, that boy, back there. You'll break the chief's heart if you don't let him put you in jail."

"Of course, let's not hurt the chief's feelings. How the hell did he find me so quickly?"

"We're all wired together on this island. Word gets around fast."

She spoke in Tagalog to the chief. Looking off into the distance, the chief frowned and unsnapped the hammer strap and closed his fingers around the forty-five's butt and lifted the weapon a little out of the holster.

However, the gun calmed Phord. With it holstered, he was at a disadvantage. Now that it was coming out, he relaxed, knowing what to do.

Phord shoved his raised middle finger into the chief's face. The chief pulled the gun out and, continuing to look away, pointed it at Phord. Phord turned his head and said, "Mariko!" Simultaneous to the chief swinging his head around to look at Mariko, Phord clamped his hand on the weapon and twisted it. It was in his hand before the chief looked from Mariko back at him. "Ow!" he said, rubbing his finger and wrist. He still would not look at Phord.

Aiming the weapon at the chief, Phord got behind the wheel, lowering his butt on what turned out to be stuffed Naugahyde, not GI steel.

Mariko had climbed out.

"Get in, Mariko"

"You think I'm crazy?"

Phord put the jeep in gear. "Mariko, please, come on." She looked at the chief. She looked at Phord. She raised and lowered her hands and sighed.

"Okay," she said. "Why am I doing this?" She got in beside him and put her face in her hands.

"You don't have to go with me, Mariko."

"Just go," she said into her hands. "Father Baum should see me now. What a laugh."

Driving off, Phord saw in the rear-view mirror the chief giving him the Filipino two-fingered, *you-lowly-dog* gesture.

5

Baum is gone.

"*Mister Marine ... helps me*".
"*Don't worry, Sweet. I'll bring help.*"

He went out onto the apron of the ancient gun porch where the social was going on under a string of many-colored paper lanterns and a vault of tropical stars. Officers from the SEATO countries and civilian dignitaries were making conversational din, draining booze from crystal stemware, and chewing on finger foods got from tables against a stone parapet, interspersed with rifle loops, 70 feet above rocks and breakers. Standing by an ancient, spiked, 19-inch Spanish naval gun was Ajax, Ajax in his field utilities regaling a group of young officers.

"My friends, some of our United States Army Airborne friends haven't shown up tonight. Are they boycotting the party and playing this game under protest? Their silent whining – which is sometimes not so silent, my friends – is the sex trickling down the leg of this exercise."

"Sir, there's a girl in a back room. She's in trouble."

Driving a Mighty Mite in drizzle, McCabe went across a hardwood-planked bridge, the fore and aft sections missing cross-planks. Going onto the bridge then going off, he had to guide the tires down log stringers, a kind of low-wire act. Racing across the bridge and bouncing up a steep hill on the other side, McCabe was hardly aware he had performed a kind of miracle of driving, having focused on missing steamer-trunk-sized boulders flanking the road.

At the top of the hill, the road ran between two Mangyan huts with cogon grass roofs, rainwater guttering off thatched window-flaps propped by bamboo poles. A half dozen women and children in each hut were gathered at the windows watching him pass, their broad, yellow-black faces impassive.

Just beyond the huts, the road forked, the left going through marsh grass, the right an open strip of churned mud, both swallowed by jungle. McCabe stopped. He couldn't remember Baum coming to this fork during the fun and games last night. If he took the wrong road, he'd end up lost, burning daylight.

He got out. Pulling up the hood and spreading out his poncho, he splashed through liquid mud in the rain. Someone spoke sharply inside the hut.

An old woman with a stump that ended above her elbow used her remaining hand to knock the flap-props free. With a rustling of cogon grass, the flap closed over the window. Before it did, he saw a young girl's face. It reminded him of the face of a girl in a second-floor window when he was leaving the Lower East after his father shot himself. Two weeks after the funeral, his mother had picked him up in her station wagon to take him to live with her and her second husband in Atlanta, Georgia.

Now, seeing the little girl's face beside the old woman brought back that recollection of driving out of the city beside his mother and the little girl looking at him out of a tenement window.

The hut he approached stood on poles, a five-foot, hemp-strapped, bamboo ladder leading to a bamboo door. From the hut came a robust odor of close-packed human habitation, flavored with a strong fish odor. He grabbed the rain-slick ladder-rungs and lifted himself up and just before he lifted the window flap and looked inside heard the snick-snack of a forty-five racking a round.

McCabe knew that sound — a sound burned into his soul. He heard that same sound when he was fifteen and sitting outside the door of his fifth-floor, ghetto walk up, clutching the white paper pharmacy bag with three bottles of the blue, 200 mg, morphine sulfate tablets, thinking: *suffer, you bastard. You made me suffer. You made Mom suffer. Now you suffer.* His father was behind that door waiting for the pills, his combat wounds on fire. And then behind that door, the metallic snick-snick. The shot. McCabe bolted into their apartment and saw on the floor beside the window in the East River light his father loved to paint in, the body and what was splashed against the wall.

Now, separated by thousands of miles and many years from that experience, he slowly backed down the ladder. The crack and the whop in the air beside his ear came simultaneously. The movement of air was a gentle kiss on his temple. Passing just a few inches closer, the round would have struck his mastoid bone, and his face where the round exited wouldn't be there — or at least wouldn't be recognizable as a face.

Needing to dive for cover, McCabe forced himself instead to stand there. The old ghetto street trick: pulling a Caro Palo in the face of bad facts. Why he did that now instead of running in panic came from the *killyoumotherfucker!* code.

Adhering to the code made him do many strange things throughout his life, as it did now. He turned around, walked back to the hut, climbed the ladder and pulled up the flap. He looked into the shifting dark with the outflow of zoo-odors now mixed with the odor of a fired forty-five. He spit. His mouth was dry, the gob hanging off his chin, representing as much Caro Palo as he could muster now.

McCabe took the road that paralleled the sea. The drizzle stopped and bolts of sunlight stabbed mists shimmering off the road and the flanking foliage. The muddy track turned into pavement of sorts, cracked and mealy WWII asphalt, hastily poured out and steamrollered by Seabees, possibly under fire.

On the side of the road, five men were pushing and pulling on a stuck-in-mud carabao cart. Tethered by loops of rope-reins running from its nose ring over and under the swept-back horns to a wooden yolk rigged to the cart shafts, the carabao stood there, vapor rising, flies circling, exuding its typical, eternal passiveness as the men struggled mightily. McCabe remembered a lecture titled "Welcome to the Philippines" given a week before by a Navy lieutenant to the Marine officers in the wardroom of the Valley Forge, a WWII aircraft carrier with a wooden flight deck, converted for helicopter operations, that carried Ajax's battalion to Far East ports-of-call. "When they're wild, water buffalo are the meanest bastards on the block. They'll rip you a new asshole soon as look at you. On a per capita basis, they kill more people on these islands than snakes. But when they're tame, they go Gandhi. Non-violent in the extreme."

The men got the cart rocking, the driver flicked the carabao with a thin stick. The carabao, its tail raised, shoulders tightening, fist-sized clumps of mud flying up behind its hooves, lurched forward. The cart rolled out of the mud and onto the asphalt.

"Can I help you?" said one of the men. Except the "man" had a young woman's voice. "I'm Sister Lucia. That's my problem. What's yours?" She wore cotton work gloves, a short-sleeve, navy blue, industrial work shirt, cotton pants and canvas sandals. She had a short-side haircut.

"You're a nun?"

She removed her hand from the glove clamped in her armpit. With her bare fingers, she held up a crucifix hanging on a thin chain around her neck. "Get with the program, my friend." She slipped the glove back on.

"I'm sorry, sister. A nun you don't look like."

"Don't be sorry. People who say they are sorry often make a mess of this world." She pressed her hand against her flat chest. "You're looking at Vatican Two. Or more precisely, Father Baum and Vatican Two. Which a lot of traditionalists have their balls in an uproar over. Excuse my French."

"You're from the states?"

"Sure."

"Cleveland, Ohio, I bet."

"How'd you guess?"

"The Cleveland accent. I used to live in Cleveland."

"Are you bragging or complaining?"

McCabe tried to laugh but couldn't. His hands were shaking and his mouth felt stuffed with dried weeds – the effects of being shot at. Throughout his life, he was aware he scared easily. That's why *killyoumotherfucker!* helped. "You can't know that Cleveland accent unless you live there then leave. You don't hear it when you're there. But when you go away and hear it, it's unmistakable."

"Yes, Cleveland, Ohio. The Mistake by the Lake. Except for the Browns. We won the championship last year, and we'll win it all this year too if we can get the blocking up front and fill in the holes in the secondary. I presume you're here with the Southeast Asia Treaty Organization."

"Yeah. I guess you've gotten a load of us running around these boondocks shooting blanks and being critiqued with umpires with white bands around their arms."

"Can't wait till you military types clear out. The chopper noise. Troops all over the place. Whores imported from Manila. 'Get outa here SEATO and don't let the door hit you on your back on the way out,' is what I say. But I guess it's better than war."

"Can't make the comparison. I've never been to war."

"I heard one of your Marines was killed. A colonel or something."

"Our battalion commander. Shimada killed him. You know about Shimada?"

"Of course! The War is over. He doesn't know it. So he keeps on killing. We must love him. But we must capture him. Or worse! By the way, what're you doing out here alone? I see you're a first lieutenant. Don't you have blanks to shoot?"

"Decided to look for Father Baum instead. Help him with Shimada. Is this where he lives?" McCabe pointed to an old stone archway that opened out on a courtyard with a big tree and, behind the tree, a one-story, rattan-walled house. The house had an open veranda and a corrugated metal roof. A dozen children were playing in the courtyard. Three women watched over them.

"Yes, but he's not here now. Of course, even when he's here, he's not here. He doesn't belong to us but to the people."

"Okay, but in his skin, where is he now?"

"In the hospital. Getting sewed up. Getting his cracked skull x-rayed." She watched his reaction. He didn't react.

"How do I get to the hospital?"

"Take this road for about three miles. You'll see it on the right. We sisters wanted to go see him. But he sent word he wants no visitors. He wants us to continue his work. He says the work is more important than his corporeal body." She bowed her head and pinched the bridge of her nose. She raised her head and dropped her hand and looked at McCabe, her eyes wet, defiantly wet. She was young and rather pretty. "Last night Father Baum was beaten up at the bridge. Evil people want to kill him. But you can't kill love. His love lives in all of us. Father Baum's love inspires us to live the work through Christ we are called to do by being better than we are. With Father Baum leading us in Christ our work is consecrated. We've had our setbacks. Shimada killed the child. The bridge action has fallen apart. The logging is starting up again. But he says we will win in the end by holding fast to love. He'll be a saint one day. I've seen his miracles." She raised fingers to her mouth and shook her head. "You didn't hear that. I didn't say that." She crossed herself. "He's taught us so much!"

"What's he taught?"

"Nonviolence. He's taught that nonviolence keeps us in control. He taught us violent systems don't know how to respond to nonviolence. He taught us nonviolent change lasts longer than violent change. He taught us nonviolence can help win the loggers to our side. But most important of all, he's taught us to love. He doesn't deserve what they've been doing to him. He told us many times, 'We must suffer like our Lord suffered if we are to stop suffering.' But still it is hard. It's hard to see him suffer so much. His suffering makes us all suffer. "

"I was there last night at the bridge."

"You were?" She grabbed his hands and squeezed them lovingly. She looked into his eyes. "You were at the bridge when he was beaten up?"

"Yes."

"Bless you! Bless you!" She dropped his hands and kissed his cheek. "Did he lie down in front of the truck like we heard?"

"Yes, it was one of the bravest things I ever saw."

"Oh, yes, he's brave. But he's so much more. He is love. He is love manifest in our corrupt flesh. Go see him in the hospital. I can't. He won't let me. He wants us to continue the work. But he might see you. Go to him. Tell him to hurry back. He told us many times he is not long for this world. He told us that his death will be a feather in the wind compared to the work with the people that must go on. Go see him and tell him to hurry back – but only when he is well."

McCabe began driving off. "Oh, lieutenant ... lieutenant!" He stopped and she came running up. Sister Lucia said smiling through tears, "Get Shimada. Capture him or…" She leaned in close and whispered, "…kill him."

"We'll see." As he drove off, she shouted after him, "Go Browns!"

The hospital was in a house like Baum's house, one-story, with a wraparound veranda, but this had a straw roof. McCabe stopped the Mite and walked past a square of plywood with a red cross painted on it. Somebody had sloppily painted a question mark in the upper right quadrant. On the veranda, there were a dozen or so people, old and young women and children (no men) were eating fruits and vegetables laid out on a blanket on the walk boards. At the end of the veranda, a woman in her Sunday best, a white blouse and white skirt, toothless, a walnut-sized growth on her cheek, was frying meat on a grill over charcoal burning in an iron catch pan. Inside were more women and children and a few men. The men were sitting on folding chairs around the walls, and the women and children sat on the floor, eating food spread out on blankets. Bubbly coughing. Children crying. Fried meat and hospital odors.

"You're here to see Father Baum?" said a tall Filipino in a white lab coat. His black hair fell over his ears and the back of his collar. He had a wild look in his eyes, one of which was slightly crossed. On rope sandals, he walked with great self-confidence to McCabe and thrust out his hand. It was covered with a rubber glove that had several brown stains. McCabe didn't take that hand. "I'm Doctor Lopez. I'm the head devil in this hellhole."

"Doctor, is the Father here?"

"Which Father?"

"Baum."

"So you're an American Marine. My brother was a Marine. Killed at Tarawa. A botched job. No high tide. Higgins boats hung up on the coral. Leathernecks attacking through hundreds of yards of waist-deep water. The Marines are experts at botching jobs. But it's the lance corporals and corporals and sergeants who have to UN-botch the jobs their superiors create. Follow me. I'll take you to Father Baum."

They went down a long corridor flanked by doors opening onto views of patients under mosquito nets in various stages of consciousness on Army-issue cots, most surrounded by family members. McCabe sensed the food odors giving way to the odors of urine, feces, and carbolic. The doctor said, "My brother was a mess steward in the officers' wardroom in the Navy and wanted to get on a fast track for his American citizenship. Then he stupidly joined the Marines and died a Filipino citizen."

McCabe, resisting an urge to pinch his nostrils against the odors, said, "Was Father Baum hurt badly?"

The doctor shrugged. "Father Baum's like my brother. My brother put his life on the line to become a citizen. Baum's putting his life on the line for the Mangyans. My brother was a mathematical genius. He was studying calculus and trigonometry when he was fourteen years old. He was going to be a doctor. But the botched job at Tarawa took care of that. He was a lot more intelligent than Baum. Baum's a little stupid if you ask me. Well, all Germans are stupid. They're smart but stupid too. Stupidly, Baum wades in to help the Mangyans. But it's a botched job. There's too much money in the forest for it NOT to be cut. Eventually it'll be cut. Baum's just putting off the day when it's cut. Millions of dollars to be made, on one hand, and the wellbeing of half-naked savages on the other hand. Who's going to win? Do the math. Even my math genius brother couldn't do the math. He joined the Marines. Flunked that test. Of course, Baum doesn't do the math either. Oh, that's strange. Baum isn't here. Where's the Father?"

The doctor had stopped by a room whose window looked out on a small scrap metal yard, surrounded by concertina wire. On a cot, sheets and a blanket were neatly folded and stacked. No one was in the room. "Ummm, Baum was here an hour ago."

"Is he all right?"

"Who?"

"Baum."

"Oh, the Father. Yes, he's all right. A few cuts and bruises. A cracked skull. That won't stop Baum. It should stop him. It would stop me. But not him. Baum can't be stopped. That's his big problem. Baum won't listen to reason. Like he took Vatican Two and ran with it to its illogical conclusion. Vatican Two said nuns could exchange their habits for normal clothes. Baum told the nuns under his jurisdiction to do just that. A lot of people around here are scandalized. They like their nuns dressing like nuns. A lot of people say these nuns look like sluts. They don't say it outright. At least, I haven't heard those words. But that's what they're thinking. I know what they're thinking. And it's all Baum's fault. Baum won't listen. Like he won't listen to those who tell him to give up his bridge action. The political and military powers here on the island and in Manila have pleaded with him to give up the action. Think Baum will listen? So last night, he gets beat up again. And he'll get beat up in the future because he won't listen. And the trees will be turned into gold and the Mangyans will leave their forest home for the delights of eating from trash heaps in the Manila slums ... the blood, the cracked skulls, the broken bones, the killing of a little girl by Shimada ... all of it will come to nothing. Well, how about that? Baum is gone. Checked himself out without my say-so. Probably went back to the bridge or up into Mangyan country or maybe the fortress. Sometimes in a cell in the fortress, he does a shortened version of fasting for forty days and forty nights. But I'll be seeing him again. He'll be back. We've got a bed for him for the next time he gets beat up. Or a tray in the morgue. Just like we have a tray in the morgue for Shimada. They're both already dead. They just don't know it yet. They'll either kill each other or somebody else will kill them. Either way, they'll come here. To a bed or to the morgue. I'm sorry, did I introduce myself? I'm doctor ... oh, I did. I'm losing it, losing my mind. Like Baum, I should be outta here myself. Back to the states. I'm Filipino but an American citizen. I got what my brother didn't. Got my medical degree in the states and came back here to help the poor. Useless. Useless. Baum and I – Baum and Shimada – all useless. Why are you looking for Father Baum?"

"Shimada is why."

The crossed eye stared at McCabe. "You poor bastard." He waved his latex-gloved hand as if McCabe were a fly to be shooed away. "He conned you too. What makes you think you can capture Shimada on Baum's say-so?"

"Not capture. Kill."

"Smart guy! The Japanese government, the Philippine government, our local government, the islanders ... they've been trying to get him to come out of these mountains for two decades. You'd better bring your whole Marine battalion to do the job. And it still won't be enough. Sorry, I must go. You find Baum. The violence inside that German makes for the nonviolence outside. Excuse me, I have to go back to trying like hell being useless."

They walked back to the porch. McCabe said, before stepping off, giving way to an old woman who, with mouth bloated with betel-nut juice and coughing hard, came up and pushed aggressively past him: "Where might I find him?"

"The bridge for starters. Maybe the fortress. Okay, smart guy, how many Marines you bringing to do the job on Shimada?"

"Only One. Me."

The doctor started to speak but then closed his mouth. For once, he had nothing to say.

6

Phord goes in circles to get somewhere.

Phord stopped the chief's jeep at a fork in the jungle road. "Byrne would love this, stealing the chief's jeep, being a fugitive. *Woh-who-ey! who-ey! who-ey!* Okay, which road back to boy?"

Mariko pointed to the road on the right. The road angled through tall trees that rose like flying buttresses overhead.

Phord drove through jungle broken up by cattle pastures then came to a village, larger than any Phord had seen. It was composed of low-slung structures of sheet metal, bamboo wattling, cement blocks, rough-cut planking, all flanking a potholed, asphalt street. As they entered the village, she touched his arm with her fingers. Tender touch, with the same wonderful, Mariko tenderness she held his face kissing him for the second time.

"Stop here," she said.

Phord pulled up beside a plaster-walled structure with a red neon-sign BAR above the door. The structure stood out from the others on the street not only because of its white-washed walls, browned at street level from the side-splash of passing vehicles, but also because of its prison-like thick, wooden doors and shuttered windows.

"What's this, Mariko? Where are we? I thought we were going back to the boy's village."

"We're where we are."

Jeeps and buffalo carts passed on the street, people staring at Phord in his Marine utilities and Mariko in her evening dress, wet gauze dangling from her waist and breasts.

Two men stood beside the door, apparently waiting for the bar to open. Their mouths drooped, and their prominent Adam's apples in their unshaved necks bobbed as they swallowed, thirsty for the first drink of the day. Mariko spoke in Tagalog. They laughed, and she laughed back.

"You know these guys?"

"All my life."

"What's this? I don't like this. Why'd you take me here? Back to the boy, Mariko."

"No, you go back to camp. The boy'll be all right. Anyway, you'll never get to see him. I'm sure the chief called ahead. Police will be waiting for you at the boy's village. Take this jeep back to camp. Walk away from it. The chief'll get it back. Go back. You don't belong here. You don't belong anywhere except with your clueless Marines."

"You're making me jumpy. You know this place?"

"My home. I've lived here all my life. Look, you insulted the chief. You embarrassed him. He'll get back at you. I know him. He's as bad as they come. I'm going to get cleaned up and put on fresh clothes then I'm going to Father Baum's place. Take this sea road straight back to your camp."

"What are you going to do there?"

"That's between me and Father Baum."

She started off toward a two-story house set back in trees across the street from the bar. Unlike the shuttered-windowed, barred-door of the bar, the house, sided with split-bamboo wattling, had open verandas on the ground and first floors and open windows.

"Mariko, wait. What's going on?"

From the second floor of the house, a woman screamed. Phord saw a round, brown face framed in the window. The face disappeared. Footsteps raced down inside stairs. Through the door, across the veranda rushed an elderly woman, dressed in the cotton blouse, skirt and bandana of the locals. She came right at Mariko, screaming and clawing the air – stubbing her toe on a motor scooter, intake manifold lying discarded in weeds. Clutching her foot, she hopped momentarily, then clawed at Mariko's dress. Mariko did not move, hands at her sides. A portly man in a wheelchair came out onto the veranda. He had close-set eyes and thick hair spiked at the temple from sleeping with his head continually on one side. His eyes were bleary, and sleep-drool glittered at the corner of his unshaved jaw. He was grinning and gesturing with a hand, two fingers of which were locked, paralyzed, against the palm, gesturing as if to say to the woman, *let her have it!*

The familiar voice called from behind him. "Hello, my sweet."

"Where's my money?" Mariko said, pulling the ripped chiffon over her breasts in a nonchalant way as if this woman ripping her dress was a common occurrence. The nonchalant movement of her hand contrasted with the hardness in her voice, hardness Phord had heard only once before.

Phord turned around. There was Makisig. Phord had not heard him approach. He had come up behind him on silent, guerrilla feet. Ignoring Mariko, he removed his aviator glasses and stared at Phord out of that face. He said, "Hello, my sweet. Top 'o the world to see you here."

7

McCabe finds the sweet uses of being stuck to a tar baby.

"Mister Marine... helps me."

"My friends, the mistake the Army made was agreeing to allow Marines to be the aggressors on this exercise. So my Marines capture the Army Airborne commanding officer when he goes out to his hole to shit. Why's he getting upset and saying it's not fair? That officer had no idea that you take people out by waiting for them to come to their shit holes. And the fact that we ambushed those poor bastards from reverse-slope spider holes three meters away and tore up their boots and put holes in their legs from the blank-wadding... is that my Marines' fault or the fault of lousy flank security?"

"Sir, about the girl in the storeroom, the girl in trouble..."

McCabe stopped at the bridge Father Baum had lay down last night under the wheels of the truck. It was a Bailey bridge with cross-braced steel, clamped transoms, and plank stringers, thrown across the river decades before by the invading Americans.

A guard with slung M-1 stood at each end. One of the guards turned toward McCabe. His hollow-cheeked face made McCabe stare. It looked just like the face of the man who had walked up to McCabe all those years ago and changed his life forever. At the time, he was five or six years old and playing with tin hellcats in the backyard of his Cleveland duplex. The man came out of the back door, his mother behind him. She said, "Colm, this is your father."

Back then, McCabe had been waiting for as long as he could remember for his father to return from war. There was a photo of him on his mother's bureau, a full-cheeked, handsome young man in civilian coat and tie with kind eyes under thick eyebrows that seemed to speak directly to McCabe: *I know you and I love you, and I'll be with you soon, and we'll never be away from each other again.*

This was not that man. This man standing before him in the October heat and the weedy smell of Lake Eire was not the man in the photo.

This man wore a Marine uniform with sergeant's stripes. His cheeks were sunken under high cheekbones, eyes blinking frequently with a watery rage.

"You're not my father," young McCabe said. He went back to playing with his airplanes and waiting for his father to come home.

Now, sitting in the Mite staring at the guard—same face, different man—McCabe remembered those words he spoke as a child. It was his father, changed by the war; but even living with him for years in New York, a deep part of him had a hard time accepting him as his real father. Even now, he felt that doubt.

Fifty meters up-stream was a pile of rubble, burned to clots of rain-soaked ash-lumps with spikes of scorched metal sticking out like bristles on a hedgehog. McCabe surmised this was Baum's supply dump for the bridge-action, torched by the logging syndicate.

A bare-chested, lanky man in GI trousers and flip flops was pushing a wheel barrel heaped with ash to the river. He upended the wheel barrel, and the trash spread out in the slow-moving water in sooty eddies. The man pushed the empty wheel barrel back to the pile, grabbed a long-handled shovel, took a swig from a bottle of San Miguel at his feet, then a swig from a bottle of Jack Daniels beside the San Miguel, shoveled ash into the barrel, dropped the shovel and pushed back to the river.

A big truck with chainsawed-and-scaled, primeval logs crossed the bridge. One thug, holding the sling of his weapon with one hand waved the truck on with the other. The truck, its 1940's cab mud splashed, its roof caved in apparently from a falling tree, drove up the broken asphalt road McCabe had just come down. McCabe smelled the sappy odor of freshly cut wood.

The wheel barrel man motioned with his finger held carefully against his stomach out of sight of the guards. McCabe got out of the Mite and walked over to him.

"*Magandang umgaga*," McCabe said, using words from the phrase book given to him aboard ship by the Naval officer after his *welcome-to-the-Philippines-don't-get-the-clap* lecture.

"Get out of here, my friend," he said.

"You're American?"

"A Flip. But I used to live in Bakersfield, California. Hell hole of the world. At least that side of the world."

"I just got here. Why get out?"

"You're here looking for Father Baum, aren't you? The Father's not here. Do the same. Be not here."

"You're drunk."

"Of course. But not dead. Like you'll be soon. Or so fucked up from a beating that you'll wish you were."

He waved his arm in a curious way, a stringy, well-muscled arm smeared with soot. "The guards can't hear me. But they can see me. If they think we're friends, I'm fucked. So, I'm pretending to tell you to get out of here. Though I'm your best friend." He smiled, no front teeth but a face, if he had front teeth that, with a couple of cheekbone adjustments would have gotten good reviews for a leading-man screen test. He waved his arm and pointed as if telling McCabe to leave. "See the man who's coming up to the guards?" he said in a low voice, looking at McCabe, not at the guards. McCabe looked at a man who appeared beside the guards. He wore black trousers, a white shirt, and black tie and had a pen protector in his breast pocket. He was looking at McCabe and talking to the guards and rhythmically punching his palm with his fist. "They're talking about you. They're wondering what a Kano is doing here. Especially a Marine. They're jumpy as hell. They know the Father'll be back. He'll be back with a stronger action than ever. I'd join them, but booze is my wife and there is no divorce in our future. You know about Shimada?"

"Yes."

"The Father says the Marines are going to help get Shimada. He's telling people to get back to the bridge." He started walking away, speaking to McCabe behind him, waving his arm. "Go three miles down the road by the river. You'll come to a gas pump next to a red shack. Go inside the shack. There's an old man with a blind eye. He's called Cesar. Tell him Pedro sent you. He'll tell you where the Father is. God bless Father Baum, the poor, drunken, horny bastard."

McCabe drove down the river road, lined by trash-clapboarded shacks, to the gas pump by a cinderblock shack, slapped over by cheap, red paint, the raw concrete showing in patches. Inside, in damp air thick with odors of grease and metal filings, were stacks of new, used, and worn-out auto parts. From behind the shack came the voice of an old man, singing a song or simply complaining in a sing-song way. *"Lulu ... lu ... lu lulu ..."* Apparently coming from an outhouse carrying newspapers, he was startled when he saw McCabe. He wadded the papers and threw them in McCabe's face. His lips caved into a toothless mouth.

"Father Baum. Have you seen him?"

The old man bent over, a faint cracking in his spine, long hair growing from his temples (he was bald on top) swinging across his face and picked up the paper wad and cocked to throw it again at McCabe.

"Baum," the man said with the same ferocity with which he threw the wad. With a claw of a hand, black with grease, grabbing McCabe's sleeve, he drew the lieutenant into a back room of the shack where ledger books, papers and auto parts were piled on a desk. Beside the desk was a small safe, its door open. The old man snatched a leather pay pouch from the safe's depths. It was unzipped. He opened it wide and upended it. Nothing came out.

"Baum took your money?"

The man threw the pouch at McCabe. It sailed over his shoulder.

The old man kicked the pouch. McCabe saw he was missing a big toe, keloid scar tissue capping the stump. Wincing from the pain of arthritic legs that wobbled as he walked, he went outside to the gas pump, a metal hand-pump apparatus topped by a glass tank and a glass bowl. The bowl was painted with the same cheap red used on the cinder blocks, but a Texaco star showed through. He shouted a few Tagalog words toward a willow-wattle shack beside the cinderblock one. A barefoot girl of about ten came out and in baggy pants and a dirty, T shirt stepped to the old man. She had red hair, a brown face, and a thin nose broken to one side. Her eyes and mouth were sneering.

The girl said to McCabe, "Cesar said Baum took the money."

"Father Baum, you mean?"

"He's no father to me," she said in easy English. "Is he father to you?"

"Who's your father, girl?"

"Take a guess, you bastard American."

"Where'd you learn gutter talk?"

"From my bastard father. He speaks gutter German. Do you want me to speak German?"

"Go ahead."

"I can't. He never taught it to me."

"Why did Baum take the money?"

The girl and old man exchanged words. The girl said, "Fuck him.

And fuck you."

"Soap will help your mouth."

"Try it, asshole."

"Where did Baum go?"

"To get more money."

"Money for what?"

The girl and old man spoke to each other, the old man getting angrier, and the girl putting her hand on his arm to calm him. She said, "Uncle says supplies."

"Supplies for what?"

The girl's laugh was a sneer. "He's going to stop the trucks again. He says the Marines will kill Shimada. He says people can go back to the bridge. He says he'll pay Uncle back."

"Does Uncle believe him?"

"Yes, Baum will pay him back. Baum never lies. Uncle will get his money back. But he's still angry. He says he could have gotten all the money he wanted from Makisig."

"Who the hell is *Mak-sackg*?"

"Makisig, you stupid bastard. *Mah-kay-sig*."

"Will Baum be looking for Mak-sig?"

"Makisig! *Mah-kay-sig*."

"How do I find him?"

"Who?"

"Mak… whatever his name is."

"Makisig! Makisig! Can't you speak fucking English?"

"Where is Father Baum?"

"Go fuck yourself looking for him."

"Get in. I'll pay you to take me to Father Baum."

The girl defied McCabe by turning on her heel starting for the shack. McCabe grabbed her arm. The blade of the butterfly knife suddenly twirled in her hand, swinging on its pivot pins, snapped into sight. Making a practiced move with her wrist and the ball of her shoulder, the girl flicked the blade at the underside of McCabe's wrist, nearly slicing an extensor tendon. McCabe let go and stepped back, admiring this creature of poverty who could bring out a knife seemingly from nowhere.

"Check this out. Where the hell do you pull that from? A little tiger you are. Where'd you learn to use that knife?"

The girl jerked her wrist and the knife clacked closed. She slipped it deftly into a pocket scabbard strapped behind her back.

McCabe pulled an MPC note from his wallet. He pulled the ends, snapping it. He raised it above her head. The girl leaped, her fingers raking the air. "Take me to Father Baum, and it's yours."

"Okay, asshole." With a sweep of her arm, she grabbed the note. She folded it, compressed the fold between her thumb and finger, then reached behind her back and slipped the note beside the knife in the scabbard.

"Tell me, are you Baum's kid?"

"Go fuck yourself." The girl hopped in, pivoting, and leaping athletically, just as a moment ago, she had spun in a ballet-like way on the ball of one foot and the heel of another to whip out the butterfly knife. *"Go! Go!"* said the girl, pointing. McCabe saw the gas needle next to E.

Sliding her dirty little hand back and forth, the girl signaled to turn off the river road. The track, deep tire marks in mud, went into jungle dense with shiny, large-leafed vines sporting red, spear-shaped flowers and smelling of VapoRub. Just as McCabe thought the track would end in a wall of foliage, like the wall Baum had driven into the other night, the foliage parted, and they drove into an open field where a few mangy cattle grazed on weeds.

"Which way?"

"Straight." The Mite bounced violently in suddenly swampy ground strewn with big rocks—McCabe, careening from side to side, feeling a light touch inside his utility jacket. The girl was out of the

Mite and running.

McCabe stopped, jumped out and sprinted. She was swift. He ran for nearly a hundred meters before he caught her. He grabbed her arm and spun her around. He pried at the tiny, dirty hands, speckled with bug bites. The girl kicked at McCabe's balls.

"Drop the wallet."

"I'll break your face, asshole."

McCabe pressed his thumbnail hard between the tiny knuckle joint. The girl yelped and kicked and kicked... and McCabe was remembering, remembering leaving New York in the station wagon and the girl's face in the window.

McCabe let go. "Okay, keep it." The girl snatched it out of the mud and ran off. McCabe returned to the vehicle. The girl ran back. Tears made paths in the dirt of her cheeks.

"Take your wallet back, sir. Will you be my father?"

8

Counterpunch!

Phord found himself the guest of honor in Makisig's bar.

Three more of the unshaven, unlovely, and unloved joined the two early-openers; and shots and beers flowed—*on the house*, Makisig ordered, *in honor of our distinguished guest*. The men laughed a good deal and clapped the "honored guest" on the back and urged him to drink up and performed their bar-feats, one touching the end of his nose with the tip of this tongue, the other taking out his glass eye and dropping in his beer glass, the third trying to do a toe-touch but being a bit ahead in alcohol-intake did a face-plant and lay there laughing

Makisig was the convivial host, greasing the conversation, laughing a lot even when Phord could see nothing funny to laugh at. Shortly, Makisig announced he had paid enough, the guest was not that distinguished to merit more than one free drink per drunk. The men gladly switched to paying. Doing so, they rather forgot about Phord, who taking small sips from a bottle of San Miguel was waiting for Mariko. The men gossiped about their local affairs, the price of a water buffalo, a house in town half-burned down, the ways of making a few extra bucks selling things to the SEATO troops.

Phord watched Makisig through all of this. He was the same

Makisig whom he had first met. The "Top 'o the world!" Makisig. The happy psychopath. Phord got the "happy" right away (the "psychopath" coming later) when he first met Makisig shortly after the battalion landed on the island.

Phord had driven Ajax to a social event in a large, open-air house in town and was sitting in the battalion commander's Mite outside the house waiting for him to come out with a female on his arm or instructions for Phord to get a female for him when Makisig came out and approached the vehicle. It was the first time Phord had seen Makisig; the man's face startled the corporal as if a Grade B movie monster jumped out of a 3-D screen, but the slight, temporary shock was replaced by the good cheer Phord would invariably come to feel in the Filipino's lively presence.

Makisig pressed into his hand a tumbler of mint gin fizz bedecked with spirals of lemon and lime peels, cooled with crushed ice, and topped by a tiny, paper umbrella. "I'm on duty," Phord said to this stranger whose dark, twisted limbs contrasted with the white, untucked barong tagalog made of pineapple fibers. "Your duty is to drink this, my sweet." When Phord brought the fizz to his lips, the glass cold in his fingers in the hot, tropical evening, and took only a small sip (taking duty seriously), Makisig said, "Top 'o the world!" And a partnership was born.

Going into business with Makisig wasn't so much to get money for himself but to take care of the troop's needs while earning money for his destitute, crippled mother. Through all his subsequent interactions with Phord dealing with the girls and the troops, Makisig remained the same, top-'o-the-world madman. No challenge confronting the two was too daunting for Makisig. When the first fuck-hut Makisig rented fell through because the owner, the mayor, wanted more money and threatened to shut the operation down with the help of his three-man police force if that money wasn't forthcoming and if, by the way, he didn't get a cut of the proceeds, Phord got schooled on leadership. As

Makisig reported this, a barely detectable ripple passed across his rock-formation features. It took Phord a few moments to realize that the man was laughing and that Makisig had reframed the predicament as a joke.

"Nothing I can't handle, my sweet." How he handled it, Phord did not know, but as it turned out they got the same hut with police protection thrown in to boot and no apparent take on the mayor's part. Phord came to understand Makisig's reframing technique as a defining experience of his life. He knew that being the guest of honor in the bar was just another Makisig reframing—to what end he did not know.

Makisig was filling a shot glass from a whiskey bottle's pouring spout, the patron holding the glass with one shaky hand and wiping his thirsty mouth with the back of the other, when light from the suddenly opened door made Makisig's gold earring sparkle. Seeing Mariko come in, Makisig said something to the patron who was downing the whiskey in one gulp. The patron clomped the empty glass on the countertop where the locals playing hand-slamming dice games over the years had left dimples with their rings in the rock-hard, swamp-wood surface. With a wobble, he turned on his swivel stool and stared at Mariko walking toward them. Phord saw in the drunk's wet eyes that her beauty hit him in the gut to the extent he, the drunk, might be in love with her.

Her eyes narrowed in that angry way that made her look exceptionally beautiful. "Why are you here?"

"I don't know. Why get angry about it?"

"Didn't I tell you how to get back to camp?"

"Yes."

"Don't give me your goodbyes excuse. Haven't goodbyes already been said?"

She wore thong sandals and a blue, sleeveless, O-neck jump suit. Her lavish, black hair was washed and half-dried and combed behind her shoulders. This was a new Mariko, the old Mariko in the black, strapless belonged to the social on the fortress's gun porch, to the finger foods, the dignitaries, the lanterns drifting like moons against the night sky, the drinks, the fragrances of the beautiful escorts' perfumes and bath salts.

This Mariko in the simple getup, sans makeup, hair blowzy, this Mariko dazzled more than ever. As she gazed at him faintly amused, amusement that pointed to a deeper understanding of something in him he did not want to understand, he knew why he didn't go back with Byrne. If he was in love, it was unlike any love he had ever experienced. It was love like a phantom-limb pain of the soul.

He leaned toward her. She raised two fingers to her lips and shook her head slightly, warning him off. He dropped his hands to his sides and drank in her beguiling presence, a faint, delicious grinding sensation in his chest.

"Remember, my sweet, one hundred percent for me rips me off."

"Makisig, take me to the boy. I won't feel right till I know he's okay. I can get our battalion doc on the case."

"Forget about the boy. I'll take care of the boy. Anyway, the boy's doing fine. You knocked him out. But he's up and around. He's fine. Everything is fine. I'm seeing to it."

"How do you know?"

"I know everything."

"He's a war hero," said Mariko. Her strange smile when she said "hero" made Phord think she knew far more about Makisig than he would ever know; and what she knew was not pleasant.

"Haven't you figured out that I know everything on this island? I'll talk to the chief. I'm sure his fingers are itching to turn the key on the jail door you're behind. So, I've got to straighten things out with him before he lives his dream. Don't get arrested. Don't go to jail here. You won't get out with all your body parts where they should be."

"He'll take care of the boy and the chief," Mariko said. She said this to Phord but was looking at Makisig. A darkness under the surface of that look puzzled Phord.

Phord said to Makisig, "If I hurt him badly, I want to help. I couldn't live with myself if I can't help."

"Excuse me while I sing the Marine Corps hymn," Makisig said. "But it's a done deal with the boy. He's okay, and you're in the clear."

"You're sure?"

"Done deals are my specialty."

"Let me see him."

"You calling me a liar, Marine?"

"You know me better than that."

"I'll take you back to camp."

"Which means I'll never see Mariko again."

"Is that so bad, my sweet?"

"I don't know, Makisig. I'm still trying to figure it out."

"Do your figuring on the way back."

"I don't have to go back right away."

"You Marines won't stay forever on the island."

"Staying on this island with Mariko might not be such a bad thing."

Makisig looked long into Phord's eyes. The skin under the Filipino hero's eyes twitched, and he clicked his dentures. "Okay, my sweet." He looked at Mariko. She looked back at him. Phord thought she nodded, but he wasn't sure.

"Datu," Makisig called to a curtain at the end of the bar. A pug-nosed man with a deep chocolate face, darker than any Filipino face Phord had seen, licking a cold sore at the corner of his mouth and rubbing yellowish sleep-crust from his eyes, pulled the curtain aside. There were two contrasting aspects to him: one was his face, like the mug shot of an axe murderer itching to murder again and two, he held the curtain bunched in his fist at his throat like a bashful teenager caught naked in the shower. "Wake up and take over. The guest of honor and I are off."

"Off where, Makisig?" Phord asked.

"Where you can think it over. Not going back is a serious thing that must be thought over."

"So is leaving Mariko. I'm not going without her." He made that decision only when he spoke it now.

"Mariko will come with us. She'll soothe your feelings while you do your thinking."

Phord looked at Mariko. She was looking at Makisig.

"Where're you taking me?"

"Bali Hai. Your special island."

Gripping the wheel with three fingers on one hand and two on the other (the only fingers that worked in hands repeatedly broken by the Japanese), he said cheerfully in a sing song, "Come with me! Come with me!"

Having left the chief's jeep in the village, Makisig was happily driving his own with Phord riding shotgun. Mariko was in the back.

They drove off the paved town road and onto a red-dirt road and up a long hill, the side of the road crumbling into gullies. People clad in rags worked grain fields. The huts were a slapdash of sheet metal, plastic tarps, grass thatching, salvaged wood, and tar paper. A view of the sea opened as the jeep reached the top where a shack on poles leaned over a miniature open-pit mine smelling of pigs. Makisig stopped at a fork in the road. To the right the road dipped into jungle. To the left the road ran into jungle but toward the sea. Mariko said something. Makisig took the left road. He steered around a pothole that could have swallowed the jeep, the tires ejecting clods of rim-mud into its depths.

He blasted through a rotten tree trunk that had fallen across the road, a cloud of winged termites bursting from the rot-smelling wood. He said, "I was captured because I lost my focus and once slept in the same place twice. Let that be a lesson for you." He laughed—or Phord took that strange sound from the Filipino's once broken larynx to be a laugh.

The jeep jostled down a steep hill. The sea disappeared as they rode through forest. "I can see." Over his shoulder, "Mariko, do you see a road?" He did not have to speak to her in English. McCabe felt the English was not for Mariko's benefit but for his, McCabe's.

Mariko said nothing. Phord turned around. When his eyes fell on her, she averted her gaze.

"Help me, my sweet. Get out and help me find a road."

Don't, Phord thought but did it anyway. "What do you want me to do?" He went around to the front of the jeep where Makisig stood.

"Walk this trail with me. Let's see if it gets to a road."

Makisig walked into brush, Phord behind him.

Makisig had his forty-five out from his shoulder holster.

Counterpunch!

Phord grabbed the gun, pivoted, and struck Makisig's throat with the blade of his hand. Makisig gagged and fell backwards. Makisig was down, gagging, face growing blue. Phord stood over him, pointing the forty-five between the Filipino's running lights.

Phord said, "This a joke? Are you crazy? Don't ever do that again." His face twisted, Makisig clutched his throat. "Let go of your throat. I'll help you breathe."

He hopped away from Makisig as the blade came up, slashing his trouser leg, scratching his thigh. Choking, gagging, Masikig jumped to his feet and underhanded the knife. Arms windmilling, dodging from side to side, Phord stumbled backwards. Makisig let out a weird noise: *lulu-lulu-lulu-lulu*. He stabbed at Phord's eyes then circled the knife skillfully under Phord's protective hand and jabbed at his chest.

Phord never ran from a fight. But this was no fight. This was outright murder. He ran. Makisig jumped on his back and clamped his throat in the crook of his elbow. He would have buried the blade into a kidney, but Phord stepped in a hole and somersaulted through a massive spider's web, flipping Makisig off him.

Phord ran again. Makisig wasn't following. Phord looked back at

Makisig on all-fours scrambling into bushes speckled with bright red, cherry-like fruit. The gun was there! It had been knocked out of his hand when he hit the ground. Phord dove into the bush. Makisig got to it first, pointing it at Phord. Before he pulled the trigger, Phord rolled against his arm, pinning his hand, grabbing the gun. Makisig, panting, spit blood from biting his tongue into Phord's face. *Lulu-lulu-lulu-lulu...* Phord sensed those were the sounds he emitted when the Japanese torturers did their worst. Phord twisted the forty-five against the breakpoint of Makisig's wrist. Phord screamed *lulu-lulu-lulu-lulu*. Phord and Makisig shouted *lulu-lulu-lulu-lulu* into each other's faces.

    Rolling back and forth in muck, they turned into mud monsters. Makisig spat mud and blood into Phord's face. Makisig's dentures showed in his mud-splashed face. He bit at Phord's nose, teeth clicking on empty air while Phord's thumbs felt for Makisig's eyes. Makisig shouted as Phord dug his thumb into an eye socket, releasing vitreous humour. Makisig's knee shot up against Phord's testicles. Phord vomited. Phord pushed his thumb into the other eye socket, pushed through something feeling like thickened onion soup up to his knuckle bone. Makisig roared and stood up and, hands clamped on his face, spun in circles. He tackled Phord's legs and pushed his face against him to bite his testicles. Phord kneed Makisig's head, and Makisig fell backwards. Phord was on top, digging his thumbs into Makisig's trachea.

9

McCabe learns a truth he wished was a lie.

"Mister Marine ... helps me."

"My friends, the Chinese human wave issue is a crock. Sure, they attacked in waves, but they did it intelligently. At the Chosen Reservoir -- I was there, I know – at the Frozen Chosen, the first night-attack wave assaulted us Marines silently, without shouting, shooting or explosives, using bayonets. If silence and bayoneting didn't work, they'd throw concussion grenades behind rolling mortar barrages or blast away with burp guns under machine gun fire. Then the next waves came. They were far more intelligent than the Japanese I fought."

"Sir, the girl ... she needs help."

"Fuck the girl, Colm. She's drunk."

"What took you so long?" Father Baum said as McCabe, winded from climbing half a hundred stairs, came into the stone-walled, stone-ceilinged cabinet. His back to McCabe, the priest was kneeling below a wooden crucifix hanging by a wire from a nail hammered into the mortar-joint of the north-facing stone wall. Beside the wall was a window, its iron bars corroded by centuries of rain and salt wind. There was a cot with a blanket, a wash basin, a water pitcher, a chamber pot, an M-1945 field desk with foldable stool, and a double-nozzle, ceramic oil lamp on the desk. If McCabe spread his arms, he could almost touch the walls. "You're breathing too hard for the climb, lieutenant. Are you out of shape?"

"How did you know it's me?"

"It can be nobody else." Baum stood up, closed his eyes and sucked his breath and lightly touched the bandage, splotched with patches of both dried and fresh blood. "Coming here is what you have to do. *Sie haben keine wahl.*" The tips of his fingers tenderly examine bandages wrapping his head. "*Es ist dein schicksal.* Your destiny is to come looking for me. Your destiny is to find me."

"And what's your destiny?"

"Being in the Hitler Youth, and its Weltanschauung, there was only one destiny for me and others like me. An early death. But I guess the universe had other ideas."

"Cut the mysticism. I thought you were a practical German." McCabe noticed the corners of the priest's eyes exuded pus from conjunctivitis contracted from this ministering to the Mangyans who were plagued by it.

"The practical part is that most people around here know I come to the fortress now and then to fast and contemplate. And the mystical part is that, whether you know it or not, the Spirit led you here – just as I knew it would."

"So, who was your guru?'

"Rommel, of course. What people don't understand about Rommel is that he was truly a mystic, and he made mystics out of the men he led. Let's get down to business. I know you don't like me, but professionally speaking, you're here to kill Shimada."

"Or capture."

"No capture. Kill. You can't capture him unless he wants you to. If he doesn't want to be captured, you'll have to kill him."

"And nonviolence?"

"Violence is never the answer. Except when it is. How were the accommodations last night? I got taken to the hospital. You and Father O'Toole to jail."

"Not five stars."

"Of course, you got out right away. They're not going to hold a couple of American Marines in that *himmel*."

"O'Toole's Navy, not Marines."

"Here. Let me show you something." Baum bent over his cot. He winced and straightened up and touched the bandage.

"Take that fractured skull back to the hospital."

Baum looked at McCabe, zigzagging lights in his eyes. "More important things face us than the condition of my skull. Please get that material from under the cot."

McCabe dragged out a mass of papers. The papers were sandwiched between two boards of rosewood, smudged with the oils of thumbs and fingers, the spine bound by loops of raw hide.

"Kindly put it on the desk."

Hefting the mass, McCabe asked, "Catholic papers, father? By the way, what order are you? "

"The order of tears, poverty, and love."

"That's a long way from tanks, desert, and flies."

"And the food, my young friend. Don't forget the food. Like the cans of strange meat with the letters AM that came from Italy. So tasty, we called it '*Asinus, Mussolini*' – 'Mussolini's Ass.'"

McCabe plopped the papers on the desk. He lifted the board, and there were newspaper and magazine clippings, maps, photos, letters in English and Japanese—a trove of information on Shimada. He pushed his hands down on the papers to keep them from flying about.

Baum said he heard about Shimada almost the first day he, Baum, arrived on the island years ago, newly ordained. Shimada was the last of an original contingent of three Japanese soldiers hiding out in the mountains, unaware the war had ended. Islanders called them "devils in the mountains." They trapped jungle creatures and stole farm animals and vegetables. Now and then they shot at and killed soldiers and policemen. Their pilfering was a small fraction of common attrition on the island, the storms, accidents, runaways, disease, etc. Still, they helped the islanders conjure a myth about the soldiers. The Mountain Devils were like the child-terrorizing boogeyman—afflicting adults too. People did not venture unarmed into the countryside.

In 1954, one soldier was killed by a Philippine army detachment on training maneuvers to fight the Huk guerrillas. In 1958, a second was killed by an armed farmer. That left Shimada alone.

Baum gathered a great amount of information on the man to find ways to bring him to earth. Some of the best information came when he befriended members of Shimada's family, two brothers and a sister. They visited the island a year after Baum arrived and drove throughout the countryside with loudspeakers coaxing him to give up. Several times, they went aloft in a hot air balloon, their loudspeakers blaring, begging him to come home. They dropped leaflets and letters from his family. Shimada did not reply.

From talks with the family, Baum told McCabe he discovered Shimada was a graduate of the secret-warfare Futamata Military School. As a Japanese soldier, he was an anomaly. The common Japanese soldier was imbued with *bushido*, the credo affirming the noblest act of a soldier was to die for one's Emperor and country. However, at Futamata, the soldiers were instructed to live for one's country instead. For instance, according to bushido, by being taken prisoner, a soldier and his whole family was disgraced. Futamata, on the other hand, taught Shimada that being taken prisoner was sometimes the most effective and honorable way of accomplishing one's mission. As a prisoner, one could give false information to the enemy, help other prisoners escape, and undertake other subversive activities.

A Futamata graduate often lived a solitary life, even if he worked amid many people. His integrity was vital. Only insiders knew that the soldier was accomplishing the mission. Outsiders, even one's family, might despise him for carrying out activities that seemed disgraceful, and he would have to deal with their scorn in silence, keep humble, live simply, and keep his spirit alive.

Baum said, "There's a Japanese popular song that reflects what a Futamata graduate is all about. The words are: 'I'm dressed in rags and look like hell; but witness, O Moon, the splendor of my heart.' My friend, in matters of spirit, Shimada is more Japanese than the Japanese."

After showing McCabe leaflets, articles, and letters, Baum unfolded a map of the island, much fingered-over, the fold-creases deeply fissured. Its edges snapped in the breeze as Baum held it down against the mass of papers on the desk with his broad, tanker's hands. On the map were written sightings of Shimada's over the years: color-coded, cross referenced with tabbed and indexed entries in a cloth-bound ledger—all in Baum's meticulous German hand.

"It took Shimada about four months to make one circle around this island. Each year, he went around three times, moving with the seasonal vegetables and fruit. He moves frequently. He's resourceful. But he suffers the fatal flaw of the Japanese mind, being good at small things but bad at big picture things."

"Which means?"

"He's good at moving and hiding, but he fails to understand that somebody might be analyzing his big picture movements. We'll get him. We'll avenge your colonel's murder."

"You mean you and I will get him."

"Take this map to your boss. I'll come with you. A platoon will do the trick. No more. Of course, I'll take more if I can get it. Let's leave now."

"Leave where?"

"Back to camp. Back to your battalion commander. The one who replaced Ajax. We'll get him to break out the troops."

"Major Gord."

"Yes. Major Gord. Let's go."

Baum's thick fingers folded the map.

"It won't work. The Navy has the case. The Navy's investigating."

"I'm no Salome, but I can hand his head to you on a platter. I pretty much know where he'll be and when he'll be there. Not precisely. But precisely enough."

McCabe clapped. "Let's go. I'm ready."

"What do you mean, my young friend?"

"Just me."

"Just you? I've heard you're a pretty good leader. But being good isn't good enough when it comes to Shimada. We need warm Marine bodies in this action."

"I'm all you got. I'm all you need."

Baum gathered the papers together and squared them. "Okay, back to camp."

"I can't go back."

Baum looked at him out from under the bandages. He scratched his nose with his thumbnail. "Why?"

"I'm confined to my quarters."

"But you're here."

"I un-confined myself."

The corners of Baum's mouth drew down.

"Your Prussian-military instincts rebel against that? Look, I..." McCabe jabbed his chest with his thumb "... want to get Shimada. And I'm going to get Shimada. Ajax was killed on my watch. I'm responsible. I'll see this through until Shimada is put out of commission."

"Aren't there other reasons, my young friend?"

"What reasons?"

"Father O'Toole told me the reasons."

"Told you what?"

"Your father figure reasons or issues."

Something about Baum's features under the bandages were like a mirror, reflecting the sudden rage that slammed through McCabe. Baum's German training – *if attacked, attack!* – kicked in. He was ready to do battle. But in an instant, he checked his feelings. He raised his hands maybe mirroring his actions in the desert when the Tommies were coming. He took several steps backward. "Sorry, my young friend. That was too close to the bone. I shouldn't have said it. I'll just be satisfied that you're with me, whatever the reason. Whatever the hell-born issue. I won't mention it again." He put out his hand. McCabe hesitated. Then he shook that hand. His rage was still there but leashed. Like Baum, McCabe had disciplined his emotions, though Baum's were not completely under control as was shortly to become evident. Baum said, "Back to Shimada. We need a chase force and a blocking force. We need communication. We need coordination. We need logistics."

"That's me. The total package."

The stone walls spun in McCabe's eyes. He hit the wall, knocking the crucifix loose, then slammed onto the floor. Baum was on him, trying to apply a choke hold. His leg was wrapped around McCabe's leg preventing the lieutenant from getting leverage on the stone floor to stand. Baum's breath was hot and loud and maniacal in McCabe's ear.

Just as quickly as he had moved against McCabe, Baum let go and stood up. His features were twisted against the porcelain rigidity of his burn-scar.

"What the hell, Father ..." McCabe rubbed his shoulder muscle and swung his arm in a circle.

Baum held the crucifix he picked up off the floor. He held it as if it were the handle of an ax. *He wouldn't*, thought McCabe, backing out of range.

Baum turned around and lifting his powerful arms that filled out the short sleeves of his shirt, he hung the steel wire of the crucifix carefully on the nail hammered into mortar of the stone wall. His actions were delicate and highly focused as if he were performing surgery.

"I guess I got too close to the bone." McCabe said. Baum brought hands to his bandaged head and, grinding his teeth, rocked slightly from side to side. When he finally spoke, his voice was strained and metallic. "You, my young friend, the total package? You?"

"What the hell? Stay back."

Baum spoke slowly pronouncing each word deliberately not as if to emphasize their meaning but to put off the pain the intoning of the individual word triggered in his brain pan. "Shimada ... killed ... your colonel. What're you ... Marines ... going to do about it?"

"What got into you?" Baum raised one eyebrow, the other paralyzed being half-amputated by the edge of the burn scar on the side of his face. "The *Furor Teutonicus*."

Now Baum spoke in normal cadence, overriding the pain that, if the tempest in his eyes was any indication, continued to be excruciating. But trained to not let pain defeat the mission, he soldiered on. "You, the total package? You're nothing. Nothing! Except one thing. You can help me talk to Gord again. He doesn't get it. But he will. I'll make him. Don't you get it?"

"Don't ask for my help. I can't get near camp. I'd be arrested. My bet is Gord won't break out a single Marine to help you."

"Yes, he will if I can talk to him."

"The Navy investigators have him tied up in knots. Plus, our generals don't want the bad publicity that our troops traipsing through the jungle to find Shimada will inevitably bring. I might be wrong. If he breaks them out, then you don't need me. Go for it. And if you don't need me, you just made my life a whole lot easier. I would welcome going back and having nothing more to do in life than being confined to quarters. Which won't be for long, anyway. But if he won't help you, come back. I'll be waiting. I can't find Shimada without you. And you can't kill him without me."

Sitting on the cot, back against the wall, scrap book on his lap, nodding off, McCabe heard footsteps ascending the stone stairwell. The climber's gasping evinced the cardio challenge of those long, steep, spiral stairs.

Feeling a breeze coming not from the window now but up from the echo chamber stairwell through the door-less doorway, McCabe shook his head and blinked. Sleep-dazed, he sniffed the stairwell air that smelled of toxic mold.

Chaplain O'Toole in his sweat-soaked sateens and bloused trousers above muddy combat boots came into the cabinet—O'Toole with the bloat on the side of his face having taken on the yellowish-brown color of a poisonous blow fish that if improvidently prepared kills you when you eat it on the spot.

He bent over, drops of sweat falling from his face, and rubbed his knee. He lifted his foot and swung it fore and aft, grimacing. "Screw it. My knee is disobeying orders. I'm not making that climb again."

At first, McCabe thought that strange look in O'Toole's eye came from the rigors of the climb; but after he stood up and embraced the priest, pressing his hands into those mournful, bull-like shoulders, and said, "Have you come to sacrifice a goat for me, Padre? Or am I mixing up religions?" and O'Toole replied, "You're the goat that I'm sacrificing," McCabe sensed that look had nothing to do with the climb.

"Father, what ghost have you just seen?"

O'Toole embraced McCabe and kissed his cheek with the good side of his mouth. "You bum, McCabe." He clutched McCabe's shoulders and held him at arm's length, his troubled eye lovingly studying him. "Saddle up. It's back to camp."

"How'd you find me?"

"Father Baum told me you're here."

"Don't you know? You're still looking for me."

"Well, here I am."

"Sure, you're here. But you'll never find me. Where is Baum?"

"He's back in camp trying to convince anybody who'll listen to go after Shimada."

"Good luck with that. Anyway, that's my job. I'm waiting for Baum to come back after he inevitably fails miserably. He and I are going after Shimada."

"Are you after psycho disability pay?"

McCabe picked up the mass of clippings and raised them to O'Toole's face. "Read these. They show Shimada's for real. They show Baum knows as much about him as Shimada knows about anyone else. Here read!"

O'Toole knocked the documents out of McCabe's hands. They papered the flagstone floor.

"Forget Baum. Forget Shimada. No Baum! No Shimada! Get that into your head!"

"Padre, you look like hell. Maybe you oughta cut back." McCabe dumped the papers that didn't get knocked out of his hands onto the cot.

O'Toole snagged the corner of his mouth between his teeth and sucked on it, a gesture he made when embarrassed. "The crackback destroyed my football career but not my drinking career." With his knee crackling like a dried cornstalk being twisted, O'Toole helped McCabe pick up the remaining papers and put them on the stack on the cot. "Sorry, McCabe. I get ahead of myself too much. But this is special, you and Baum and Shimada. Look, the exercise has been canceled. The battalion has been ordered to pack up and ship out."

"Because Ajax got croaked?"

"No, something else. Troops are coming in from the field. Ships are moving closer to shore. Let's go."

"Once Father Baum comes to his senses that I'm his only hope, we're crossing the line of departure."

"Are you listening? Major Gord hankers to see you."

"I love him too."

"ONI is wondering where the hell you went, McCabe. We'll go together to see Gord. I can help paper this over. You're too good a leader to have charges against you. But the bomb is falling. Be somewhere else when it hits. Come with me now. Talk to Gord. Talk to ONI. Get them on your side. Let's go!" O'Toole went out the door, his sleeve catching on a cast iron pintle-and-pin mortared into the stone casing – all that remained of what had once been a strap-hinged door.

McCabe got up, closed his hands around the ancient bars, corroded to an almost treacle-like brittleness, and looked out at forks of sunlight breaking through lowering clouds and scissoring in oblongs of yellow across the purple waters. "Didn't you hear me, Padre?"

"Hear what?"

"Do I have to say it in German? I don't know German, but I'll say it. You said you speak a little. Maybe German you'll understand. *Auf Wiedersehen.*"

O'Toole unhooked his sleeve and stared at McCabe. The wind blew his rather long, unmilitary hair, back and forth across his forehead, black hair with streaks of red, indicating the genes of Vikings who pillaged and raped his Gaelic forbears.

"Colm, listen. Before we shipped out, I had to get swimming qualified. Jump into the deep end and paddle a short distance. Simple. Easy. But not for me. I told them I'm a freak of nature. My body sinks like a lead safe. The instructors insisted. In I jumped. Down I went. Right to the bottom. Three of them had to haul me out. Never got qualified. But here is what I learned that might help you. Do what you fear, and you're blessed with new opportunities."

"So, you jumped in. What was the new opportunity?"

"To open the hearts of the people in charge. Not just for their understanding but also for mine."

"I don't get it. How can you learn if you're dead?"

"Good question. Of course, you'd ask it. I can't speak for you. Only for my experience. Getting up the gumption to jump in helped me later relate to the troops in ways I couldn't have before jumping in. Colm, helping you get out of this mess you're in is taking a lot of talk and prayer on my part. But it's also going to take you doing what you fear."

McCabe said, "Pray for me the way the Pope Clement prayed for Giordano Bruno when his jaw was clamped shut with an iron gag and an iron spike driven through his tongue before they burned him at the stake."

"Man acts, but God loves. Don't laugh. It's not the joke you think it is."

"Did God love my father blowing his brains out?"

"I've prayed for your father too, McCabe. He's why you're in this mess. Not him. But how he died. And the linkage to Ajax."

"I told you how he died."

"Colm, you told me how he died. You told me where he died. And you told me why he died. But here is something you haven't told me. It's the secret of the whole fiasco with you and your father and even Ajax: it's clear and simple and maybe you don't know it – at least consciously. You're scared."

"Who isn't?"

"You've been scared since your father killed himself. Being scared has made you angry. And it's made you stupid. Not all the time. You're smart most of the time. Just some of the times. But those times caused a lot of wreckage."

"How about you? You're real smart, aren't you? You're real smart swallowing the party line about God and the trinity and all the rest."

"I believe in the Black Dog. I believe in what happened with a priest and an altar boy and wine behind a locked door in a back room of a church's basement. The Black Dog came out of that. And because of the Black Dog and what happened, what cannot be eradicated from mind and heart, I believe in love."

"I won't laugh."

"I must believe in love. There is no other choice. I believe what is not done for the benefit of others is not worth doing. So, the party line doesn't matter. You know it's not that I don't believe in God, it's that I suspect sometimes God doesn't believe in me."

"Is that blasphemy?"

"Doubt is the rock of my faith."

"Save me from Socrates. I'm not buying what you're selling. Goodbye."

Uncoiling, O'Toole drove his shoulder into McCabe's diaphragm. McCabe's head hit the crucifix. It swung on its wire but did not, as with the first priest-attack, fall to the floor. O'Toole wrapped McCabe in ape-arms, lifted his feet off the flagstones, and spun him toward the door. The rotting wood of the frame crumbled in his hand like bread. They lurched through the doorway and onto the flagstone apron overlooking the long drop down the no-railing stairwell.

"Hold it," said McCabe. "We don't have parachutes."

"You're going with me, whether you like it or not." O'Toole looked behind him at the drop. His bear hug loosened as he stepped away from the edge. (O'Toole once told McCabe that heights scared him as much as water depths.) He pushed McCabe into the doorway, sidled away from the apron edge then grabbing his web belt yanked the lieutenant down the first several stairs. Pulling him, he pressed against the stairwell wall.

"I'll go down with you. But the slow way. In one piece."

Walking down the spiral staircase, McCabe wondered whether his being attacked by two priests of different orders within a short space of time was some sort of first in the annals of Christendom.

Outside, O'Toole pointed to a Mighty Mite standing on the flat area McCabe—the tactical infantry lieutenant as always—figured would have made a good commando staging area, being immune from plunging fire from the fortress. "Get in."

Shaking his head, McCabe felt the kink in his neck caused by O'Toole's using him as a blocking dummy deepen. "I'm waiting for Father Baum. In fact, here he comes now."

Baum drove up in his beat-up jeep. Its mud-caked wheels and ripped-away vegetation flapping from the wheel wells showed his good works encompassed the boondocks. He stopped beside O'Toole's Mighty Mite but did not switch off the motor, its throbbing exhibiting various malfunctions which McCabe felt resonated with Baum's variously malfunctioning character. With a half-dollar-sized fresh patch of blood soaking his head bandage, Baum looked at McCabe out of another face.

Since McCabe had met him, he found Baum had different faces. There was the face when he first saw him in the officers' tent after Ajax's murder, the tight-lipped, burning-eyed, middle-aged Martin Luther face; there was the smiling, cruel-mouthed face he looked at drinking in the officer's club tent; there was the demon's face seen in the back-splash of the headlight as they drove to the skeleton cave; there was the forward-thrusting, sneering, avenging angel's face as he jumped him in the fortress cabinet. Now this face as Baum looked at McCabe over the hood of the jeep, this Baum-face McCabe had not seen before. It was the face of a convicted heretic climbing the execution platform and seeing for the first time the hooded inquisitor, the stake, and the red-hot tongs in the basket of burning coals.

What tied it all together was the half-face, burn scar. That remained the same in all the changes. To McCabe, it was like the unchanging magician's hat from which was pulled all manner of things. The magic was not in the things but in the hat. Yet without the things we would not know the magic of the hat. The scar wasn't magic but for McCabe it somehow held the secret magic of the man, the magic of his suffering. *Yet, on the other hand,* McCabe thought, *it was just a fucking scar.*

Though Baum was looking at McCabe, McCabe sensed, by the way the German's torso under his black, short sleeved shirt, was torqued slightly toward O'Toole, he was really looking at the American priest. Or trying not to look at him.

"Where are your wheels, my young friend?" Baum said.

"Who are you talking to?"

"You."

"I thought you were talking to Father O'Toole."

"You I'm talking to."

"My Mite's round the other side."

"Get in," said Baum. "I'll take you."

"No," said O'Toole.

"What's up between you two?" said McCabe. Not having slept since well before Ajax's murder, McCabe's thoughts had taken on a supernatural clarity. He felt he was seeing behind appearances. These two priests were talking nonsense, but on a deeper level, McCabe saw their nonsense made perfect sense. He knew they believed in—or convinced themselves to believe in—a lie. During their Sunday get-togethers, his father had convinced him it was a lie not just by his words but moreover by his very being. McCabe knew that his father's war experiences were the true realities of this world, not some invisible being, the existence of which was, as his father claimed "hooey." The remembrance of his father's passionate, consistent, and brilliant denunciations of all religions made these priests, in McCabe's eyes, liars and dupes. That was proved just a few minutes ago when they had been manhandling him for stupid reasons; now the nonsense they were talking matched the nonsense of their beliefs.

"No Shimada," O'Toole said.

"Agreed," said Baum, sideways glancing at O'Toole. "No Shimada. Back at camp, I was blocked from seeing Gord. So, you Marines won't sign up. Okay. *Es gibt nichts mehr zu diskutieren.* Nothing more to talk about. I'm packing up Shimada's dossier and putting it away in our church. Volunteers?"

"I'm in," said McCabe. "Padre, you and your knee stay here."

"Don't go with him, Colm."

"Agreed. I shouldn't. I won't. But I am."

Going into the fortress, McCabe saw out of the corner of his eye what only his supernatural clarity could see. He saw O'Toole unlovingly spit. Murder has made tricksters of us all, he thought.

Baum led McCabe through a portal in the wall through a dark passageway in which Baum farted and into a light filled hall, light coming through an iron grating in the ceiling, and then down stone steps. Instead of going up the long, winding stairway to the cabinet, he led McCabe outside.

Baum said, "Your battalion chaplain suffers from the most distressing of all human afflictions. His love lacks legs."

"Why am I not surprised you said that?"

Baum turned and looked at McCabe. He was about to speak but said nothing. He turned away. Then he said, "Yes, it's true, I couldn't get to see Gord. Your battalion sergeant major put up a wall. But that's a splendid outcome."

"Baum, riddle me no riddles."

"You Americans, massacring Indians made all of you blood simple. You say 'riddles'. I say, it's plain as death. We're going after Shimada. Plain, isn't it? Don't bail on me. You're all I got. *Qualität geht vor Quantität.* Just you and me. Stealth and focus. We might be more effective than a platoon. There's your vehicle. You drive. I'll ride. Let's go."

"You had no intention of going up and packing up the clippings." Baum said getting in. "Drive."

"You leaving your jeep behind?"

"I'm leaving O'Toole behind. He'll just get in the way."

"Smart move. You had no intention of going back up those stairs. You knew he couldn't make it up with his knee. You wanted to come out here and leave him behind. Your jeep is bait. You lied to Father O'Toole."

"Fortunately, yes. But lies often can become truths."

10

Going Native.

The corpse passed gas. Phord was sitting beside it. A minute before, its legs were kicking. Now it was still. Its head was turned toward Phord, eye sockets filled with mud and clotting blood, a spittle bubble budged from its lips, a rainbow of colors quivering on the liquid surface. The last breath had not been strong enough to pop the bubble. Phord wiped his fingers on leaves hanging off a long jungle stalk then wiped his fingers on his trousers. The odor of intestinal gas hung in the air.

Mariko handed him the gun and the knife. His fingers closed around them, but both weapons fell to the mud. "I don't want them."

He stood up, testicles aching, and gagged, bile trickling into weeds at his feet. Wiping his mouth with the back of his hand, he heard the glass-breaking sounds of a small stream. He breast-stroked through foliage. The stream ran clear over yellow leaves that looked like feathers. He took off his mud-and-blood-soaked shirt, peeling it like adhesive from his burnt chest hairs. He stepped out of his muddy bloodied trousers. Just above the knee was a squirt of Makisig's intraocular fluid. He knelt beside the stream and with shaky hands, splashed mud off his face.

"Mariko, where were you? Couldn't you help stop him?"

Mariko dropped his clothes into the stream and stomped on them with bare feet then wrung them out and spread them out on a flat rock where vapor rose from them in sunlight.

Shivering, he said, "Let's get him back to town." She stood beside the stream, hugging herself. "Snap out of it, Mariko. We must report this. Mariko." Ripping vines out of the way, she went back to the corpse and stood over it. She made the sign of the cross – the Filipino way, quickly around her nose and chin, ending with briefly touching thumb to lips. She returned to the vehicle and started it and drove into thick undergrowth. The wheels sprayed mud. She switched off the motor.

"Get dressed," she said. It was the first time she had spoken to him since before he killed Makisig, and her words were sharp and clear in the moisture-laden air. His clothes, still damp, plastered against his skin.

She grabbed the feet. The feet in open-strapped sandals were lumps of once-broken, badly healed bones. Phord realized the blinding pain Makisig must have experienced just walking. He thought: *The Japanese broke him. You can't endure the pain he must have endured without being broken. That's why he was mentally cracked. That's why I had to kill him.*

Mariko dug her heels into the ground and tightening her grip on the ankles heaved back. The thing that was once Makisig moved like a block of stone, flattening grass and crushing red-and-yellow mud orchids. Her sandal strap broke, and she fell backwards, landing on her butt. He pulled her to her feet. He got his hands under corpse's armpits and said, "Lift the legs again." She picked up the feet. The unexpected slack-weight made the body slip from his hands. The dead man hit the ground and rolled over on his face. There was faint crunching of glass. "Again." Hefting the body into the jeep well, Phord saw shattered aviators sticking out of a front pocket, the glass shards spilling out and tinkling on the fender.

Well-practiced in driving jeeps, she athletically jumped behind the wheel and hammered the gear shift skillfully backing up then going forward to the road Makisig had just driven down.

"The other way," Phord said.

"No."

She gunned it. The jeep dropped into a gorge—trees closing overhead, darkness closing in—then up the other side into sunlight. The sun was setting in an uprush of purple-orange clouds over the sea. As the jeep bounced over vines, thick as a man's arm, Phord heard thumping from the body in the well. "Stop," he said. She pulled over. The thumping had been the corpse's forehead hitting the flange of the tailgate.

He removed the corpse's jacket and wrapped it around the head and got back in. A jeepney was approaching. and she drove off the road and waited for it to pass.

"Let's wait for dark before going on."

"Why?"

"We don't want to be seen."

"We're going back to town. Isn't town back the way we came?"

"Yes."

"Let's go back"

"No."

"Why? We're going to report this. So, what if we're seen?"

"The electric cure is why."

"The what?"

"In our country, people get the electric chair. It's another American gift to our nation."

"Self-defense."

"For you, yes. You'll be handed over to the American government. For me it'll be the chair. Or twenty-five years at least in Manila's rape prison. President-for-life, Ferdinand Marcos and his thugs rule this country. Your self-defense claim would be laughed at. Their word is law. Marcos was a guerrilla leader, or at least he says he was, just like Makisig. So Makisig was well-connected. You bring his body back, and if the Marines don't take you into their loving arms, you'll be jailed. Probably wind up with a bullet in the nape of your neck. Attempted …" She air-quoted. " … escape. And nobody could do anything about it. Even your president Johnson."

She parked in an area away from the road but open to sea wind. They watched clouds come up and a storm come on, gray curtains sweeping the darkening ocean. In the gloaming, with the rumpus of songbirds around them, he held her hand, not really wanting to touch her and knowing she felt the same.

The birds fell silent. The air felt strangely pressurized against his throbbing testicles. The storm made landfall. Foliage tossed wildly as wind and rain hammered up the hill. A sheet of rain smacked the windshield. Wind-blown rain hit his face. Branches cracked, and leaves rattled. She removed her hand from his and turned the ignition switch.

"Let's do this."

The rotting fish odor enveloped him before he saw the shack. It showed as a chocolate blur through wipers in the rain-slashed beams of the headlights. The odor got stronger as he ran hunched against the rain to double doors. She walked head high, arms swinging casually, not bothered by the downpour, as inured to the elements as Maskisig. The doors were secured by a rusted padlock big as a fist. She fetched a key from under a cement block beside the door and opened the padlock and swung the doors open, letting more fish odor out. She went to the rear and struck a match from a waterproof canning jar of matches on a worktable and lit a hurricane lamp and brought it forward.

"You know your way around here."

"It's my uncle's. I used to help him fish during the summers in between school."

There was a cobalt blue, 30-foot, slant-bowed banka with outriggers and horizontal planing fins. Just aft of amidships, an outboard was bolted to a block of wood. On the walls around the boat were ropes, nets, and buoys. She grabbed a bow rope and pulled the banka, which was amazingly light, down a wooden ramp to the sea, keeping the bow back from the heavy surf. Rain drummed on the boat's nylon canopy.

She returned to the jeep. "Help me."

They dragged the corpse to the shack, Phord gagging. Makisig's kick in his balls was a gift that kept on giving. With rope from inside the shack, she made a whipping around the dead man's legs, laying the rope and wrapping the long end then making a bight in the short end. In the final turn, she passed the long end through the bight and secured it with a double hitch. Struggling mightily, they dumped the corpse into the outrigger. While Phord dry heaved, she brought over three concrete blocks from the shack, looped ropes around the neck, the waist and both feet which she threaded through the block-hollows and tied with bowline knots. She put the lantern back in the shack, keeping the flame lit and the doors open then came back to the boat.

"Shoulder to it," she said. The boat, stuck in sand at the end of the ramp, wouldn't move. They pulled the dead man and the blocks out. Released of that ballast, it floated. She climbed in and grabbed the pull-cord handle and swung her arm. The outboard engine started.

"Get me out into the surf."

He pushed on the aft-pointed stern. The boat moved forward. A curling wave hit the boat. He was knocked down against the corpse rising and falling in the water.

"Can you haul him back in by yourself?"

"Sure."

He got some of the body onto his shoulder but tripped on the ropes to the blocks and fell forward. The swallowed salt water stung his adenoids and throat.

"You're useless." She jumped out and together they re-loaded the boat with the body and the blocks. They climbed in, and she throttled up and turned the bow into the waves. In the heavy surf, with the hopeless cutwater and lack of spray rails, the boat shipped water. "Start bailing," she said. "Or we'll go nowhere fast."

"With what?"

"The plastic bucket under your seat."

Built to be paddled in relatively calm waters, the banka had little reserve buoyancy forward. The outboard power tended to dip the bow into waves rather than ride them. Her uncle had installed aft planing fins that helped get the bow up a little but not enough for the seas tonight, so Phord bailed, out of breath and his shoulders feeling cracked. After a half-hour's plowing through chop, she throttled back.

She shouted words, smothered in wind blowing her hair across her face. He shook his head and cupped his hand behind his ear, holding for dear life to the gunwale with the other as a big wave violently tipped the craft. She pointed to the corpse. She pointed at herself then pointed at the engine and jabbed her fingers at the bow. He guessed she was indicating she had to keep throttling to keep the bow headed into the wind.

He grabbed the windings and heaved the body over the side. He heaved two of the three cement blocks over. Picking up the third, he neglected to see the rope attached to one of the overboard blocks. That rope was wrapped around his ankle. The block sank, the rope went taut, and his leg was pulled over the side and bent backward. The block, being attached to the corpse and the other block, was too heavy to pull in.

He swung his leg over and pushed himself into the water, intending to slacken the rope to free his ankle. Slack wouldn't come. The rope tied to the block in the craft was looped around the taut rope. Then he made another mistake. He threw that block over. He thought the buoyancy of the water would loosen the rope enough to get his thumb under and free his ankle. But the rope around his ankle tightened. He was now attached to three cement blocks.

Water closed over his head. The next intake would fill his lungs.

Death was not just on him; it was inside him, an instant away. His hands slipped off the gunwale. His lungs filled – not with water but air. His head broke the surface of the water. His forearm was being squeezed. Mariko had gripped his forearm and kept him from going under. He was clutching the gunwale again.

"What the hell?" Her face was right up against his.

"Rope, Mariko. My ankle."

She let go of the throttle and holding to the gunwale, jumped in beside him. Before she went in, he saw she had a knife clamped between her teeth. Then she was underwater holding his waist against her with the crook of her arm. He felt a sawing against the rope around his ankle. The downward drag pulling him under snapped. She came up, gasping, "Darling, get in, goddamnit." Freed of the rope coils, he heaved himself into the banka. He noted she had called him darling. He did not know why.

"A set up. What else could it be? Makisig takes me into the boondocks. Boom. What I can't figure is why he wanted to kill me. It wasn't money. I didn't have more money to give him."

"He deserved to die. He wanted to die. It's like he pointed a gun to his head for years. Your finger pulled the trigger."

"I didn't exactly shoot him."

"You know what I'm talking about."

They were sitting in the little room by the light of a dim electric bulb in the dark of the morning behind the main house across the street from Makisig's bar, washing down with gins and bitters a meal of pig, rice and roots she had skillfully cooked.

On one side of the small room was a closet with many-colored night dresses and stylish shoes. Beside the closet was a dressing table with a three-view mirror and foundations, moisturizers, concealers, ointments, powders, blushes, eyeshadows, lipsticks, creams, mascara, brushes, isopropyl, combs and brushes. The other side of the room was another country with jeans, sandals, simple, cotton shirts and skirts, cork boots, several Filipino long-billed trucker's caps on wall-pegs. The room was equipped with an efficiency kitchen, refrigerator, and compressed-air constructed rattan furniture. A toilet and shower were behind a door in the back. "Indoor plumbing was put in when I became a cash cow." There was a bed beside a window.

When they first arrived, she had advised him to shower and go to sleep. She showered too, drying her hair with an Egyptian cotton bath towel by bending to one side and cocking her head in that special way of hers that so endeared her to him. The towel, taken from a five-star Manila hotel, had gold bars and gold logo that accented the sorghum bronze of her face. Lying on her on the bed after he showered, he closed his eyes and dug his thumbs into Makisig's windpipe, pushing through something hard then something soft in the old guerilla fighter's throat. He woke, sweat soaking the freshly cleaned cotton pillow slip she had put on for him. Her naked body pressed against him, she stroked his forehead. "You were moaning. I'll get you a drink and make you a meal."

He was hungry but couldn't eat much. He quickly downed a tumbler of the gin drink but felt no kick.

"A set up. What else could it be? Mariko, why did you just sit there? Why didn't you help me?"

"First man you ever killed?"

He wondered why did she ask that? Was she in cahoots with Makisig? He asked, "Have you killed before?"

She came around the table and touched his cheek lightly with the backs of her fingers and brought her fingers to her lips and kissed them where they had touched him. "If my uncle hadn't had that fishing knife spring-loaded on a bracket under the transom, I wouldn't have been able to cut you out. You'd be digesting in sharks' bellies."

"Answer me. Have you killed?" She didn't answer. "I think you have killed, Mariko. Why didn't you intervene? There's a lot I don't know about you."

"I told you a lot. I told you more about myself than I've ever told anyone. That's enough."

"What about Shimada? You're Japanese, or at least half. Did you secretly bring him food and medicines? Did you fuck him?"

"Don't try to figure out what needs to be left alone. Makisig is no more. Know where we dumped his body? My uncle calls it 'shark alley.' Water going between two rock outcroppings over coral attracts lots of fish, sharks especially. Hammerheads galore. Now he's being digested. Forget him. The important thing now is I've got to get my due."

"What? Your due?"

She sat down and reached across the table and took his hands and brought them to her lips. "My body was the goose that laid his golden egg."

"He pimped you out?"

"Why is that a question?"

"Because I'm asking it."

"Asking what you shouldn't come to know is a bad way to live."

"I want to know everything about you."

She dropped his hands and hugged herself as if chilled. "If I told you, you might get sick to your stomach."

"Try me."

"I'll tell you the surface stuff. Then we'll shut up about it."

"Tell me all the stuff."

She looked at her hands and thought for some time. When she did speak, her voice was strained as if she was admitting to a long-held secret. "I told you about my lovely childhood."

"You said your mother hated you, but not why."

"You want stuff? Okay, how's this? When the War started, my father went to the jungle to fight the Japanese. A Japanese official moved into our house. He raped my mother for three years. That's me, product of a Nippon father. Motherly love for me was not her thing. A lot of beatings over nothing was more her thing. Understand? Now we get to Makisig. I grew up in the house across the street from Makisig's bar. As a child, he had his eye on me, though I didn't know it. When I was ten or so, he paid for me to go an American Catholic school in Manila."

"That's why you talk the way you do."

"Nothing to brag about. In fact, something to be ashamed of. I was from boondocks. The other students were from wealthy families. They hated me. I hated them. When I got breasts and pubic hairs and had acquired an American way of walking and talking and looking at the world, he took me out. He bought me classy clothes and cashed in."

"Didn't you know what he had planned for you?"

"You're so stupid! No, naïve. Naïve is worse than stupid. You think I thought Makisig was a saint? My mother knew. My father knew. I knew. Even though I was a child, I knew." She stood up and started pacing. Then, "My first trick was with a wealthy Japanese businessman in Manila. I was in my early teens and a virgin. He had a soft prick but it was stiff enough, and I bled all over the Five Star hotel sheets and scared the hell out of me. Afterwards, I cried and cried and scrubbed myself with bleach. Makisig's investment paid off. Starting with that one man, he earned more in a year than his bar and government pension provided. We camped out in Manila months on end. Now you know about me. If I were you, I'd clear out."

"Go on."

She placed her hands on the table and leaned toward him and said close to his face. "Shut up. Enough said. No more."

"Don't you understand? It doesn't matter what you've been through."

"Oh, yes it does. You don't know. You don't want to know."

"I want to know everything."

"Oh, you do, do you? Stupid, naïve American. Get your life's lessons from Hollywood. Things in my life would make your hair stand on end."

He got up and came around the table and grabbed her shoulders and shook them gently. She let him do it, amused by his overboard emotion.

He said, "I told you a lot last night. But there's a lot more. My father deserted when I was young, and my mother worked three jobs a day … emptying bed pans, cleaning windows, doing domestic work and a little pro wrestling, slaughtering poultry. I was ten or so and complained about our hardscrabble, mac and cheese, lousy furniture, peanut-butter-and-jelly life. She took me to the slaughterhouse where she worked. She said, 'You think chicken comes from plastic packages? Look.' She jammed a fowl upside down into an aluminum cone. She stuck a knife through the bird's lower jaw and into its brain. Then she cut off the head. 'Minimum wage I get for killing hundreds of chickens a day. The only job I can get for now. Sorry to hurt your delicate feelings.' The next day I got a job shining shoes. I gave her all the money I made. She went into professional wrestling part time but got crippled in her last bout. Mostly she stays at home now. She gets what I make. Back then, me and my sister Sarah ran the streets. Though I never asked her, Sarah maybe did a little prostitution on the side; because now and then she came up with money gotten from I didn't know where nor care to find out. Once, we carried off the television past our mother sleeping on the couch and got 12 bucks for it. I gave her the money. She needed it more than I did."

Mariko laughed. He loved her laugh. It was bright and vigorous and healthy; yet there was an underlying viciousness to it that made him doubt himself. She sat down at the table and put her head in her hands. She raised her head, and the look in her eyes was something he did not want to see but felt compelled to face. "My body did not belong to me but to strangers … dirty, nasty, brutish strangers. I had awful dreams

– though waking dreams were worse. Then I saw *Breakfast at Tiffany's*. I wanted to be Holly Golightly ... I wanted to be Audrey Hepburn ... singing "Moon River" on a fire escape in New York."

"But you said Hollywood is a poor excuse for reality."

"I've learned to make my reality. I was beautiful. I knew that. Holly Golightly (Audrey Hepburn) was beautiful. She knew it. I had suffered. Holly had suffered. I knew I was nothing. She knew she was nothing. I would go to New York and find Holly by becoming Holly. I would find me ... the real me ... the me that wasn't a bucket for ejaculation. Holly and I would be one. We were one."

He squeezed her hand and kissed her lips and took her lower lip between his teeth and sucked it gently. She pulled back and looked at him, at his eyes then at his mouth then at his eyes again. She touched her lower lip with the tips of her fingers.

"Does this come under the category of better-late-than-never? I thought you might be gay."

"There's a principle involved. But you wouldn't understand."

"You hateful Marines landed, and you came into my life, and I keep trying to get rid of you the way Holly threw the cat out of the cab into the rain. Your killing Makisig changes everything. I don't know how. I haven't thought it through. It just does. But one thing, I intend to get what Makisig got through me. It's mine now. It's my due. Do you want to see my stash?"

"No."

"It's under the floorboards under that sink over there."

"I'll take your word for it."

"You can count it. Nearly four thousand dollars. It's in a metal box. Greenbacks. Makisig was always paid in greenbacks. I never wanted to count it, but it's there."

She moved toward the sink. He reached across the table and clutched her hand. "Don't."

"Don't get pissed."

"I'm not pissed. Getting pissed is useless now."

"No, better yet ... get pissed about it. It's something to be pissed about. I'm pissed about it. I'll always be pissed about it. Like I'm pissed I can't have children. Several fucked up abortions. Don't you think I'm pissed about that? Being pissed is my guardian angel. It's going to help me get what's mine."

"Where's *his* stash?"

"In metal boxes under the floorboards in his bar. Kind of dumb but Makisig hid them where thieves would go to first."

"Does anybody else know about them?"

"I don't think so. He lived alone. He doesn't have a family. Couldn't get it up after what the Japanese did to him. In fact, he wasn't left with much of anything to get up."

"I thought he was fucking you."

"You're so naïve. He's done worse things to me than fucking could ever do. I would welcome the fucking if the other things were stopped."

"I don't understand."

"You don't want to understand. As far as I know, I'm the only one who knows about the stash. Except maybe Datu."

"It's yours. Let's get it."

"Don't get involved in this."

"I'm not involved in this?"

"All your *semper fi* bullshit has blinded you to what life really is."

"He really needs it now, Mariko, doesn't he? I don't want any of the money. I just want you to have it."

"You don't know where getting it is going to lead."

"Let's get it and get on with our lives."

"What'd you mean *our* lives? When did you start thinking *our*?"

He peered out the window. The rain had stopped. Dripping water made hollow thwacking sounds on some metal object just outside the window. She opened the door. "Your clothes are soaked. I'll be right back." She went outside. He heard her walk to the front of the house and open and close the door. Shortly, the front door opened and closed again. Her footsteps came back. She opened the door and came in. She held flip flops, red cotton trousers, and a white shirt. The trousers and shirt had the pressed-down look of being folded years ago. They smelled of naphthalene.

"Wear these until we get your Marine clothes dried."

"Where'd you get them?"

"My father's. He never used him. When he came back from the war, people gave us a lot of clothes – far more than he would ever need. My mother doesn't like to throw anything away. We've kept them in storage all these years."

He stepped into the red pants, pulling the drawstrings to tie them.

"They almost fit you. My stepfather is big for a Filipino."

He slipped on the white, short-sleeved shirt. It had an open neck with three buttons down the front. She stepped back and looked him up and down and laughed.

"My authentic *katipunero*. Here, one more thing." She wrapped a red bandanna around his neck. He knocked it away. "No. Wear it. Trust me." She tied it.

"Okay, Mariko. Let's get this done." He opened the door. She closed it.

"It's not that easy. We've got Datu to consider."

"Who's that?"

"Datu ... Makisig's caretaker. He's old and ugly and a helluva knife fighter. Taught me how to use a knife. No family. Family killed in the war. Never married. Too ugly. Too poor. He lives alone in a backroom. Keeps the place going when Makisig's gone. I'm not taking all of the stash. I'll give most to Datu. But I can't let him see me take what's mine. He'll kill me. Datu has killed for Makisig. And he'd die for Makisig."

"Where is he now?"

"He's there. That's the problem. He's always in and around the bar.

He doesn't ever leave except to get supplies. There's only one thing to do. I've got a plan. You in?"

Phord saluted comically. She looked grimly at him.

Mariko went out to the jeep and came back. She had Makisig's forty-five and the knife. He had forgotten all about them. She sat down at the table and pushed a cracked suspension to one side. She sat at the table for a long time, staring at her hands gripping the edge.

She nodded and twisted the corner of her mouth, seeming to decide something. Getting up, she went to a small workbench, got a can of *Hoppe's #9* solvent and a can of *Birchwood Casey* gun oil and sat back down, removed the magazine, retracted the slide, checked the action, stripped the weapon, cleaned. and oiled the parts, and reassembled and re-holstered it. She cleaned and oiled the knife. She put knife and pistol in a drawer beside the work bench.

She said, "Let's sleep. We have to be fresh. We should get a few hours' sleep before I'm ready to go. Come to bed."

He untied the drawstrings to get the waist-material slack over his hardness. The sheets felt cool and clean and welcoming against his bare skin. Before she turned off the bathroom light, he watched her body through the transparent gossamer romper she put on. In the dark, her fierce embrace was like a treasure he lost by neglect and found by accident. He pressed his lips to hers, remembering the kiss she gave him in the hut by the sea. She moved her lips to one side by a small degree. His lips followed hers, but she lowered her head. He raised his hand to cup her breast. She gently removed it, kissed it and lowered it to his side.

"Mariko, what's wrong?" She did not reply. "Mariko, last night, with no love making, I thought you figured I'm queer."

"'Making love. Is that the right way to describe what you didn't do?'"

"Don't think I didn't want to."

She touched him. "Your titi rubber stamps that."

"I didn't do it because I never did it with Ajax's girls."
"So, I was Ajax's girl?"
"That's the order he gave me at the social."
"Am I Ajax's girl now?"
"What do you think?"
"I think we shouldn't. I think we should try to sleep."
"And if I love you?"
"Don't kid yourself."
"And if you love me?"
"What a laugh. Let's not do what you think I am. We need sleep. We have important things to do. And ugly things."

He lay awake, staring at the lighter darkness in the dark of the window that looked out on Makisig's bar. She held him long and desperately; and eventually he heard her breathing smooth out and grow heavy. A high-strung weariness spread through his body like a warm tide. Then he heard a cock crow. Her room swam into view. The light in the window had increased so he could almost see outside into the street. *Why am I here?* She was lying beside him, her hair sprayed across her face. He raised up on an elbow. He had been asleep without knowing it. She opened her eyes. She came wide awake immediately and looked at the window.

"Good morning."
"A military morning, Mariko. Dark before dawn."
"Jump off time, my love."
"Love is it now? It wasn't a while back."
"I hope your sleep got you bright and cheerful. You'll need it."
"Bright maybe. Cheerful, no. What's your plan?"
"Listen. Makisig says Datu doesn't sleep well. Nightmares of the war. We can't take the chance he'll be asleep. We have to do this when he's up and about. Wait here. I'll go in first. I'll leave the door ajar. Look into the bar from here. There's a light at the back of the bar in front of a bead curtain. That's Datu's living-hole. I'll go in and tell him

about a supply issue Makisig was having. I'll tell him Makisig wants me to see his supply ledger. He's got a stack of these ledgers for Makisig's bar. They go back years. When he starts looking through a ledger, I'll come to the door and signal for you. Get inside and close the door behind you. I don't want anybody in the street looking in. Be fast. But quiet. If Datu sees you, he'll kill you. Makisig's stash is under the bar. Roll the keg aside, and you'll see a finger-hole in the floorboard. Using that hole, lift the floorboard. You'll expose a cavity where there should be three or four metal boxes. They're filled with cash. Take them out. Put the floorboard back. Then get the hell out! The boxes are small enough to carry them all. Carry them back here." As she spoke, she dressed. Phord dressed too. Though not the neckerchief. "Got it?"

Phord nodded, skeptical but inspired by her natural confidence.

At the door, she said in that hard voice she used with Filipino men, *"Don't screw this up."* She crossed the street. From a key on a ring of keys she got from a wall hook behind her worktable, she unlocked the bar door and went inside. Standing in her open doorway, Phord looked across the street into the door she left open and saw a light burning behind a bead curtain in the back. The shadow of someone crossing that light showed on the floor. Mariko came back to the open door and raised and lowered her hand. Phord crossed the street and went inside. He closed the door behind him and went to the bar. He could hear Mariko talking in Tagalog behind the bead curtain. Baritone voice replying.

There was a table beside the door and a sign nailed to a post.

CHECK GUNS	SURIIN ANG BARIL
KNIVES	KUTSILYO
AT THE DOOR	SA PINTUAN

Two rows of cantilevered pegs were sticking out from the bamboo-matting wall. Hanging by one peg, showing in the glow of the electric light bouncing off the floor under the beads, was a leather belt. Attached to the belt with ring-clips were horned-leather sheaths with the protruding butts of three butterfly knives.

Phord went around the bar and, feeling with his hands, found the wash tub and the aluminum barrel beside it. He knelt on the boards and tipped the barrel and rolled it a little way to one side. Unable to see the floor in the dark under the counter, he patted around searching with his palms.

The floor was wet and sticky and smelled of rancid booze and rodents. His finger found the hole, and he lifted the floor section. It came up with a grating noise and with an up-rush of decay stink.

The beads parted, and Datu came into the bar. Heavy footsteps, asthmatic breathing. Phord recollected that Makisig had asthma too. The footsteps went to the door. Phord heard a butterfly knife being slipped from its sheath. The knife opened with a metallic smacking. Mariko came into the room and began arguing with Datu in Tagalog. They went back through the beads, and she kept arguing with him. Phord reached into the space beneath the floorboards. He felt around with his hand. He took a prone position and kept feeling around. Then he put the floor back, rolled back the barrel, and while Mariko was still quarrelling went outside and across the street and back into her room.

"That was close," she said when she came back. "He heard you back behind the door. That's why he came and got his knife. I had to argue him out of what he was seeing and hearing. I almost didn't. Where are the boxes?"

"No boxes. I moved the beer barrel. I lifted the floor. I searched under the floor. Nothing."

She gripped his arm. "What? You really checked?"

Her voice had a strange tone like an echo.

"As far as my arm would reach. There's nothing under that part of the floor."

"He told me the boxes were there. He told me that if anything ever happened to him they were there and I was to get them."

"Nothing's there."

She thought for a long while. Her beauty as she suffered in her thoughts had the look of almost-darkness. "Oh, the poor man. The poor, poor man!"

"I thought you'd be pissed."

"What would Father Baum do? Would he be pissed?"

"I don't know. I don't know Baum."

"He will see the love inside Makisig that the poor man tried to live by. I must see it too even if nobody else sees it. And seeing it is also a betrayal."

"I don't understand."

"Of course. He was never your pimp."

Mariko retrieved from under the floorboards a large metal box. She replaced the boards and opened it and handed him the box. "Count up, please." He took one look at the bricks of greenbacks secured with number 14 rubber bands and closed the box and handed it back. "No," he said.

She upended the box. Money rained down around him. The bands broke on several of the bricks, and single fifties and one hundreds flew. Phord scooped them up and put them in the box.

"Mariko, are you okay?"

She got the forty-five and sat down and field stripped it and reassembled it, talking to herself under her breath, her eyes half-closed. Since she had already field stripped, cleaned and reassembled it an hour or so ago, Phord figured this activity might be a meditation, a prayer with recoil spring and barrel bushing instead of rosary beads. After she replaced the pistol in the drawer, she faced Phord and said, clearly, calmly, "It's settled. I've thought it over. I know what I'm going to do. I'm going to apply for my visa to the states. But first I'm going to see Father Baum. I need his guidance now."

He knew there was trouble because the situation was ordinary. They were driving down a jungle track heading toward Father Baum's Catholic outpost, Mariko behind the wheel, through shrubs that gave off odors like smelling salts under towering mahogany trees. Sunlight spangled in treetops while the jeep pushed through dim, leaf-filtered light.

They came upon a stopped jeep. Two young men crouched beside the right rear tire, one had his ass-crack showing above his trousers' belt. A half hour before these young men had passed them on the track. The path was wide enough for one jeep, and the driver hit the horn and pulled around, waving gaily, bouncing through fiddleheads ferns, and then sped off. Now stopped, their jeep blocked the track.

Phord said, "Go around them, Mariko. Keep going." She stopped. "What the hell? They're working on a tire that isn't flat."

"I see that. But it doesn't matter. Father Baum once stopped for me when I needed help. He didn't know me. But he stopped to help me. I should stop for them."

She switched off the ignition. He put his arm across her. "It's okay. Let me go." She pushed his arm but he kept her blocked in. "Okay, listen. A couple of years ago, I broke down on a lonely road. It was called 'Robbers' Alley.' In fact, it was this road. Middle of the night. He stopped and gave me a ride. That first time I met him taught me to always stop to help." She pulled away from him and got out. "It's a lesson for you too, one of many lessons you haven't learned yet."

As she spoke, the men came over. One, short, wiry and the color of mahogany sawdust, looked worried; the other was chewing angrily on a long, scraggily mustache. He had a pugilist's ears. Their hands were empty. There were no tools beside the wheel. They looked neither at Mariko nor Phord but at the suitcase and a metal box Mariko had tossed in the back.

They exchanged words in Tagalog. Mariko got behind the wheel and drove around them. They waved as she drove past, smiling, thumbs-up.

"What help did they need, Mariko?"

"It's the help all the young men of this island need. And it has nothing to do with fake flat tires."

A few minutes later, they appeared in the rear-view mirror. They came up quickly and the driver hit the horn. Mariko pulled over. They pulled around her but instead of going on, stopped. A jungle thicket pushed up against the road. Mariko, unable to plow through that thicket to go around them, had to stop. They got out and came over. For the first time, Phord saw that one of the men, the short, brown one, had a stoma and was smoking a cigarette, inhaling and blowing the smoke in a long plume out of the hole in his throat.

They conversed in Tagalog. Throat-hole spoke with an esophageal quaking, closing and opening the stoma with his thumb.

"What's up, Mariko?' Phord asked.

The friendliness she showed the men was replaced by that impatient annoyance she often directed toward Phord. Her face was defined by the eyes of her Japanese father, the double-lids, epicanthic folds, the Filipino/Austronesian features of her mother, and a mysterious, brown light-skinned European look. That combination resulted in Phord (and Makisig) seeing an amazing beauty while some locals saw ugliness. "Piss off," she told him.

"That American school taught you well. Look, if these characters find that out you have ..." He was about to say, stupidly: *"... shit loads of money"* but saw her shake her head. Like all Filipinos he met, they probably understood at least some English.

Throat-hole went to the back of the vehicle, the bouquet of Aqua Velva wafting as he passed Phord. He stopped and, narrowing his eyes and scratching the back of his head with a Phillip head screwdriver that had somehow appeared in his hand, he contemplated the suitcase and box. Tobacco smoke filled the moisture-laden air and a whistling came from the hole as he chain-smoked the butt in and out. The other, Ears, biting his mustache as if it were gristle, joined him. Throat-hole put his hand gently on the box. Phord noticed he had a gold wedding ring.

Phord dropped his hand slowly upon Throat-hole's hand, pressing the hand down on the box, compelling the young man to drop the Phillip head to use his other hand to smoke or talk. The released screwdriver clanked on the box and rolled onto the jeep's floor. It fell through a rusted-out hole in which the differential housing and brake lines showed.

Ears sidled up against Phord so that in this jungle with no other people in sight, the three of them crowded together as if they were going through one door. The box, the color of gun bluing, and the suitcase, a pink, expensive, metal Samsonite, incongruous in this poverty-ridden area, focused their attention.

Throat-hole freed his hand from under Phord's and with that his thumb opened the box. There was a loud click as the latch came up. He pulled the lid up a few inches before Phord slammed it back in place. But that few inches revealed greenbacks. Seeing those greenbacks, Throat-hole had pinpoints of light dancing in his eyes. Christmas in the tropics! He tried to open the lid again, but Phord slammed it shut. The closing lid pinched a small piece of thumb. Throat-hole pulled his hand back, closed his lips over the thumb, and sucked the nick. "Ouch," he said. He took a drag on the butt in the stoma, looking at Phord with friendly confusion. Ears grabbed the ends of the box with both hands. He had sucked the end of his mustache into his mouth and was chewing on it so hard his upholstery-stuffing ears moved up and down. Phord put one hand on the chest of one and the other hand on the chest of the other and pushed slowly. He didn't want to push too hard. He didn't want to make this scene worse than it was or could be by triggering a free-for-all which, two-against one, he might not win. Both leaned into the push. They would not be moved. Feeling a tingling behind his eyes, Phord said, "Mariko" in a voice higher than he wanted it to be. He realized, surprised, he was calling her for help.

Mariko didn't disappoint. She was standing beside them, the cleaned and oiled forty-five in hand. She pointed it at the ground. At first, the men didn't see it; but when Phord spoke her name, they looked at her and saw it. Her eyes gazed levelly upon them, warm and friendly.

Throat-hole clamped his thumb on his stoma and belched and quacked something in Tagalog (or English, Phord didn't quite understand the words). His finger held in front of his partner's face signaled *let's go*. Ears blew his mustache out of his mouth, they walked back to their jeep, got in and waved in an *we'll-all-be-great-friends* way and gave their celebratory thumbs-up and drove off. As they disappeared behind foliage up the road, Phord saw Ears talking into a military surplus PRC6.

Mariko backed up, doing that expert thing with the gear shift, and headed back the way they came.

"You saw that bastard with the radio," he said. "I'll bet he's calling friends."

She got more speed on the narrow road than Phord was comfortable with. A wild water buffalo ran across the road in front of them and out of sight into brush; then it came back onto the road, stopped and faced the jeep. Tall at the shoulder as Phord's abdomen, its gray-black coat mud-splashed and fly-blown, its enormous, backward-curving, crescent-shaped horns raked with deep fissures, it shook its head, pawed, and woofed.

She braked and wrenched the wheel. The grill smacked the buffalo head on. The jeep swung off the road, its right front wheel hitting a depression. Vines and leaves spun in Phord's vision. The jeep was on its side. On his back, catching his breath, he saw on the road the buffalo's legs sticking straight up, kicking. The animal's bellows were like human screams.

Down the road came the grinding of a jeep motor and then another. Two jeeps were approaching. Additional interested parties, apparently colleagues of Throat-hole and Ears, were speeding their way.

11

We have Shimada!

"Mister Marine ... helps me."
"No, sir, she's not drunk."
"To hell with the girl, lieutenant. Don't go back to her. Go straight back to camp."

"Here comes the most amazing woman in the world," said Baum.

"Not interested," said McCabe.

"Through her we get Shimada."

"I want to meet her."

Baum drove them out of undergrowth into the amphitheater-shaped area beside the end of the bridge. No one was there. No guards, no logging company thugs, not even traffic. It looked as if there was a halt to the logging. Baum stopped the jeep in litter scattered around the truck-tire-flattened weeds. The litter tumbled down the banks beside the abutments into the tanned-leather-colored, slowly moving water.

He got out and kicked angrily at an empty pack of Marlboros. It was a rather athletic kick—though not too robust he being cognizant of his aching head—getting torque with his hips and swinging his leg in a compact arc. (O'Toole told McCabe that Baum had played semi-pro soccer in Germany before the War.)

He muttered, "*Gegen dummheit gibt es keine pillen.*" He squinted at McCabe. Baum had a way of frequently talking German to himself under his breath, getting annoyed when others caught him doing it. A private person with private wounds, he disliked being spied on. "Sorry for the German," he said. McCabe knew he was not sorry only irritated that Phord heard. "It's an old saying. *There's no pill for stupidity.* These loggers are so stupid! Money makes them stupid. Most islanders are too poor to afford a whole pack of cigarettes. They buy one stick—or one-half stick—at a time. Loggers get wages to buy their cigarettes in cartons. To them, the island's a trash dump. Look at this crap they threw around here. Logging poisons land, people's hearts, people's souls. But some people are not poisoned, and I'm going to show one amazing woman the way to Shimada. And with Shimada gone ..." He swept his hand at the trash in the weeds and down the embankment. "We're kicking stupidity in the balls."

He drove to the river and came upon a dozen or so mounds under green, plastic tarps secured with galvanized-steel pegs. The mounds were arranged in two neat rows, the pegs lined up precisely as if positioned by a carpenter's snap-line and pounded in at the same angles. This was Baum's supply dump for the non-violent action. The linear protrusions in the tarps showed the supplies under them were neatly stacked. McCabe hadn't thought that logistics would be part of Baum's actions. Now he saw that a great deal of thought and care had been put into this. He remembered O'Toole saying that Baum had told him about fighting with Rommel in the desert and that it was "... a tactical heaven and a logistics hell." Baum cut his logistical teeth in hell.

Baum stopped, got out, walked to the river and bent over. McCabe saw the priest's abdomen rising and falling and heard the noises in his throat. His vomiting was loud and violent. Baum did things with a heavy, peasant's hand. He spat and wiped his mouth with his hairy forearm and picked up water in his cupped hand and wiped his arm and turned and walked back to McCabe. Black circles around his eyes showed in contrast to the ghastly white of his face under the bandage. He put his hands on the hood and leaned against the jeep.

"You know what? You might not be such a bad guy after all. Maybe I can understand why you're making such a big impact with the poor on this island."

"Same with you, my young friend. When we first met, I thought you were all hat and no cattle. That's what they say in Texas. But I'm changing my mind."

"Why don't you lie down?"

"Nein."

"Moving around like this could get your brain bleeding."

"No time to waste." Two H-19 Chickasaws buzzed low over the trees.

"They're heading out to sea," McCabe said. "The battalion's clearing out. It'll take a few days to clear out completely. That gives us a little time. Do we have enough time?"

"Who knows, my young friend? Nobody's been able to capture or kill him for two decades. We've got at most two days. What did your Lincoln say? The occasion is piled high with difficulties."

"The world has been changed many times with a just few minutes action."

"Yes, even just a few seconds. But not with an AWOL lieutenant."

"I'm not AWOL. AWOL means you're not going back. I'm going back."

"You Americans ... a mystery wrapped in an illusion." Baum scratched the back of his ear under the bandage and scuffed his sandal in the dirt. "Picking cotton was the only time I thought I understood Americans. Since then, the mystery, the illusion deepens."

He said, "No mystery. Ask O'Toole. He seems to know all about why I'm here."

"O'Toole is also a mystery."

"O'Toole's a mystery to himself."

Baum clapped his thick hands. They made a distinct pop. "Let's stop flapping our jaws, as you Americans say. Come on."

McCabe followed Baum down between the tarps. They gave unto a six-sided, stove-jack-equipped, general purpose Army tent. "Here she is," he said.

McCabe looked at Baum, not where he was pointing. A moment ago, the color was drained from his face; now a bit of red (Baum's skin was light and freckled) was coming back to upper patches in his cheeks. His eyes, tearing up from vomiting, were clearing. His resilience interested McCabe who figured it was a characteristic that enabled him to transform himself from soldier to priest. He looked where Baum pointed.

Out of the mosquito net opening of the GPS tent stepped an elderly woman. She wore a half-sleeved black dress that reached to mid-calf. Her shoulders were broad, her hips slim. Her hair was pulled back so severely (tied at the nape of her neck) that it had an oily shimmer. Her forehead was big, her eyes small and her chin even smaller. Something about the straight line of her mouth, some low-burn cruelty, made McCabe wary.

"McCabe, this is Tala."

McCabe held out his hand. Tala looked at his hand then at his eyes. McCabe lowered his hand. He swallowed a little knot that had gathered on the back of his tongue. The cruelty was not just in her mouth but in her eyes too, deep in her eyes. Yet her expression mocked him. He touched his thumb to his nose and wiggled his fingers.

"Why mock her?" Baum said. "She knows as much about Shimada as I do. She knows the Japanese." Tala looked at Baum, and the skin beneath her eyes pulled down. Baum put his arm around her shoulder and pressed his fleshy lips along with a three-day growth of whiskers against her cheek. He said something in a low voice in Tagalog, and she looked at Phord and raised her hand to shake. He took her hand in his. It was limp and dry and somehow had the same communication of malice as her mouth and eyes.

She spit gently in his face.

Baum got in front of the woman and pressed his hands against McCabe's chest.

"Let's talk, my young friend."

"Don't push me like I was going to do something to her."

"I'm not pushing. I'm pulling."

McCabe walked to the riverbank wiping his face with his sleeve.

"She's the best, McCabe. The best. I can't do without her. She's been with the bridge action since the beginning. The powers sent thugs to destroy the supplies. But she fought them off. She might have had help. I don't know. She's small but fierce. The lazy beasts figured it wasn't worth the effort to go against her. So, they let the supplies alone until they could figure out what to do with her. Her husband fought the Japanese in these jungles. He was wounded and the Mangyans saved his life. She'll do anything for them. Her help at the bridge against the loggers here has been great. Without her, we can't get Shimada."

"Manners would help."

"When you lose a war, then talk about getting manners. You don't know what it means to lose a war. That's why I can't understand you Americans. You're the winners. I can't understand that. So, you're cursed. Of course, I'm cursed too. My country lost. And it's cursed. Her country lost. Understand?"

McCabe nodded he understood, though he didn't.

"Don't blow smoke. You don't understand. I don't expect you to. You can't understand. You know what losing was for her? Before the war, she was young. She was beautiful. She had two ardent suitors.

Then the Japanese came. Her parents were killed. Her suitors became guerrillas in the jungle, and she was left alone. A Japanese official moved into her parents' house. He lived there with her for three years. Maybe he raped others too. She won't talk about it. Why should she? So, she can spit in your face. That's her manners. That's her right. Spitting in your face is like knowing that the knife and spoon go on the right and the fork on the left. Now let's get to work."

Back in the tent, the woman was sitting at camp desk writing. When Baum and McCabe entered, she picked up the paper and handed it to Baum. She began writing on a new sheet of paper. Putting the paper in his shirt pocket, Baum said, "Let's go, McCabe."

"Where?"

Baum walked to the jeep. Usually, his actions were slow and deliberate, mirroring the heavy, muscular aspect of his physique, moving as if he willed himself to be conscious of that action before he took it. Now he walked in a quick, jerky way.

McCabe, following Baum, stopped when he heard the woman call him. She held out a sheet of paper. He came back and took it out of her fingers. In block letters, she wrote, KILL HE NOW.

"Kill who?"

The woman didn't answer.

"Who should be killed?"

The woman was silent.

"Shimada?"

McCabe balled up the paper and threw it down. He followed Baum. They took off up the river road.

"She's really very beautiful," Baum said. "Don't you agree?"

"Hard to see her beauty through the spittle."

Baum took the paper out of his shirt pocket. "Take it, my young friend." McCabe took it. "Read it." The woman had written map coordinates. That's all. McCabe handed the paper back. Baum kissed it and held it up triumphantly. The paper snapped in the air stream.

"Shimada's there?"

Baum winked at him. It was done with the eye that was on the burned side of his face. A spear-tip-shaped patch of skin, smooth as melted sugar, extended from his temple to his jaw like a half-mask. Though the burned-to-a-crisp skin stopped at the edge of the eye, that eye when winked communicated the experience of nearly being burned alive in his tank. "We're not home free yet. First, we must see the Crazy Guy. This paper is where. He'll tell us when."

"Who's that?"

"The other suitor. The one Tala didn't marry. He was captured by the Japanese. He didn't have Mangyans to save him. He knows when Shimada will be at those coordinates."

"He's still on the island?"

"Never left. He owns a bar beside Tala's house."

"How can he be crazy if he owns a bar?"

"Oh, he's crazy. You'll see. Nobody can survive what was done to him and not be crazy. But maybe crazy will get Shimada. Sanity hasn't." He stopped and touched the bandages. "First, I have to clear for action."

He unwound the bandages from his head. They were bloody and smelled foul. The wound ran from the side of his forehead back into his temple where a patch of hair had been shaved off and several dozen stitches applied. The wound-margins were swollen, blood and pus leaked between cracks in the scabs.

"Coagulation's good. Maybe some infection."

"I've seen worse, my young friend. Stigmata is good for what ails you." From the floor well, he picked up a blue, cardboard box with a red cross and removed cotton bandaging and a brown bottle of hydrogen peroxide. He soaked the cotton with the peroxide and dabbed it on the wound. The bubbling and hissing were dramatic. "Afraid I'm going to ask you to put a clean dressing on. You had first aid in your Marine officer's training?"

"What the hell do you think?"

"I'm not talking about training. I'm talking about training. Training when hot metal is flying, and assholes are puckering. Nobody's fired at you in anger, my young friend?"

McCabe remembered the forty-five going off at the nipa hut. He remembered the gun pointed between his eyes in the candy store when he was a boy and a junkie robbing the store had pulled the trigger. There was a click, a misfire. Twice guns were pointed at him and the trigger pulled ... but not in the kind of anger Baum meant. "Not to my knowledge."

"Kindly do the honors."

McCabe folded a triangular bandage into a cravat. He placed the base just above Baum's eyes and brought the tail over and behind his head. He crossed the free corners over the tail, tied them in a half knot, and tucked the tail behind the half knot.

Baum tentatively felt the bandage. "It's stable. Good job, my young friend." Baum walked onto the bridge over the spot where he had laid down in front of the truck. He dropped the bloody wrappings into the slow-moving water.

"How did you get the coordinates?" McCabe put his hand on Baum's shoulder. "I guess I should call you partner – though I might break out in hives saying it."

"One more thing to understand about Tala." Baum's jeep jolted slightly as a front tire hit a shallow pothole. The jeep veered off the muddy-sandy road. Baum stomped the brakes. The vehicle stopped, its radiator sticking in a bush with bright orange berries. His head drooped; his thick, healthy teeth showed in a horrible grimace.

"Father," said McCabe. "What the hell? Are you okay?"

Baum ground his teeth. His thick fingers slapped the top of the steering wheel several times. After a while, he raised his head. He looked at McCabe. His eyes were bleary. "I must tell you this."

"Get back to the hospital. That was just a minor bump the jeep hit.

Something is wrong with your skull. You could croak."

Baum said through pale, stiff lips. "Urgent that you know this."

"Know what"

"Know that Tala had a daughter by the Japanese official."

"What's that have to do with Shimada?"

"Wait. Wait. Let me finish." He reversed the jeep back onto the road and stopped it.

"We've got a lot more bumps ahead. You won't make it."

"Says who? *Sagt wer?* Listen. Listen! The daughter became a prostitute. She worked a lot in Manila."

McCabe said, "Manila prostitutes were imported for the SEATO exercise. I might've run into one. I raided their fuck hut."

Baum shifted into first. But he didn't let up on the clutch. He looked down the road. He said, "Tala's daughter also lived on the island. I know her. When she's free, she helps me minister to people around the island."

"Is this a Filipino thing? Prostitutes doing double-duty with the church?"

"Don't be dumb, my young friend. My heart breaks for what she has to do." Baum drove slowly. "I figured there might be a connection between Tala's daughter and Shimada. She being half-Japanese. I have no proof, but I think she might have secretly taken him food, medicines, and other supplies. Shimada had to have help. Existing all these years on his own without help from an islander was impossible. She's the logical choice."

Baum steered between a half dozen potholes. "When Shimada killed that girl and our action collapsed, I asked Tala's daughter. She denied it, of course. I knew even if she did know, she wouldn't tell me. So, I got with her mother, Tala, and Crazy Guy. Being the girl's pimp, Crazy Guy was plugged into her body and her thoughts. There wasn't anything she wouldn't tell him if he pressured her enough." Given his pain, this was a long speech for Baum. He was silent, gathering his energies to say more. Then, "He maybe got out of her the place she and Shimada might meet again. Yesterday, he had radioed Tala the coordinates. He said he would send another radio message about the time. Then, nothing. *Nichts.* He's gone dark. Anyway, we have the coordinates."

"But not the time."

"We have Shimada, McCabe! We don't even need two days."

"We need the time."

"We have him! The time will come. I wish we had a Marine company to get him. Just you and me ... I don't like it. But I must live with it because *das Eisen schmieden, solange es heiß ist.*"

"What?"

"Strike while the iron is hot."

"Pinning your hopes on Tala's daughter is a joke. How long have you known her?"

"Years."

"Why didn't you get information from her on Shimada in the years before?"

"I wanted to. But the time was never right. Now it's right. The Marines are here. Your commander's been killed. The daughter is back from Manila. Shimada is in the area. Tala's upset by the girl being killed and is gung-ho about helping. The people need to get motivated to re-start the bridge action. Today, the stars are aligned."

"I don't like your plan, Baum. It stinks. But the crazy thing is, I've come to like you. I don't like you, but I like you. Or maybe I like that we share the same need. Or maybe it's just your spunk I like."

"Whatever that means."

He steered the jeep through a village of grass huts and plywood shacks. A burned-out hulk of a jeep stood beside a shack with scrap metal walls and a roof made of double-folded tent canvas.

"By the way, what's Crazy Guy's name?"

"Makisig, my young friend."

12

Katipunero!

Mariko lay face down beside Phord in blue flowers. (Groggily, Phord wondered at their beauty and why they didn't give off perfume.) Mariko's arm was stretched out and twisted unnaturally, palm up, fingers plucking the invisible strings of an invisible harp.

The jeep's motor was running, gasoline smell in the air. He crawled through plants from which almond-shaped bulbs grew that, when brushed, split open to let out a caramel-like liquid. He reached under the steering wheel column and switched off the ignition then crawled back to Mariko.

Her eyes were open but not tracking. She sucked spittle, swallowed hard. He helped her sit up, head lolling. She said something in Tagalog then said, "Bloody hell."

With the backs of his fingers, he brushed her hair off her face and kissed her cheek. "Where are you hurting?"

The water buffalo, on its back kicking, bellowed. Mariko got to her feet pushing Phord's helping hand away. "Poor thing!"

Three jeeps approached. They stopped in front of the water buffalo. Eight men got out. One, taller and lighter-skinned than most Filipinos, pointed a forty-five.

Jerking his arm to keep the weapon aimed between the beast's moving-target eyes, the man pulled the trigger. Pieces of horn flew into the weeds. Then there was buffalo bellowing and men shouting and forty-fives going off. The animal, energized by the lead pumped into it, struggled to its feet, then was rewarded with a shot to the lungs. It keeled over, blood pouring from its mouth, stretching its neck back in one, last feeble attempt to gore, its shoulders and high quarters in death spasms. The odors of gun smoke and blood mixed with the gasoline smell and the smell of defecation. The men's heavy breathing peppered the silence. They looked surprised at what they had done.

Driving a jeep attached to a rope around the horns, the tall one pulled the buffalo off the road, legs up, bloody carcass steaming. Half a dozen thumb-length, stomach worms were corkscrewing out of the open, tongue-flapping mouth, escaping this corpse like rats deserting a sinking ship.

The men stood in a circle and conferred, glancing at Phord and Mariko. Then they walked over, fanning around the two.

Throat-hole and his pal Ears were there. Throat-hole fell to his knees in the flowers and snapped open the box. He wasn't smoking now. Greed triggered temporary abstinence. Phord kicked at his face but was grabbed by three men and pulled away. Ears stuck a forty-five delicately under Phord's chin.

When he first joined the Marines, he heard that the forty-five had been invented to stop the Filipino Moros fighters during their insurrection against the Americans some 60 years before. Before battle, the Moros tied their testicles with copper wire, the pain ejecting them into an altered state of consciousness. They bound their limbs tightly with cords to reduce bleeding. Charging the skirmish lines, they might have been shot many times by the .38 pistol issue of that day but continued attacking, lopping off a few American heads with their krises before expiring. The forty-five was the answer, knocking the attackers on their asses so they couldn't kill when almost dead. Now history had come full circle: the Filipinos had the weapon—Phord saw many locals packing it—and this one was his personal, historic blowback.

With cold metal against his throat, Phord tried unsuccessfully to swallow. Mariko, standing beside Phord, was empty handed. Her forty-five was in the jeep.

Throat-hole opened the box. The men, dirty, unshaven, their eyes wide with grotesque eagerness, crowded forwarded.

Mariko slammed the lid shut and sat down on the box and hugged her knees. She was dressed in what she called, *"my embassy outfit"*, a simple, white cotton blouse, brown-black slacks, and chic sandals—a simple but classy look. With her hair pinned up, two tresses falling over her shoulders, modest makeup, and the proud, intelligent look in her eye, she appeared to be the daughter of a noble Philippine family. Mariko was an expert at taking on appearances that suited the situation though; however, now with her clothing ripped and stained, and some of her hair spilled out from their pins, she wasn't quite embassy-presentable.

The tall, light-skinned one stepped in front of Mariko and raised his hands. The men halted. A few of them stepped back, giving him room. They fell silent and awaited his word.

He looked down at Mariko, his legs spread, fists on hips, grinning the pirate-captain-before-his-beautiful-young-captive grin. (Probably derived from the same Hollywood movies Phord had seen.) His eyes were black and slightly crossed (though when looked at from another angle, they were normal), his hair perfumed, a gold crucifix glittered on his hairless chest. He spoke to her in Tagalog as if to order her to bow down and kiss his horny-nailed feet clad in leather, tire-rubber sandals.

He flicked his fingers in her face, indicating she should stand. His gesture showed he was used to being obeyed. She did not move. She stared at him.

The leader turned to the men around him and said something in

Tagalog. They laughed, not so much, it seemed to Phord, because what he said was funny but in deference to him.

Mariko picked up a mechanic's rag that had shot out of the somersaulting jeep. She got to her feet and raised the rag to his face. He pushed her hand away. She pointed at his face and said something Phord didn't understand. He shook his head. His heavy-lidded eyes closed slowly as he mulled over what she said then opened quickly. He dropped his hand and nodded. She stepped toward him. He took one backward step. His mouth grinned, but his eyes were alarmed.

She dabbed across his face, removing flecks of buffalo blood. He closed his eyes, disliking her attentions but putting up with them. Phord saw him as handsome, but when he looked at him from a different angle, he was—like the change that came over his crossed eyes—ugly. She tossed the rag into weeds. He wiped his face with the back of his hand then cracked knuckles of that hand

Mariko spoke to the men, turning slowly to look into the eyes of each as if she spoke only to him. Some dropped their eyes. Others looked at her then looked at the Pirate Captain to see how he was reacting to her words. They listened with reluctant interest, she casting a spell upon them practically against their will.

When finished, she turned to the leader and with her fingernail flicked off a tag of blood she missed with the rag. It was a gesture that was an odd mixture of endearment and taking charge.

The leader snapped his fingers and pointed at Ears. Ears who still held the gun under Phord's chin, protested in Tagalog. He nonetheless lowered the gun.

Phord swallowed, but saliva wouldn't go down. He spit it out. He tried to take a deep breath, but his lungs felt strapped. The top of his head seemed to be coming off.

Throat-hole and Ears shouted in Tagalog and pointed at the box. The young man placed his hand on Throat-hole's face and pushed. Throat-hole staggered backwards. Burping in his stoma, he grabbed the forty-five out of Ears' hands. Glaring at the Pirate Captain, Throat-hole lifted the pistol. There was a dangerous ripple in the Pirate Captain's eyes, like that barely visible ripple on the surface of water when a croc's eyes and nostrils appear. Intimidated, Throat-hole dropped his eyes and lowered the weapon.

Ears stepped forward, fists under his chin in the peekaboo style of Floyd Patterson. Taking advantage of the peekaboo's susceptibility to overhand punches, the Pirate Captain swung wildly. His knuckles made an unhappy sound on Ears' skull.

The Pirate Captain clamped his hand between his thighs and turned in a circle. *"Owwww,"* he said. He pushed Ears—wobblily, goggle-eyed, clutching the top of his head—out of the way and spat orders. He clamped his injured hand under his armpit. The gang crowded around one side of the jeep and pushed. The vehicle swung upright, gasoline squirting, suspension sounding like a hacking cough. He exchanged words with Mariko.

She said to Phord: "He wants us to keep on our way and forget this ever happened."

"What the hell did you say to them?"

She shrugged. Phord walked off, stopped, untied the flyless, katipunero pants and urinated. His urine spattered in army-ant mulch at his feet.

"*Juramentado*," the Pirate Captain said.

"What?"

"She's *Juramentado*."

"What're you talking about? What'd she say to you?" Phord pulled the pants up and re-tied the drawstrings.

"*Juramentado!* Keep away from her. *AAAH!*" The Pirate Captain removed his hand from his armpit and shoved it under Phord's eyes. His knuckles were swelling. *"Broke!"* He clamped the hand back in his armpit. He stomped and thrust his head back and shouted to the sky, *"AAAH!"*

Mariko started the engine. It cranked but wouldn't start. She got out and lifted the hood and bent under it. "Start it up."

Phord got behind the wheel and turned the key. "Stop!" she said. She adjusted fuel lines. "Okay, start it again." The engine cranked. "Stop!" She adjusted spark plug wires and carburetor choke. "Okay, again!" After a moment of cranking. "Stop!" She slammed the hood and stood there leaning on her straightened arms, head bowed. She said to Phord: "The rollover probably screwed up cylinder compression."

"What's that mean?" He knew nothing about engines.

"Nothing good."

She spoke to the Pirate Captain. He listened, alternately blowing on his knuckles and clamping his hand in his armpit.

He gave orders. A young man came up behind Mariko, carrying the rope used on the buffalo carcass. Though his skin was light, his hands clutching the rope were black from working in soil. He looped one end of the rope through the jeep's tow bar then looped the other end through the tow bar of the gang's jeep.

Her jeep was towed back to town, she sitting behind the wheel, Phord beside her. The parade of four jeeps, carrying Mariko, Phord, and gang members, circled around the oval plaza with its mowed grass, its half dozen palm trees and its bronze bust on a concrete podium of a hero that looked a little like a young Makisig. They made their way to the outskirts of town. She shouted a word Phord did not understand. The jeeps stopped abruptly outside a plywood-sided shed. With one hand, Pirate Captain untied the rope then threw the rope into the back of his jeep. He shouted to the men, *"Vamanos!"*

"Wait," Mariko said. Mariko opened the box and brought out greenbacks and counted, peeling bills which she held in one hand with the thumb of the other hand, licking it at intervals. She offered the bills to the leader. He shoved them away.

Mariko handed the bills to Throat-hole driving the jeep. Throat-hole reached for them but drew back when the Pirate Captain shouted a Tagalog rebuke.

Mariko folded the bills and inserted them into the Pirate Captain's shirt pocket. One hand in his armpit, he pulled them out with the other and swung his arm. They fluttered to the ground. The jeeps drove away.

Phord, picking up the bills, said, "Why pay them off?"

"They helped."

"That money's been ripped out of your soul. Nobody has a right to it but you. They were ready to kill you for that money. Now he threw it back in your face. What changed? I don't get it."

"You wouldn't. Help me get this jeep in the shed."

They pushed the jeep into a dirt-floored shed. There were wall-to-wall tools. Lizards scurried in the rafters in the dark. She lifted the hood and turned on a portable, electric work light. She removed the valve cover, unscrewed bolts and stuck them into a piece of old cardboard. She re-threaded the bolt holes and re-torqued the cylinder heads, straightened bent valves with a ball peen hammer and flathead screwdriver, and re-set the cam timing. She turned on the motor and cocking her head and squinting listened. "Running rough, but it'll get me to Father Baum's outpost." It was nearly midnight by the time she left the shed, closed and locked a broad, metal-strapped, wooden door and went to a room in the house Phord had been to earlier in the day. They showered in a small, clean bathroom with rose-colored tiles on the floor and walls. Then she cooked a meal of fried, salted fish and rice. Eating, they downed tumblers of her special herb-flavored gin drink.

She said, "We'll get a few hours' sleep. Then I'll head for the Father's in the morning. And what about you? Back to camp?" She pressed her fingers to his lips. "Stop. Say 'love' and I'll scream."

He pulled her hand away. "How about this word, *juramentado*? Where did you pick up that word? Do you know what it means?"

"No."

"It's Spanish for a Moro who kills Christians. The word means 'oath taker.' Don't you know the Moros? You Americans fought them at the turn of the century. They're Muslim Filipinos. Fierce fighters. No one has been able to really conquer them. A Moro goes Juramentado when he takes an oath to kill Christians. He goes through rituals and bindings of his limbs, shaves his head, shaves his eyebrows, dresses sometimes in white then makes a surprise attack, sometimes on a lonely road, sometimes in a crowded public place. He knows he is going to be killed in the process. He welcomes death. Death means he'll go to paradise."

"The gang leader said you were Juramentado."

"He's a fool."

"Fool enough to believe what he said. What did you tell him? They were all set to take the money and maybe do bad things to you. But your words stopped them in their tracks."

"Stopped him. Stopped the leader. Didn't you see what he was wearing?"

"No."

"A crucifix. There's no mystery to what I said. I told him it wasn't my money. I told him it was God's money. I was taking that money to Father Baum's outpost. I told him if he took it, he would burn in hell. But that wasn't the only point he understood."

"And that was …?"

"There's no me without that money?"

"But you were giving them some money."

"Why am I not surprised you don't understand? The things that look complicated to you Americans we Filipinos see as really very simple. Without New York … without Holly Golightly … there's no me. The leader knew that. He didn't know what New York means to me, of course. But he sensed what the money means to me. And what I would do to keep it. He also knew if he wanted it, he not only had to kill me, he had to kill you too. He couldn't just kill me and let you go. Killing me, a Nobody, he might've gotten away with it. But killing you, he'd be killing a Somebody. Maybe a couple of the others would have been willing to kill you and me. But he had that crucifix, and he had his mortal soul and he had his power over the gang."

"He didn't have to help you by pulling your jeep here."

"Christian charity? Who knows?"

"But to throw the money back in your face? Crazy!"

"It's a Filipino thing. You Americans worship money. But for Filipinos ... at least those who haven't been too Americanized ... there's something more important than money."

"What?"

"You didn't see it when he threw the money back?"

"No."

"Then you'll never see it."

"Educate me."

"He admires the Juramentado way. Though he doesn't know what it really means. What it means is simple; and it's this: life is death. Every college sophomore knows that. But you have to live it to know it. For me, the meaning of that money is death. I died countless times earning it. If it goes, I go."

"If we married there would be no problem. You love me, Mariko."

He clamped his hand on her mouth as she screamed. She tried to bite it. He dropped his hand.

"Go on. Keep screaming." She fell silent. Or maybe she hadn't screamed. He thought she had screamed. He heard her scream. But now that she was silent, he wasn't sure. Her silence was a kind of scream. She said, "Love? Don't talk to me about fucking love. You don't know about love. You don't know about anything."

"Mariko, I remember seeing that movie you love so much. It didn't make much of an impression on me." As he spoke, Mariko got the forty-five out of a holster hanging by a web belt off a peg by the door.

She placed the weapon on the worktable and stared at it. "But I remember it now. Look at Holly at the end. Holly after she threw the cat into the rain. She had to admit her feelings for Paul. Her feelings were her destiny. And she finally gave into them."

She stared at the forty-five, her fingers drumming lightly on the tabletop. She got up and walked in a circle around the room then came over to Phord.

"Living here with me, your paychecks to your mother will be cut off."

"I'll make money some other way. My military pay is a fraction of what I can make in civilian life. I can always sell. Maybe we can move to Manila. My mother will get all the money she needs."

She stopped in front of him. "*Feelings*, you say? *Foolishness!* I say. You want feelings? You want foolishness?"

She kissed his mouth and slipped her hands under his shirt and sat him down on the bed and licked his lips and bit them softly, untying his drawstrings and stripping off the pants.

"You're the first one on this bed."

Wrapping him up, pressing with her heels in the small of his back and rotating her hips, she brought him quickly to ejaculation. As she did, she looked into his eyes, inviting him. He saw that aching invitation in her eyes but felt it in his groin and in his bones.

Then her legs were off him and she pushed away and was on her feet and across the room and down on the floor in the corner embracing her knees.

He went to her and cupped her chin in his palm, but she would not raise her head.

"Mariko, what's wrong?"

"Is that all there is? What a laugh."

"What happened?"

"I don't know. It's the concussion. I'm thinking crazy thoughts. Oh, I've solved the problem."

"What problem?"

"You."

"Problem? I'm the solution."

"Finally, I know how to get rid of you."

He lifted her to her feet. She rose, her limbs slack. If he had not held her, she would have dropped back to the floor. He walked her to the bed. There, she pressed her face against his neck and held him with a new passion. So beautifully confident with the men, she now trembled and wept like a child in the night.

She woke him in the dark, on top, straddling, death-gripping his shoulders, rocking in a frenzy, her body madly surging, dark hair flying, at long last crying out, her cry like the sound in the first moment when two automobiles impact, a metallic crunching crack, inhumane cracking sound coming from her throat – then silence, sweat plopping on his chest. She collapsed on him, sweaty breasts, struggling for breath as she tongued his lips.

"Get rid of me, Mariko? What're you talking about?" She pressed her face against his neck in the private space under his jaw. When her breathing evened out, she rolled off him and lay spread-eagled staring at the ceiling. "Answer me. What're you talking about?" A tress of hair lifted as she blew it off her face. He said, "We both of us changed since we came together." She turned her head quickly to look at him – yet said nothing. "I thought you were just another one of Ajax's girls. That's why I wouldn't touch you. I never touched any of Ajax's girls. I couldn't. I couldn't because I hurt for them. And hurt for Ajax too. Maybe nobody else knows about Ajax but me – me and his ex-wife."

He pulled her hands covering her face aside. There was so much he did not know about her. Not despite but because of her having revealed a lot of herself, he felt she was hiding a lot. Opening her hands was like opening a door to her real self. For a moment, he thought he saw that self in her face in the dark. But the moment passed, the feeling left him. Seeing in her face was a door he could not open prompted him to speak of another closed door, Ajax. Speaking of Ajax, he felt, would help him speak of her. And bringing Ajax into her might bring her out to him —or bring him out to her. "You see, Ajax wasn't always like this. Up until he was wounded in Korea he was happily married, true to his wife. But he came back loaded with shrapnel that surgeons couldn't remove. He was changed. The shrapnel had damaged him so he couldn't control his itch. His wife couldn't satisfy him. They had no children. They divorced. When she found out what I was doing for Ajax, she looked me up at Camp Pendleton and told me about him. She said he was sick and needed treatment, but nobody knew what treatment would help. And people don't know his other side. Sure, he was mean and tough and often became a frenzied minotaur scaring hell out of his subordinates, but there was a side of him … like when I saw him in his dress blues change a tire for an old lady at night in a driving rain. He'd give homeless on the street all the money in his wallet. For years, he's been anonymously donating most of his paycheck that he didn't send to his ex-wife to needy enlisted families. In combat, he sacrificed himself many times for the lives of his troops. There are scores of Marines alive today because of him. On the island, he risked his career by shooting in the air during a melee at a basketball court, saving more Marines."

"You know what that means?"

"What?"

"Nothing."

Later, after they made stormy love again ("What do you Americans say about 'opening a can of worms'?" she laughed) and slept again, he went into the bathroom. She had gone to the toilet earlier and had written on a piece of paper on the toilet lid. "Blocked. Need plumber. Use outhouse."

He slipped on his Filipino pants and shirt. He remembered when he first donned them Mariko grinned—a look of genuine affection replacing the usual look on her face when she interacted with him of constant, low-grade suspicion—and called him *"my true katipunero."* Then he realized that look reflected more than affection. He realized with a mild buzzing behind his eyes, a feeling that always preceded a bout of depression, she loves me, what a shame.

Katipunero .... He guessed the word had a special, emotional meaning for Filipinos. Wearing the clothes, he felt the same urge that came over him when he was standing on a high place. The urge to jump, afraid the wanting to jump transformed into needing to jump. The fear now was the same. He was afraid he did not just want to be a katipunero, he needed to be.

As he did with many of his fears, he plunged into it. Though he was simply going outside to urinate, he tied the red cloth around his neck. He would piss in katipunero style! A new sales pitch in action! Closing the door softly behind him, he felt this katipunero could live on this island that he had begun to love and never go back to the states.

Not knowing where the outhouse was, he walked up the narrow street between empty, slap-dash market stalls, his sandals slapping on wet pavement, his shirt and neck-rag dampening in jungle mist.

The stars were dimming, though even at this stage of early light, they were bigger and brighter than the stars in the states. Unable to find an outhouse, pissing into trash in the back of Makisig's bar, Phord saw a figure come out of the shadows. It bumped into him. The figure had a strange, sour-vanilla odor. Light flashed in his eyes, bright parabolas spinning before his face. Phord knocked the flashlight away. He pushed the figure.

"Holy shit!" said the figure. "It's corporal fucking Foid."

"Who the hell are you?"

"Lieutenant McCabe. You're under arrest, asshole."

13

Death is the close of Phord's sales pitch.

"Mister Marine ... "
"Forget the girl, McCabe. Don't mention her again. Go."

You're a gift tied in ribbons dropped in my lap. I've wanted to hang your ass for a long time. What're you dressed like a clown for, corporal?"

Like a knocked-out boxer coming to and wondering why his opponent's hand is being raised in a ring filled with people when the last thing he remembered was touching gloves at the start of the fight, Phord found that he was standing at attention. Enveloped by this strange odor, the odor of sour vanilla, he thought: *The odor of an American!*

"Sir, I —"He shut his mouth. There was nothing to say. Being at attention and emitting "Sir ..." said it all.

Yet as a katipunero, he knew there was Mariko and his life with her.

"You motherfucking, shit bird, malingering, thieving, traitorous, fuck-up ..." McCabe shut his mouth and breathed deeply, once, twice, three times. The repetition of deep breaths indicated an acquired skill by someone who badly needed that skill. The bill of his soft cover came down almost over his eyes which raged in the quickening light. "Okay. I'll deal with you later. First things first. Tell me, do you know a Filipino named Makisig?"

"Yes, sir."

"He owns this bar, right?"

"Not sure, sir."

"Where the hell is he?"

"How should I know, lieutenant?"

"You've gone native."

"Is that what it looks like?"

"What am I looking at? What do I see?" Phord did not answer. "You're hanging out here, right? You ought to know Makisig or know of him."

"No, sir."

"*No sir.* What the hell does that mean?"

"I don't know, sir."

Phord saw a white balloon floating toward him. Then he saw it wasn't a balloon but the wrappings of a head bandage. A broad-shouldered, squat man with a head bandage stopped in front of Phord. In this fairy land of mist and first light and flashlight beam whipping about, Phord could not clearly see the man's face though he sensed it was ugly.

"I'm Father Baum. I'm looking for Makisig too." The man pronounced "father" with an "aw." Phord thought: *Father Baum? Mariko's Father Baum?*

Phord felt he had woken up and gone outside to piss but was still dreaming: Lieutenant McCabe suddenly come out of nowhere asking about Makisig; Mariko's Father Baum in a head bandage standing before him. Maybe he was dreaming he had killed Makisig, and the dream was like the remembrance of a favorite movie having a stronger hold on him—like *Breakfast at Tiffany's* for Mariko—than reality.

"Good for you."

"Makisig owns this bar," Baum said.

"That's interesting."

Phord saw he could easily take off, dash around the corner of the bar and down the street into the jungle at the end of it. He could lose this crazy lieutenant in the jungle then later circle back to Mariko. His quads contracted—but he did not move.

"Maybe he can help," Baum said. "A little help is better than no help."

McCabe trained the light on Phord's face. "This shit bird help *us*? Ha. Ha. You're a shit bird, Phord. Always have been. Always will be."

"Thank you, sir." Phord said and meant it.

Phord liked McCabe. The troops, who had disparaging nicknames for each of the officers, called McCabe "Train Wreck." He got the moniker for having his car crushed like a tin can by a Santa Fe locomotive when it got hung up on tracks in an Oceanside onion field after he tried to take a shortcut back to his apartment following a late-night booze-and-philosophizing session with Father O'Toole. The name wasn't reproach but tribute. "Train Wreck" was just another name for "hard charger." For instance, as a company commander before Ajax selected him to be camp guard commander on the exercise, he acquired a *semper scrotus* rep. In Camp Pendleton, he led his company on a 35-mile hike with field transport packs, a mission Gunny Lawler called, "whacked out." A good number of the troops dropped out, several wound up in the hospital with heat exhaustion. A congressman complained, and due to the old military rule of "shit flows downhill," there was a festival of high-ranking officers getting their asses handed to them. Ajax, the recipient of a royal chewing out by the division commander, might have relieved McCabe except he loved the lieutenant like a son and the troops loved him like the second coming of Chesty Puller.

Baum said, "If Makisig hasn't shown up by now …"

"You German?" Phord said.

"Accident of birth," said Baum. "And time."

"Without us knowing the time," McCabe said, "we're screwed."

"Screwed?" said Phord.

"We're looking for Shimada," said Baum. "You know who Shimada is?"

"Of course."

McCabe said, "What'd you know about Shimada?"

"Everybody knows about Shimada."

"Bullshit. You don't know about Shimada."

"The Devil in the Mountains. That's what I know about Shimada."

"You don't know he killed Ajax."

"You're right. I didn't know that. I was wondering who killed Ajax. I'm kinda outa the loop."

"There's a loop I'm going to get you into, Phord. Marine-brig reveille starts at oh dark hundred with pushups then double-timing in place – all before chow. That's the loop for your ass."

An early morning breeze brought animal stink from the mechanics' shed. Last night while Mariko worked on the head bolts and valves, he had washed buffalo hair, meat and grease off the grille. She had closed the shed door to keep her electric light from attracting nosey neighbors, so the air was like an anesthesia mask against his face. Sweat dripped from his face into the pink plastic bucket, flesh and hair floating on the surface of bloody water. Sponging off the grill seemed to make the odor grow stronger.

"Just you two going after Shimada? What do you want from me?" After a moment, he added, "sir."

Baum said, "*Zeit*. Time. Makisig gave us coordinates. But not time. When we have map coordinates and time, we can be where he might be when. No guarantee, but it's the best hope we have. Makisig's key to us getting Shimada."

Phord didn't know what the German was talking about. But he did know that with McCabe involved, another "train wreck"—whatever that might entail—could be in the offing. *Hot dog!* Phord thought Byrne would say. Byrne would love this mess.

"Time I know," Phord said, not knowing what he meant.

McCabe's laugh was a murderous bark. "Who told you?"

"Makisig," Phord let slip.

"You said you didn't know him."

"I mean I know him."

"So, you know him."

"Not like you think I do."

"Do you know him or not?"

"Show me the map."

"Don't change the subject. Do you know him or not?"

"I do and I don't."

"Cut the crap. You said Makisig told you something."

"You don't need Makisig. You might need me. Show me the map."

"To hell with the map. What about Makisig?"

"Stop wasting time," said Baum. "Get the map out."

"Phord's a bullshit artist."

"The map, lieutenant."

McCabe looked at Baum. He looked at Phord. Then he looked back at Baum. Phord saw that McCabe had a quick, efficient way of sizing someone up. That quick-read proclivity would translate into speedy decision-making under fire. "Okay, but he's blowing smoke. Come here, Phord."

They walked to a Mighty Mite parked behind the bar beside Mariko's jeep. Apparently, they had just arrived. Phord smelled its hot aluminum engine block and frame. It didn't smell like the steel of a normal jeep. To him, that odd aluminum smell was the smell of American Marines and vertical envelopment.

Lieutenant McCabe got out a map from his M1938 dispatch case, hanging from a shoulder strap, and opened it on the hood and trained the moonbeam on it and all three men brought their heads close together and stared.

"Makisig gave us these coordinates that Shimada was supposed to show up at."

"Of course," Phord lied, not knowing what he would say next. Having cut his salesmanship teeth by keeping the men in his mother's life at a distance and by selling odds and ends on the street to help keep his family out of utter poverty, he was most convincing when he did not know what he was saying – or at least what he was going to say next.

"Why do you say, 'of course'?" said McCabe. He was innately suspicious of declarative statements. On the streets, they were often accompanied by violence.

Phord said, "Well, isn't it obvious?"

"Enlighten us, asshole," said McCabe.

In the gooseneck beam, Phord saw the stiffening of lieutenant McCabe's forehead and cheeks and the drawing back of his lips from his teeth. He had heard the lieutenant had grown up in a tough part of New York; and he guessed his defense was a quick-release temper. It was mostly bluff, he figured, though dangerous too. Phord's bet was he could combine the lieutenant's temper and his wanting to get Shimada to create a slingshot of circumstances propelling him to get clear of these two. He didn't know how it could be done, what those circumstances would be, but he was confident it could be done—though he had to be careful doing it.

Phord said, "Shimada doesn't just want to fight. He wants to keep on hiding. Big difference. He's been holding out for twenty years and can easily go another twenty. These coordinates show how."

"It takes a great talent to be such a shit bird," said McCabe.

"You see where those coordinates are," Phord said, forcing the confidence he lacked into his voice. "At an intersection of two jungle roads connecting the inner island economies with the coastal economies. I'll bet a lot of Shimada's pilfering over the years happened in this area."

"*Du hast recht,*" Baum said.

A tight wire in Phord's chest loosened a little. This might work—whatever "this" was and whatever "work" meant—if—if he got this priest to back him up. He had the stupid face of Van Gogh's Potato Eaters. And his German seemed as stupid as his face. "Note the trails feeding out of this area back into the mountains. I'll bet there are more trails than this map shows. They're Shimada's bug-out routes. He could grab his take on the roads and then bug out over many mountain trails and nobody would be the wiser. I'm sure he had many other such attack-points around the island, but this is the one closest."

Talking, Phord felt buttery warmth radiating up his throat to the back of his tongue. When he had this feeling, he knew he could talk his way out of any mess – or if the occasion warranted, into it.

"Tell me something I don't know," said McCabe. "Like when."

"You mean when he's going to be there? That's obvious too. Don't you see it?" Phord didn't see "it" either. He not only didn't know what "it" was, he happily didn't care. The contours on the map smeared into one another as the flashlight beam faded. "Shit," McCabe said. He slapped the moonbeam against his palm.

"Didn't you bring fresh batteries, my young friend?" Baum said.

"Hell no."

Baum said nothing. McCabe said, "Don't give me your Teutonic-efficiency crap." These two reminded Phord of a married couple who hate each other but stay together for the kids: the "kids" in this case being their shared desire to get Shimada. McCabe said to Phord, "Okay, when …?"

Phord said, "Well, the way I figure it …"

"Get your umbrellas out. It'll be raining shit."

And great shit it'll be, thought Phord. He knew a con was simple: you just had to figure out what the mark wants then support him in getting it—for your own ends. "The way I figure it, if you go there now …"

"Don't use the word *you*, use the word *we*," said McCabe.

"Sir?"

"We meaning all three of us. You're going with us. *We is you too.*"

Phord said, "You. We. It doesn't matter. Now is what matters!"

"Stop playing for time. Get to the now. Which is the when."

"I told you. It's obvious."

"I'm stupid," said McCabe. "Make me smart." Mission impossible, Phord almost said, though he knew the lieutenant was smarter than most officers he knew, despite his temper being a quick-acting stupid pill.

"It's got to do with the moon. Phases of the moon." Why that came out of his mouth, Phord didn't know. He was always at his best jumping off a cliff and constructing his wings on the way down.

"Total bullshit," McCabe said. *I agree*, thought Phord.

Phord said to Baum: "He usually moves at night and only when the moon is at certain phases." Phord had learned that if he was trying to convince several people at once, he went after the person who looked more easily convinced. Convince that person and then get that person to convince others. His most persuasive words came not out of his mouth but out of the mouths of people he had convinced.

"Let's go," said Baum.

"Are you crazy, Father? He's fucking with us."

"Going where he tells us is not going to hurt us, my young friend." The tight wire in Phord twanged. Something was wrong. The priest sounded convinced, but Phord doubted the German was convinced. There was something hard and unyielding and ultimately unconvinced about this man. Phord thought the person the priest showed the world was a fake. "Let's go. The worst we can do is find nothing. The best we find Shimada. So what, who gives us the information? Finding Shimada is all that counts." *You don't believe what you're saying*, Phord thought, though he did not know why he thought it. It takes a salesman to know a salesman.

"I don't like it. It stinks."

"I don't like that it's just you and me going after Shimada. I don't like that I don't have a platoon of Marines to help. My young friend, you don't have to like it. I didn't like lying down in front of that truck on the bridge."

"A helluva lot of good it did."

"Had to be done. A cracked skull isn't too bad a price. Our Savior paid a worse price. This'll probably lead nowhere. The odds are against us. But they might be better odds than I've had in a long time."

Lieutenant McCabe turned to Phord. "You're coming with us."

"Let me get some things."

"You're getting nothing."

"It'll only take a few seconds."

"Now."

Phord looked at the door to Mariko's room across the street. His *aye, aye, sir* felt to him like the words of a body-snatching stranger.

With McCabe behind the wheel, Baum riding shotgun, and Phord in the back, they drove off, headlights illuminating the same road Phord and Mariko had been on. A ground-hugging animal's eyes burned red in the glare on the side of the road.

"Sir, don't go this way."

"Shut the hell up, Phord. The map doesn't lie. I know how to get there."

"It's not safe. There're other roads. I've heard this is called 'Robbers' Road'. There might be gangs down there."

"Phord, shut the fuck up!"

One of Phord's rules of salesmanship was to know when to shut up and let the customer talk.

"Aye, aye, sir."

His silence was one of his best sales pitches – and, as it turned out, one of his worst.

14

The foolhardy death.

"Sir, she's hurting."
"I said GO, lieutenant."
"Aye, aye, sir."

When the battalion first arrived on the island three weeks before, the officers were invited to play the locals in a goodwill basketball game. Taking place on the town's concrete basketball court, flanked by shaky wood-and-iron grandstands packed with howling locals, lit by floodlights on rusty towers, and using a tin contraption with revolving gear wheels that showed the score. As time was running out with the score tied, a short, buck-toothed center ripped the ball from Lieutenant McCabe's hands, elbowed him in the neck, took three steps without dribbling, straight-armed another then leaped, feet spinning, for a layup. The multiplicity of fouls committed by the center occurred right in front of the ref; a pudgy Filipino with bottom-bottom glasses, a crossed-eye and a brown nose that turned purple when he blew his whistle which was looped around the neck of his striped shirt with a 14-carat gold chain. He stared curiously at the play through those glasses then when his nose changed color he let fly with whistle noise, signaling not a foul but the basket counting, the locals winning, and the game over. The end of the game wasn't the end of the action. Descending triumphantly from the layup, the center had his buck-toothed grin wiped off his face as a Marine cut his legs out from under him and another Marine kneed his chin. He was unconscious before he hit the concrete. During the subsequent bench-clearing, stands-clearing melee, the Marines received a cultural lesson. The locals disdained battling with fists, preferring instead to use extraordinarily long, spring-loaded butterfly knives.

Lots of shouting and shoving and dramatic flipping of the butterfly knives—the whirring of the long blades and clacking of the counter-rotating handles in the skillful, brown hands—before Lieutenant Colonel Ajax poured his special brand of oil on those troubled waters. He walked out onto the center of the court, pulled his forty-five out of the hand-polished, Spanish leather holster with the curlicues AA (Alfred Ajax) carved into the flap, shoved the automatic above his head and pulled the trigger. Ordered by this commander's intent, the officers immediately broke off and returned to camp.

Now, after the basketball game and the shot in the air, after the murder of Ajax, with the SEATO exercise canceled either because of the murder or other circumstances, around which rumors were flying, Corporal Phord and Lieutenant McCabe found themselves in the boondocks, watching Father Baum die.

Their Mite was pulled off the road and Father Baum lay on the ground, enveloped by gunshot odor. He had a sucking chest wound. Pressing a compression bandage against the wound, McCabe recalled – not knowing why – Ajax's fabulous shot into the air.

Stretched out in giant sword ferns, Baum raised his broad, scarred hand—burned like the side of his face after his tank ran over a Bakelite mine in the desert—and opened and closed it in front of his eyes. Gazing at that hand, his eyes under his head bandage burned as if it might hold the answer to a question that long troubled him.

With the same motion he used kneeling before Baum, McCabe unholstered his forty-five and held it out to Phord who snatched it and disappeared into brush.

One side of Baum's chest, rising and falling with shallow, rapid breathing, was swelling. His blue finger tapped the air above the clerical collar lying across the open neck of his blue shirt. He ripped the collar off its studs. McCabe stripped off his jacket and skivvy shirt and pressed the shirt against the lesion. Through the cotton, he felt flesh quivering. His face blue, Baum emitted a small, strangled noise that caused the back of McCabe's neck to prickle.

"My fault, Father. Stupid to go down this road. Hang on."

"Listen," Baum said.

"Don't leave me. Do you hear? Don't leave me!"

Running through dozens of zigzagging orange-and-purple butterflies, Phord quickly caught up to Ears. Seeing he couldn't outrun Phord, Ears stopped and jerked his arm, raising his forty-five as if to throw a right-hand lead. For a moment, a point-blank shoot-off was in the works. Just like when Mariko cut the rope off his ankle in the water beside the bank, Phord felt death pressing on him. But the forty-five plunked at Ears' feet in a patch of pink-and-white orchids as his hands shot over his head.

"No shoot! No shoot!"

Blood hammering in his ears, mildly surprised Ears spoke English, Phord pointed McCabe's forty-five at man's chest intent on emptying his clip.

The accompanying silence was broken by Throat–hole meters away flailing through the jungle out of sight making a getaway.

Tears flowing, nostrils discharging, Ears dropped to his knees. A butterfly lighted momentarily on the top of his ear. He thrust supplicating hands fore and aft over his head. The top of his head had a large lump, the swelling scalp showing white in his black hair, the product of the Pirate Captain's overhand punch. Phord emptied his clip—into the air. Ears ran off.

Phord returned to the jeep, mortified he couldn't bring himself to kill Ears.

Naked torso splattered with blood, McCabe got to his feet. He shook his head slowly, decisively from side to side. He said, "His last word was German. I didn't understand. *'Craw'* ... something."

Looking at the corpse, McCabe not knowing why had this strange remembrance of Ajax on the basketball court firing over his head. There was a deep connection between this dead body and that shot, but McCabe did not make it consciously until long after he left the island, and he saw a squad of dead Marines that had been a few minutes before cut down by a single mortar round that exploded in their midst. In that future time, coming upon the gore, he remembered Baum's corpse and Ajax's shot and for the first time understood. He put his head in his hands and wept – not only for the Marines but for what had been lost on the island as evidenced by that shot.

15

Mariko leads.

Eleven hours later, Sister Lucia stopped the jeep near the bridge. She said to Phord beside her, "She carries her coffin on her back. But with style." The sister pointed to Mariko. Mariko was standing some fifty meters away in front of a tarp-covered supply dump upstream of the bridge. She wore a quarter-sleeve chambray blouse, blue chinos, and sandals. Her hair was in a French braid. She was speaking to eight locals grouped around her, speaking in that enthralling way she spoke to the thugs, chopping the air with her beautiful hands, looking levelly into the eyes of one person then another and another. Sister Lucia said, "Look what's in people's eyes when she speaks. Her style is beauty and grace and words that fit the emotional moment. But in the end her style doesn't matter. It's what's on her back that counts." Sister Lucia dragged her thumbnail, split, the exposed tissue painted with iodine, across her jugular. "Heartbreaking."

Downstream where the river road broke out of the jungle, a jeepney stopped. A riot of smashing colors, like an enormous flower emerging from the trees. Three locals got out and hurried over to listen to Mariko. Behind the jeepney, a jeep with four locals was approaching.

"Yes, heartbreaking," said Phord. "Though maybe not in the way you think."

"You don't see it. You don't see the mortal danger she's in. The Filipinos call it 'carrying a coffin on your back.'" The nun wore faded jeans and a workman's shirt. She had a thick neck, the back of which was mottled with patches of sunburn-induced hyperpigmentation. Her brown, bowl-cut hair was sun-scorched blonde at the tips. Her eyes and eyelids were red from weeping. "She's taking over Father Baum's job and working people up against the loggers. I'm sure she'll get more people to listen to her. But here's the trouble: she controls her say but not what people do after she's had her say."

"What'd you think they'll do?"

"Don't know. But I do know what Big Money will do. Father Baum is the example of what Big Money does when crossed. When he was a common priest, he was left alone. But finding his style organizing against the loggers got Big Money's ire. On the island, we say, 'Catch a snake with your enemy's hand.'" Phord immediately thought of Mariko standing by while he choked Makisig's life out of him. "The robbers were the hand that killed the man who was a snake to Big Money."

"Sister, I don't want to keep you from your duties."

"You wanted me to drive you here, Marine. That's my duty. My question for you is, when can I drive you back to your unit? I gave you this ride because you said you were going back."

Sister Lucia's man's hand, calloused and sun blackened, came down on Phord's forearm. Her smile became a grimace. Her face, pale under the sun-brown and drawn by the weeping that started when McCabe and Phord had brought Baum's corpse to the church that morning, changed in a moment from pretty to a little ugly.

When Phord was three years old and living in a Los Angeles barrio, a neighborhood man had a Halloween mask, green and fanged, that when donned made Phord, thinking he was facing a demon, cry; and when removed prompted the child, seeing it was not a demon but his neighbor, laugh. With the mask on the neighbor, Phord cried. With the mask off, Phord laughed. Mask on, cry. Mask off, laugh. This change in the nun's face, this clamping of her hand on his forearm, showed as stark a transformation in her appearance as the mask had prompted in his neighbor all those years ago.

Sister Lucia said, "We'll get them."

"Get who?"

"The bastards. Excuse my Spanish."

"You know who did it?"

"Of course. I went back to the place the father was killed at. I saw their abandoned jeep. I know who that jeep belongs to. They're notorious thieves. Now it's murder, and it's the chair. Not pretty. They'll get gauze taped over their eyes to keep their eyeballs from popping out of their sockets when the switch is pulled. After you brought his body back to the church this morning, you and your lieutenant friend wrote reports. Those reports are their tickets to the chair." She clamped her hands to her face. "Oh, Father … Father …" She sobbed into her hands, rocking back and forth. She dropped her hands and took several deep, shuddering breaths. She turned her agony-filled eyes on Phord. "Okay, out with it, Marine. What're you doing here? You told me you wanted to come here. So, I gave you a ride. But if I leave, how can you re-join your unit?"

"Re-joining might not be in the cards."

"What's this? Desertion?" She wiped her face with the heel of her hand and leaned toward Phord. "Give me the skinny."

"Too complicated to explain."

"Listen to me. Don't trash your life, young man. Get an honorable first."

She lifted the metal crucifix hanging off her neck over her head. Her fingers beckoned for his hand. "Look, I'm not too smart. Getting a Masters in sociology from Miami of Ohio made me stupid. But think of me as a little smart giving you this." The metal made his palm tingle.

"I can't take this. It's yours."

She kissed his closed hand and signed a cross over it.

"Remember, you're not alone. You walk in Christ's light." She pointed at Mariko speaking to the people. "Maybe you can take the coffin off her back. Let's stop the killing." As Phord started walking, pocketing the crucifix, she said, "Wait, please."

He came back. She beckoned at his pocket. He took the crucifix out. She took it out of his hand and placed it on the chain around his neck. She kissed the crucifix. "Thank you, sister." He coughed to remove a catch in his throat. He turned around and went toward Mariko. He saw she was heading into the Army GP tent. Several locals she passed outside the tent clapped. Tala, weeping, hugged her daughter and kissed her cheeks. And just a few hours ago, Tala was ripping off Mariko's dress. Mariko gently pushed Tala out of her way and walked into the tent.

Phord made his way between the people toward the tent. Seeing how her words brightened their faces, Phord thought, *she's dangerous.*

Before entering the tent, he felt a soft blow on his shoulder. Phord swung around and faced the young man who had bumped into him: the rooster neck, the big hands and small wrists, and the forearms as skinny, smooth, and hard as baseball bats. Most of all, those small, black eyes that he didn't see until now.

The same young man Phord decked.

"You're okay, I see," said Phord. "Well, that takes a load off me." Phord held out his hand, and when the young man wouldn't shake, Phord raised his hand to his temple then lowered it in a smart salute.

The young man spoke in Tagalog to the people, sputum flying from snarling lips. Clearly, he was carrying a lot of anger toward Phord.

"Make a hole!" Phord commanded. The people opened a path. A sandal-clad foot pushed in front of his boot. He tripped on it and took several stumbling steps before regaining his balance. Ignoring the perpetrator, he went into the tent.

In the cathedral light, Mariko was making checks with a pencil on a sheet of paper on a clipboard. Startled seeing Phord, her eyes narrowed in that reflexive suspiciousness he had come to know in her so well. She put the pencil between her teeth and stepped toward Phord. Glancing at the crowd outside, she stopped. She removed the pencil, and said, "Where the hell did you go last night?" Her angry words did not square with the look in her eyes, which made Phord think for the second time, *she loves me!* And for the second time, the thought depressed him. Sweat ran down both her cheeks. The heat inside the tent was stifling.

"Shanghaied. I'll explain later. Mariko, why are you here?"

"Why are you not here?" He lifted his arms. She thrust the clipboard against his chest, the spring-loaded clip pricking his neck. "Get back. People are watching. You've heard about the Father?"

"I know too much about him. What the hell? Are you leading this?"

"Me? What a laugh. Father Baum was the leader. Father Baum is the leader."

"Good trick if he can lead now."

A chinless man outside the tent with a big belly, white shirt and yellow slacks called to her. She spun away from Phord, her thick, black hair in a French braid swinging across her back, and went to the man. His chinless jaw wagged. She raised her hand. He shut his mouth. She spoke in Tagalog and pointed with the clipboard toward the distance. Apparently sent away, he walked off, his anger showing in the stiffness of his stride and in the way he slapped the air beside his hip as if slapping her away. She walked from sunlight back into the interior shadow.

"Mariko, why are you doing this? What are you doing?"

"Running scared. Trucks are coming tomorrow. The loggers are aiming to cross the bridge to get more hardwood. We're packing this bridge with bodies. Those trucks won't cross."

"Look." Phord looked where she pointed outside the tent. The group of people had broken up, and individuals were going about carrying out Mariko's directives. "The whole island is mourning our Father's death. Without him, we all must be leaders now to carry on the struggle. But we must be careful. We must do this struggle right. We must get organized. But you know what I'm afraid of? Organization and logistics are everything. Father Baum understood that but nobody else in the action does."

"And the struggle is …"

"Right now, halting the logging traffic at the bridge. Later, it means stopping the logging completely."

"Stop them at this bridge, they'll just build another bridge."

"No, they won't. They can't. If they tried, we'll stop the construction. They know that. They won't try to build another bridge. If we stop them here, they're beaten. Not for good. There'll be more fighting. But at least for now. They know it."

"They'll jail you."

"Others will take my place. Father Baum told me they jailed the marchers in Birmingham. They filled up the Birmingham jails. But the people kept coming. Non-violence paid off. Father Baum was right. The anti-logging movement can't be defeated — if it remains nonviolent."

"But Shimada …"

"Father Baum's death changed everything. Seeing what the Father risked, people are willing to risk Shimada's long arm. For the first time since the girl was killed, people are coming to this camp to sign up."

"I didn't know you had feelings for this movement against the loggers."

"I didn't. I don't. I never did. I still don't. Never will." Two men outside called to her. She called back, making a wide, sweeping, impatient gesture with her arm. They snapped-to at her command and pulled a tarp from a stack of C-rat cases, exchanging gripes but carrying her orders anyway. She said, "What a pain these two guys are. This collection of locals I'm dealing with is the full catastrophe. A lot of my work is dealing with volunteers who make loafing an art form."

Tala came into the tent talking angrily in Tagalog through betel juice out of the side of her mouth. "Another ball to juggle," Mariko said. Her head snapped forward as she spoke sharply to her mother in their language. Tala's wide, oddly drooping mouth opened, brown juice trickling out of the corner. Her face had many levels like rock strata on the walls of a gorge. On the surface, it was leathery and wrinkled deeply from a lifetime of tropical sun burns. But deeper, there were the remnants in her eyes and well-shaped cheeks and tragic mouth of an amazing beauty. He remembered Tala coming out of the house and clawing Mariko. He thought she hated Mariko for being the beauty she once had been, though there were probably many other reasons for her to hate her daughter. This dance of recriminations between mother and daughter, somewhat formal in its elaboration and intensity, must have been repeated countless times in their lives since Tala probably could never get over Mariko being the issue of the Japanese who raped her. Tala put her hand out, the veins on its back bulged like twisted rubber tubes, as if to ward Mariko off then backed out of the tent. Mariko turned back to Phord, her eyes wasted. Phord saw that just having Tala in her presence drained Mariko's spirit.

"She's got her priorities screwed up. She wants what she wants. Not what needs to be done. So, she's constantly sticking her nose into my running things. Look, I understand. This is my mother's battle. It's not my battle. It's been her battle as long as I can remember. The Mangyans took my stepfather in during the war. He and Makisig were fighting together in the mountains. The Japanese captured Makisig, but the Mangyans found my father wounded and nursed him back and at the end of the war brought him back home. Ever since, my mother feels indebted to them. My stepfather in his chair can't get much work. We've been poor as mice, but she always made sure to give the

Mangyans something, food, clothing, and sometimes a little money. She became one of the most important persons at the bridge action. But she doesn't know logistics. She just knows tactics. And what she knows about tactics is wrong. When I get this action back on track, I'm off."

"Where?"

"What do you think?"

"That's a pipe dream, Mariko?"

"Not when I do it."

"And your stash?"

"It's safe. This is what I'm doing now. I can only focus on what I'm doing now. Miss Holly Golightly and I waited for years for me to get to New York. We can wait a little while longer until I get this working. Even if … even if I use my stash to help fund this action. Don't you understand?" She held up the clipboard as a shield against him. "Lay off, please. We're not alone, you know. Let me finish. As I grew up, spit on my dress was a daily occurrence. And that's the least of what people did to me. During the day, I kept a face of stone; but at night, alone in my room, I wept long and hard. There. That was my life. That's what the name Mariko is all about. Today, I realized the people's grief over the Father's death is my grief too. I'm not Japanese even though I am. I'm them, the islanders. Even if they hate me, I'm them. I can't deny that – not when they're suffering. There's only one way I can repay Father Baum for giving me so much. To give others what he gave me."

"What did he give you?"

"You know what people think when they look at me today? *Whore. Puta. Slut. Pokpok.* What a laugh. But with Father Baum …. Just my being with Father Baum …just being in the presence of … I can't explain it. Look, there's no God. I know that. But there's Father Baum. I don't believe in God, but I believe in him. I believe in his marvelous presence. For the past few years, every month or so, I would now and then help him, and the nuns wash the sick, change dressings, feed children. Just the ordinary stuff that's so badly needed. Now and then people, recognizing me or hearing about me, wouldn't let me near them, but all the time I was with Father Baum, he held me dear. Once I showed up with Father Baum and a nun in a jungle clinic, a nurse who worked there somehow knew of me. How, I don't know. She spit at my feet and refused to work with me. Father Baum embraced me. Right in front of her. His tears wet my shirt collar. Finally, she broke down. She embraced me. She let me help. Later, she said Father Baum's embrace, his presence, had taught her about forgiveness and love, about cherishing every individual. She and I have become good friends doing good works. You asked what he gave me. That's what."

"That's why you're here?"

"This is where the Father had put so much of his work. A few hours ago, when I first showed up, I started doing little things to help. People who had left the camp after Shimada shot the girl were coming back, inspired by Baum's life and death. The trouble is, they desperately need help organizing. A lot of help. I can help. I can lead. Maybe I learned to lead by being an outsider all my life. Yes, many people still look with *puta* in their eyes. That's okay. Let them look. They need me. They accept my help. They can look that way all they want. You Americans have a saying, *'Tell it to the Marines.'* There. I've told it to the Marines. But that's not the most important audience. For years, Holly Golightly has been telling me. Now maybe I have something to tell her. "

"We'll have a great life together."

"Of course, you'd have to say something stupid as that."

"Nothing's stopping us now."

"Everything is stopping us now."

"What for instance?"

"Him, for instance."

She pointed her clipboard at the young man who was standing just outside the tent watching them. His hand was the handle of his bolo in the scabbard. Phord remembered hitting him. He remembered the jolt that went up his arm as his fist struck the youth's jaw.

Mariko waved the clipboard at him. The youth saw the gesture. He released the bolo. He turned and walked toward a group of men, rage showing through the back of his sun-blackened neck above the collar of his blue, cotton shirt.

"Watch out for him, Mariko."

"Don't worry. You see he's easy to deal with."

"No telling what these locals will do."

"Father Baum's strength is in me. I think maybe I can do this. I'm trying to get these people off violence. We must hold to nonviolence. We must keep the faith with Father Baum. We must keep to the principles of Gandhi and King that Father Baum embraced. These bolos the men carry around must go. But how do I convince them to give them up? Their bolos are pricks. They're pricks are bolos. More and more I see the mountain Father Baum had to climb. This action could fall apart any moment for one of any number of reasons. But the biggest reason would be violence. And that's what I'm most afraid of."

"You and I can fit in here."

"These people are very conservative. They hold their religion and morals dear. Plus, they dislike foreigners, especially Americans."

"Fuck them."

"You just proved my argument. It'll take a long time for them to accept you—if they ever do. And time we don't have. The trucks'll be here tomorrow."

"I'll wait till the action is over."

"Days? Months? Maybe longer?"

"There's gotta be a way, Mariko. Just a short while ago, we were strangers. Whether what we have now is because we were meant for each other or luck or blind chance, I don't know. I won't ever know. I don't care. But what's real is what's in our hands now. We can make what's in our hands now work for us."

Raised voices came from the riverbank. Two men were arguing with each other, their voices growing in volume. She rolled her eyes. "More fun." She kissed her fingers and brushed them across his cheek, then looked at the crowd watching her and dropped his hand. A feeling he could not find out filled him. "My *katipunero*. My sweet. My love. You spoke of what's in our hands. Let me speak. I told you I found the way to finally get rid of you." She looked at him quizzically. "By falling in love with you."

She went outside and thrust her arms between the arguing men and pushed them aside and spoke to them. Looking at their feet and blinking hard, they heard her out.

Phord waited for Mariko, but she didn't come back. She was busy directing people to pack supplies into two jeeps—listening, ordering, cajoling, and occasionally laughing. McCabe saw she connected personally with them.

Phord walked out of the tent. He forced his legs to take him back to the nun. She was sitting behind the wheel, watching him. Walking toward her, he felt her loving kindness enter him in a way he had not felt before. As it turned out, that love remained in his life, an antidote to the evils he would come to encounter. "You didn't have to wait," he said.

"Oh, yes I did, Marine."

Before he got in, he looked at Mariko. Now and then touching her temples, still bothered by yesterday's concussion, she was talking with three men who had just showed up.

One of them interrupted her and pointed toward Phord. She looked at him across the open ground. Her look proved her last words to him. She turned back to the men. They gathered around her to read something on the clipboard.

Left with nothing to say and no way to say it, Phord climbed into the jeep. The nun said, "Why so miserable, Marine?"

"Nothing much," said Phord. Mariko was looking at him again.

"Just a knee in the balls."

Someone called out to him. He turned around in the seat and saw the young man standing down-slope by the tent where a tongue of jungle pushed against the river. He was calling and swinging his arm for Phord to come over.

Forgetting the Marine adage that the road to hell is paved with the bones of leaders who failed to establish flank security, Phord told the nun to wait and went to see what the young man wanted.

16

McCabe learns what he does not want to know.

"H*gffgh!*" shouted Gunny Lawler, spreading his legs and throwing out his arms. Braking hard, McCabe thought the gunny looked like DaVinci's Vitruvian man except Lawler wore sweat-marbled sateens and held a clipboard with flight manifests between his dentures. The Mighty Mite's grill stopped just a few feet from Lawler's meticulously rendered gig line.

When Lawler yelled, his monstrous dentures rotated, and the clip board dropped out. Lawler caught it in mid-air with a swift snap of a big hand used to grab the troop's blouses to hold them in place for one of his patented head-butts, which he called "deep communicating." Instead of re-setting the dentures with the usual upward push of his thumb, he had developed the knack of maneuvering them back into place with a practiced jerking of his lips and tongue. *Look, ma, no hands.* Like a good grunt, he comfortably coped with calamity.

"With lieutenants going AWOL, this man's corps is getting the lug nuts on its wheels loosened."

Phord looked at the pillbox-pungency madness in Lawler's eyes, thinking: *In civilian life, two guys in white coats with a straight jacket would be coming for him.* He said, "It's not AWOL, Gunny, if you're on a mission"

"A lawful mission, I hope, sir."

"Maybe not legally lawful. But lawful in a values sense."

"You lost me. And I don't give a shit if I'm found."

"Mission accomplished. Where do I drive this junk pile?"

Behind Lawler, across the airstrip, Marine work parties were collapsing tents, folding them into strap-secured blocks, carrying them on mechanical mules along with the other camp infrastructure equipment, field kitchen gear, generators, water and sanitation gear, collapsed fuel bladders to Chickasaw choppers. The choppers were landing and taking off at precise intervals. The noise made the lieutenant and gunnery sergeant shout to be heard.

Lawler's sleep-deprived eyes checked out the identifying number on the hood with information on a manifest sheet. He dropped the clipboard dramatically to his side and looked at the sky with his famous *Lordsavemefromfuckeduplieutenants* expression. "You jammed up our loading sequence, sir. Mites went out this morning."

"Well, they can leave this one behind as a token of friendship. Hands across the ocean. Or toys for tots. Whatever works."

"At the Chosen, we put thermite grenades on the engine blocks of broken-down jeeps. Melted those fuckers to taffy."

"The engine block on this mother is a thermite grenade."

"I suggest you report to Major Gord, asap."

"Good idea, Gunny. Keep keeping me outta jail."

"Can't be done now, sir. I'll drive this to the staging area and get a lift. For it and for you."

"Hell, Gunny, don't take it personally. Nobody else was going to track down Ajax's killer."

"Yes sir. Whatever you say. You might get your kicks chasing hot hair and moonbeams. But in the meantime, this man's Marine Corps must keep on trucking."

"Was it my fault nobody but me would send me on the mission?"

"Did you track the Jap down, sir?" Lawler clicked his teeth, signaling skepticism, which, along with madness, was his normal outlook on life.

"Where's Major Gord?"

"Aboard ship. When you stand tall, be like Brer Rabbit and lay the fuck low." Lawler drove across the air strip. As he drove, he reached behind him and with his knuckles massaged pressure points on the back of his neck. It was a sort of acupuncture trick he learned over the years to keep awake whenever he was suffering from the grunt's common affliction, sleep depro. A month on the island had given him a good dose of it.

A member of one work party, helping fold a tent near the center of the airstrip, straightened up from pulling canvas and looked at the tree line where McCabe stood. He started walking toward McCabe, limping. From a distance, he looked like a Marine grunt, but as he got closer, McCabe knew that limp. The grunt transmogrified into Father O'Toole. His smile in his half-bloated face was an artifact of sadness. With his sunburned, badly-peeling face, his dirty sateens, he still looked, when he got up close, like a regular grunt—except for his Navy lieutenant's bars on one collar and the silver cross on the other.

"What is this, Padre, good works?"

"No, faith. Being useful is about faith. McCabe, you and Father Baum ran out on me."

"Think I betrayed you?"

"By their fruits you shall know them. You betrayed yourself."

"Father Baum is dead."

The rotor-wash from a chopper taking off blew a splinter into O'Toole's good eye, which teared up and blinked hard as he rubbed it with the tip of his little finger. "Say again?"

"He was shot by thugs on a jungle road early this morning."

"Why haven't I heard of that?"

"The battalion is clearing out. Communications with the locals are scrambled."

"What happened?"

"Shot through the chest."

"Wait a second. You realize you can get arrested on the spot now."

"No worry. I'm back. I'm going to see Gord."

"Follow me." He led McCabe behind a wall of foliage, sporting white bell-like flowers, their pistils looking like clappers. The two men were screened from the airstrip. "I heard what you said. You don't have to say it again. Shot through the chest? How'd it happen?"

"You know Baum and I went looking for Shimada. We came upon Phord and set off on a back road. Phord told me not to go down that road."

"Corporal Phord … you were with him? Where is he? How's he doing? I've been praying for him too. Slow down. You're piling a lot on me."

"I'll get to Phord later. Dumb going down that road."

"What the hell were you doing on that road in the first place?"

"Screwing up. Phord told me to stop. But I went on."

"Wait. Let's get back to Father Baum. Shot, you say? In the chest?"

"Let me finish. This will explain it. We met up with two thugs. Phord told me later he had a previous encounter with them. They were hanging out on the road thinking Phord might come back. Or thinking any foreigner connected with the exercise might come along that was easy pickings. Their jeep was parked half off the road, and they were fiddling with the rear wheel. The old trick. Phord told me to keep going. He said he knew these thugs. Of course, I didn't listen. I should have sped up. Instead, I slowed down. They had their guns out, and I had no chance of getting my forty-five. Phord had no weapon. Father Baum had no weapon. Phord knew them. He started shouting angrily at them like they were old enemies. He was shouting in English, of course. I'm not sure they understood him. One, the shorter one … he had cauliflower ears … raised his gun. I still don't think he intended to pull the trigger. He raised his gun almost to protect himself from Phord and his shouting. As soon as he raised the gun, Baum stepped in front of Phord. Baum had his arms out protecting Phord. That startled the thug. He pulled the trigger. It was a knee-jerk reaction. They left their jeep behind and ran. I gave my weapon to Phord who chased them. I tried to help the Father."

With a snap of his hand, McCabe snatched a gnat away from his face. He crushed it between his thumb and finger and wiped the crushings on his trouser leg. "My fucking fault. I didn't listen to Phord. Then I didn't know how to deal with a sucking chest wound. I'd never seen a wound like that. Baum had it big time. He was gasping hideously. Yet he could struggle to speak a little. The discipline it took just to say a few words. He started to tell me what to do, how to let the air out but not in, but then he stopped talking about the wound, and said …"

McCabe paused. The gnats were warming to the task. O'Toole was continually waving them away from his face in what the troops called, "the Filipino salute." As a matter of discipline, McCabe had kept his hands at his sides. Now he smashed a few with a slap on his forehead then his cheek. The blood of their comrades excited them, and their buzzing became fiercer.

O'Toole watched McCabe. Like Lawler, the chaplain was knocked cockeyed by lack of sleep. There were half-disks the color of burning-tire smoke under his eyes, and his inveterate sadness had deepened in the rough features on the good side of his face.

However, McCabe felt something was wrong with O'Toole's watching. It didn't square with the astonishment McCabe expected the priest to show. Sensing O'Toole was holding something back, McCabe kept on, "In Baum's eyes, I saw something I had never seen in my life. They were flat. They were cold. No, that's not it. They were something else. Deeper than the surface flatness, there was … I can't describe it any other way, they were asking … asking … asking …"

"I know," said O'Toole, alternating rubbing the top of each hand with the palm of the other. The backs of his hands were sunburned and peeling too.

"What do you know?" O'Toole didn't answer. McCabe went on: "Then he said … then he died. I watched him die. I watched that look in his eyes and then there was no look. His eyes were empty. No noise came from the hole. And I was left with what he said. You know what he said?" The skin beneath McCabe's eyes sagged. He was breathing through his mouth. O'Toole put his arm across McCabe's shoulder. He said nothing. Saying nothing when nothing needed to be said was O'Toole's forte.

McCabe continued, "I could have saved him, but I didn't. He was telling me how to save him, how to stop a sucking chest wound. He was strangely calm. At that moment, he was a motivated German soldier. Taking care of the wound was easy. I could've done it. He just had to tell me how. You know it was crazy but kneeling beside Baum I thought of Ajax on a basketball court shooting his forty-five into the air. I don't know why I thought that. Anyway, then Baum said …" McCabe stopped talking. The end of the sentence was stuck not just in his throat but in the deep mechanisms of his perception. "Anyway…anyway…" He couldn't get it out. He said, "We tied the Father…" (It was the first time he used the word in connection with Baum.) "… tied him to the hood like a shot deer. We drove him to his nearest Catholic outpost. God, the wailing. I didn't know how much Father Baum was loved until I witnessed the nuns, the locals reacting to his death."

That twisted look that made no sense to McCabe dug itself deeper into O'Toole's face. McCabe said, "Padre, are you listening? Listen. Listen. I must tell you. I must tell you what he said just before he died."

"No need."

"What?"

"No need to tell me."

"What'd you mean? You must know. I don't believe it... what he said. But I want you to know it."

"Keep it to yourself." O'Toole's anger changed his face in such a way the midges momentarily flew off then came back. He touched his throat with the nail of his little finger. Suddenly aware of a gesture he made unconsciously, he dropped his hand.

"No, I've got to tell you. Especially *you*, you must know."

That strange pulling back in O'Toole's expression translated into his turning away. "Padre, what the hell! You of all people must know this – that Baum said ... said ... *he ... killed ... Ajax.*"

Something seemed to leave O'Toole's body. His big shoulders drooped.

"I don't believe it, Padre. He was dying. He was confused. Why would he say a thing like that?"

O'Toole kept his eyes lowered. He did not wave the gnats away.

McCabe said, "By the way, this is for your ears only. If word got out that Baum might've killed Ajax—even though he didn't—the locals would be traumatized for years. The church and the church's good works would be torpedoed. The nuns who followed the priest and his work to put Vatican Two into action would be put out of business. And the non-violent action at the bridge would be finished for good. I haven't even told Phord. He was with us. But when Father Baum told me, Phord was trying to run down the thieves who shot him. So, I'm the only one who knows. Except, now, you." McCabe squeezed the priest's shoulder. "Padre, you're the troubled spirit. You need rest."

"Rest is not an option where we're going."

"Where?"

"Scuttlebutt is we're banging a U in the South China Sea."

"Absolute crap. Johnson promised we're not supplying American boys to do the job Vietnamese boys should do. By the way, what did you mean by this?" McCabe mimicked the way O'Toole touched his throat. Looking out from the slit between the swollen lips of skin, O'Toole's eye sparkled.

"Say what?"

"This." McCabe tapped his neck.

O'Toole's lips flattened into a hard, straight line. He started to turn away. McCabe grabbed his arm and turned him back around. It was hard moving him. If O'Toole didn't want to be moved, McCabe couldn't do it. But he moved O'Toole. Strangely, O'Toole must have let him.

"Common knowledge, Colm."

"What was?"

O'Toole shook his head, biting his lip. "The cravat."

"You know about that?"

O'Toole looked out across the airstrip. His eyes were filled with dark lights. "About what?"

"That."

"What's that?"

"You just said it."

"Said what?"

"The Spanish necktie."

O'Toole looked back into McCabe's eyes. The priest seemed to be peering into something inside McCabe he did not want to see.

McCabe said, "Baum's last word was German. *Craw* ... something. Was it cravat? You speak a little German."

"*Krawatte.*"

"Spanish cravat, Padre? Wait a minute. That wasn't common knowledge. Nobody else knew about that necktie but me. I found the corpse at oh dark thirty. I was the only one with a flashlight. I was the only one who saw the mutilation. I covered the corpse with a poncho. I didn't tell anyone. ONI was next to see the body. They flew it to a morgue on the hospital ship. ONI kept a lid on that information. Only they knew. They classified the necktie. I was told by ONI not to tell anybody. How did you know? Who told you? Somebody had to tell you. Who told you?" O'Toole's crazy eye looked deep into McCabe's eyes. The priest slowly passed his hand across his face but not to deflect the midges. "I didn't tell you. ONI didn't tell you. How did you find out? Did Gord tell you?"

"There is no answer that you'll accept."

"But there is an answer. Wait. That last word. That German word. 'Kra'... whatever. Necktie. Baum knew? If he knew, who told him?"

"Consider nobody, Colm."

"Saying nobody means Baum was somebody. If Baum was somebody, that means he saw Ajax hacked. If he saw Ajax hacked, either someone else did it or ... someone else didn't do it. If someone else did it, Baum would've turned him in or he would've sounded the alarm. No one was turned in. No alarm was sounded. That means ... that means ... that means Baum *did* kill Ajax." Hardness in O'Toole's mouth moved up into his eyes. "Oh, my God ... You knew about the necktie, Padre. How did you know?" The two stared into one another's eyes. But the seeing had gone out of both O'Toole's eyes. "Did he tell you?" O'Toole said nothing. "Tell me, did he tell you?" O'Toole didn't answer. "If he didn't tell you, how did you know?"

"Mortal sin," said O'Toole.

"Mortal sin, sure. If that's how you want to look at it. He had a mortal sin hanging over him. Doesn't your party line say confession is the antidote? Oh ... I see. You were the only priest around. He confessed to you? That's how you learned? He told you in confession? Isn't that right? Oh, sure. You're not going to answer. You can't answer. Your seal of confession. You can't tell me. But I'll answer me. He told you in some confession. Of course, Baum did kill Ajax. He killed him and confessed it to you. But when? When did he confess it? When?" O'Toole kept silent. "The only time he could've done it was when I was in the fortress. You must have met him on the road when he was going to or coming back from camp. He stopped you. He had to get it off his soul right away. You became his priest confessor. When he got to camp and couldn't get to see Gord, he came back. You and I were outside the fortress. When he came back, you knew he had killed Ajax. That's why you two were acting so weird toward one another. I said I was going after Shimada and you knew Shimada didn't kill Ajax. You knew I was going after the wrong guy, yet you said nothing. You were hog-tied by your canon law. And because you didn't tell me, Baum, Phord and I went down Robbers' Road. Baum was killed trying to save us. And Phord and I were almost killed. If you had told me, I wouldn't have gone off with him to look for Shimada. If we hadn't gone, we wouldn't have gone down that road."

"Tell me. I want to know about Phord. A troubled spirit."

"So now you'll talk. You change the subject. You won't talk about what Baum confessed to you. But you'll talk about Phord. Yes, he's fucked up. But aren't we all fucking up, even you?"

"Tell me about Phord." O'Toole's voice was so soft, McCabe almost didn't understand the words.

"He helped me get Baum's corpse back to his church. Then in all the commotion, he disappeared. Maybe permanently. Permanently disappeared is the best place for him. To hell with Phord."

"Don't give up on him." O'Toole's voice was back to its normal croak.

"Let him rot on this island."

"Maybe he needs help."

"Cut the priest malarkey. Always looking for what can't be found. Face up to what your malarkey has done." A liquid churning spread through McCabe's chest. He clenched and unclenched his hands. "If Ajax was with us, he'd un-fuck things. My trouble is, I had to get involved with the likes of you." O'Toole eyes closed slowly then opened. He sadly shook his head from side to side. "Ajax would be showing us what to do. I loved that man. I love that man. Even dead he's with me, guiding me. If you had let Ajax guide you rather than relying on your spiritual salesmanship ..." McCabe stopped and let the churning subside a little. "Oh, hell, never mind."

"Ajax ..." O'Toole said, "Ajax, you say? Baum dead. Baum a murderer. You think you know everything. Ajax, you say? Ajax? Rape. Blood. Murder. Little girl." O'Toole brought the heels of his boots together. He sang sarcastically, *"From the halls of Montezuma ..."* A partial, high-pitched quality affected his usual, raspy voice, resulting, McCabe surmised, from the shock to his nervous system resulting from Baum's death.

McCabe shook the man's shoulders. "Don't go nuts on me."

O'Toole smashed his lips and pushed them out. "I'm just trying to process this, Colm. Baum and Ajax and Phord and you. Rape and murder. It's a bitch to process."

McCabe started toward the landing zone. O'Toole grabbed his arm, "I said 'rape.' I said 'murder.'" The wind had died, and the gnats were back and so was the clattering of rotors on the wind. "The little girl..."

"What girl?"

"The girl at the fortress during the SEATO social."

"There were a lot of girls at the fortress during the social."

"You were at the social, Colm. I saw you there."

"Ajax called me there on the radio. He told me to leave the CP and come to the fortress. He wanted to talk to me. When I got there, he took me off to one side where we were alone and told me to get off Phord's case or he'd relieve me."

O'Toole looked left and right as if checking to make sure they were alone, even though they were the only ones at this end of the airstrip. McCabe leaned close to O'Toole to hear the words, "The girl Ajax raped."

"Ajax ... what?"

"The girl. The little girl in the back room."

"Mister Marine, helps me ..."

"I think I saw her. Going to meet Ajax at the fortress, I took the wrong way inside and got lost in a maze of rooms. I went through this room where this pretty little thing in a yellow, ivory-lace gown was sitting on the floor calling for help. When I told Ajax about her, he told me she was all right. He said, 'Forget her. Go back to camp.'"

O'Toole watched McCabe. The priest's lips parted and he cleared his throat. His lips closed. Then he nodded and hardened his mouth. He said, "This is what you have to know about your Ajax. Ajax saw her at the social and liked what he saw and took her into that back room and raped her. Then he left her on the floor and went back to the social. He went back to being the star of the show with the gaga, young officers. Back in the room, she bled out. A kitchen worker found her body. Filipino officials kept it quiet. This was a SEATO social. Dignitaries galore. Things had to go smoothly. President for Life, Fernando Markos, had to look good in the Southeast Asian military and social community. A murder would've jammed the diplomatic works. They got rid of her body in the night."

"Who told you this?"

"Ajax told me. At the social he took me aside and said, 'Did you see that little chicken in the corner in the yellow gown. I took her in a back room and gave her what for.' He didn't know she had died, though. I didn't know at that time she died.'"

"Why would he tell you that?"

"He was a Hemingway fan. Now and then he'd bait me like Rinaldi baited the priest in *A Farewell to Arms*. I let him. I knew his secret. I prayed a lot that he might find his way to the light. With the girl, he said, 'She loved it. She struggled but that meant she was crazy about it.' He said, 'Father, think of the delights your vows have walled you off from.' His baiting didn't stop me from praying for him."

"Ajax said that?"

"Ajax did that. If he had not been killed, I would've turned him in. I would've prayed for him and turned him in."

"Didn't he know he hurt her?"

"The more important question: *Didn't he care?*"

"What? He just left her on the floor and returned to the social? What's the answer?"

"The answer is mere gook."

"Hasn't her family complained?"

"Her family's destitute. Wearing an off-the-rack gown loaned to her, she was there for the pickings. She got picked all right. By Ajax. The family probably got blood money for keeping quiet. So now you know. That's Ajax for you. The star of the show."

Mister Marine ...
Leave her, Colm ...
... helps me ...

McCabe said, "Say again: He just left her on the floor and returned to the social. I don't believe you." McCabe started off again toward the landing zone.

"What's not to believe, Colm?"

McCabe stopped and turned around and looked hard at O'Toole. The hurt look was back on O'Toole's ruined face. Since the violence at the bridge, the swelling had made it hard for McCabe to read O'Toole's emotions; but the deep hurt now soaked through. He said, "She was young. Probably a virgin. Uterine rupture."

"I don't know. I don't want to know. Keep away, O'Toole."

McCabe walked across the airstrip through the Marines' packing-up commotion to the landing zone. The chopper had lifted off. Beside two squads that were lined up carrying their field transport packs ready for the next lift, a staff sergeant was chewing out a lance corporal. The staff sergeant's freshly-shaved, bulging cheek wobbled as tobacco juice and invectives streamed from his mouth, droplets speckling the lance corporal's boots. Lawler broke in and pointed out McCabe. The staff sergeant scowled, spit a long, brown stream, waved his hand as if shooing away gnats—though at this end of the strip, the constant propwash blew the gnats away—and continued the juice-and-obscenities rant. Lawler came over to McCabe.

"I got you on the next flight, lieutenant. The boarding sergeant owed me a favor. It's going out to the ship Major Gord is on. What's the matter? You look like you swallowed a drop of hell."

A Chickasaw came into view over the trees, blunt-nosed, white MARINES against the olive-drab fuselage, the flapping changing as the pilot feathered the blades. It came down, and the prop-wash flattened McCabe's sweat-damp, sateen jacket against his chest, stinging a tropical rash he had picked up on his pectoral a few days ago. The crew chief in an orange jump suit leaned out of the hatch and swung his arm. McCabe, first in line, hustled, hunched over, pulling the bill of his utility cover over his eyes squinting in blade-blast. He got in, the metallic grinding of the rotor head loud in the dim interior. He sat down and snapped on his harness. He stared at the Marines clobbering through the hatch and sitting down against the bulkheads. The crew chief thrust his raised thumb toward the cockpit where the pilot and co-pilot, in orange jump suits, were manipulating controls with their hands and boots. The Chickasaw's reciprocating *Pratt and Whitney* revved up.

Mister Marine ...
Leave her, Colm.

McCabe hugged himself. He jackknifed. "O'Toole," he said, "You're right. What's not to believe? You finally found me." He raised up and shouted, "Wait." He unsnapped his harness. He stood up. With both hands, the glaring crew chief made a *get-the-fuck-down-you-stupid-bastard* gesture. He had a round, flat face with a wall eye pointing toward a broken-and-badly-set nose. "Back off," McCabe shouted. McCabe pushed past the chief and jumped. The chopper's wheels were a few feet off the ground and McCabe going out of the hatch fell some distance before landing and rolling once. He walked, slapping tarmac mud off his trousers.

Gunny Lawler was supervising a Marine work party strapping down camlock-capped jerry cans on a master pallet when he spotted McCabe. On infantry-bowed legs, he sprinted to the lieutenant, sucking his finger that got pinched when, spotting McCabe, he hastily pulled it out of a tie-down ring. His herringbone twill utility jacket and the sweatband of his blocked, eight-pointed cap were marbled from rain and perspiration

"Lieutenant, what're you doing to me? I pulled strings to get you on that chopper."

Lawler raised the clipboard to throw it down. Under the bill of his cap, his eyes, a ruin-scape of sleep-deprivation and madness, locked on McCabe's eyes. Seeing what was in McCabe's eyes, Lawler rejected a show of temper with the clipboard and lowered it slowly to his side.

"Gangway, Gunny. I'm headed for town."

Lawler's lips folded inward against the dentures, and he spat blood sucked from his pinched finger. "I got enough problems. Lieutenant problems I don't need now. So, God speed, sir."

17

Love loses.

Sitting beside Sister Lucia in her jeep, Phord spotted Lieutenant McCabe walking on an asphalt road outside of town. He touched her arm and pointed. The sister drove to him and stopped.

Phord hopped out and saluted. The pain in his rotator cup and neck gotten from having just fought with three Filipino men near the bridge did not prevent this katipunero with red neck-rag from executing a precise salute.

"Need a lift, sir?"

Phord knew the red trousers-white shirt made him an outsider both to the locals and the Marines, but he didn't care—or maybe cared too much.

McCabe did not return the salute. His eyes were stormy seas, his cheeks and forehead darkening to the color of the back of the nun's neck. "I've been looking for you, corporal. Again, as usual."

"On foot?"

"All our vehicles have been uploaded. The jeepney I hired broke down."

McCabe got in beside Lucia and said: "Hurry, sister. There's one chopper left. If we miss that, we're screwed." He said to Phord over his shoulder: "We're screwed anyway. Charge sheets are probably coming down the pike. These civvies you're wearing won't help."

"I don't get it, sir. You don't have to do this."

"*You* don't get it. I *have* to do this."

"Why, sir?"

"Marines don't leave wounded on the battlefield."

"Who's the wounded? Where's the battlefield?" McCabe didn't answer. "That's bullshit, sir."

"You're right."

"So, what's the reason?"

"Have you talked to Father O'Toole?"

"No, sir."

"Talk to him some time. He'll tell you why I'm here. Better than I could tell you. He's good at finding what's lost."

Phord removed the red neckerchief and mopped his face. "Being with the First Civ Div has been a kick in the ass, lieutenant. It always gets its own."

Phord reached around the lieutenant's shoulder and held out his hand to shake. "I'd go to hell and back with you, lieutenant," he said.

McCabe looked at the hand. He didn't take it. Phord withdrew it.

"Can't hear you," said McCabe, cupping his ear. He said to the nun, "I'm glad to leave this piss ant place."

"Don't paint with such a broad brush," said Sister Lucia. Driving as if she just broke out of prison and the law was hot on her tail, the nun slammed the jeep down the jungle road leading to the now abandoned airstrip. "One of the piss ants just saved this Marine's life."

McCabe turned and said to Phord: "Is that true?"

Phord shrugged.

"It happened a while ago," the nun said.

"What happened?" said McCabe.

"A lynching Filipino style: with bolos instead of rope."

"No big deal," said Phord.

"Murder's a big deal. Tell the lieutenant what happened."

Phord rubbed his shoulder and then the side of his neck, knowing those parts of him would be stiff tomorrow. Knowing too he was lucky to get away with only a little stiffness.

They rolled up to the airstrip. It was empty now whereas just a few days ago it was crowded with soldiers, sailors and Marines, tents, and equipment. A single Chickasaw, props slapping slowly in the tropical air, stood at the end of the runway.

"Hang on," Sister Lucia said. The jeep jumped forward over WW Two tarmac, chewed up by the recent camp traffic.

"What the hell happened?" said McCabe.

Driving, Sister Lucia said, "This Marine got jumped by locals with bolos. She got in the way."

"Who's she?" asked McCabe.

"Tell him!" the sister said, looking quickly at Phord then back to the front. Phord shrugged. "Could we say squeeze? Anyway, she jumped in the way of the swinging blades. Got her arm machete-chopped. Bled some, but she's okay. Hey, Marine, what do you think? Amazing what she did for you. Bought enough time for me to get you out of there. She loves you more than she loves life."

The chopper's rotors blurred, the engine roaring. The nun braked the vehicle to a sliding stop beside the chopper. The Marines jumped out. "Wait!" shouted Sister Lucia. She got out, hurried around the front of the jeep and took one hand of each Marine into both her hands. In the motor wash, she kissed first Phord's hand then McCabe's. "Go with Christ, Marines." She pressed metal into McCabe's hand. Dog tags. She shouted over the engine roar, "This was in Father Baum's breast pocket."

Ajax
Alfred
0 ...
RH Positive
No Preference

The chopper, which had been lifting off, came back down and bounced on its wheels. The lieutenant and the katipunero corporal, favoring his arm, ran for the hatch. "Go Browns!" Sister Lucia shouted, pumping her fist. The crew chief angrily waved them in; upset, their sudden appearance made the pilot abort.

"Did you feel what I felt?" McCabe said, sitting down and buckling up.

"Feel those vibes the sister gave off?" said Phord, sitting next to him. "She's special, that nun. She radiates pure something."

"Agree, Phord. Pure love. That's what I get."

"I'd convert for her alone."

"Roger that."

With McCabe and Phord inside, the chopper went up, and the trees slipped below the hatch and became a mass of foliage spreading to the sea and the fortress overlooking the sea and the setting sun. McCabe and Phord saw the bridge near the fortress and people gathering around the end of the bridge. The two Marines saw the river spilling out from under the crossed-braced steel and cutting though the dark green of the jungle lowlands then into the wild blueberry-colored shadows of a mountain valley.

As the chopper headed out to sea, McCabe pointed. A lone figure, dressed in brown rags, sand-brown military cap, flaps down, stepped out of the twilight dark of the jungle onto the empty runway. He looked up at the chopper—then turned around and disappeared back into the foliage.

The chopper banked, and the jungle closed over the airstrip. The fortress got smaller until it disappeared in the long green line of jungle against the shore. The glittering sea flowed beneath them; and in the distance, getting bigger in the leveling sunlight, was their destination: the U.S.S. Valley Forge, a WWII aircraft carrier converted to a Chickasaw platform for carrying Marines to war.

18

O'Toole fulfills his quest.

Sixteen hours later, McCabe, was back on the island. When he flew out with Phord, he thought he left for good. But he was back again, riding not in a Marine vehicle but in a Filipino jeepney he just hired. He shouted to the driver, "Stop!"

The driver, a young man, almost a boy, pumped the brakes. Air in the brake lines made the jeepney stop haltingly. They were alone on a jungle road. McCabe opened his mouth and worked his jaw from side to side, ear canals crackling from the change in air-pressure caused by his ship-to-shore chopper ride. He reached around the driver's shoulder and pulled the key from the ignition. Dangling on the key ring were a rabbit's foot, a mystic star, a feng shui figure eight, and a voodoo love amulet.

McCabe said, "I'm driving. Get out." He turned to the only other passenger, a man sitting beside the driver. "Stay put, old man." McCabe jumped out of the back and came around the galvanized-steel side panel with its portrait of long-haired Jesus radiating tongues of psychedelic colors. "Didn't you hear me?" he said to the driver. "I said, '*out.*'" The driver, gripping the wheel, didn't move, confused by this crazed Marine in his green utilities who had showed up a few minutes before, jumping from a chopper that landed on the deserted airfield where tent town stood yesterday with all its military bustle.

McCabe squeezed the back of the driver's neck and pulled him out. "I told you to go faster. You wouldn't. Now I'm driving. Get in the back." McCabe pushed the driver by the neck to the back of the vehicle and shoved him. *"Inside!"* The driver climbed in the back and sat on the upholstery. McCabe pointed his finger in his face. "Keep cool, my friend. No tricks."

Behind the wheel, he inserted the key, started the engine, and stomped the pedal. As his foot pressed down, a faint tremor caused by sea-legs ran up through his calf. The jeepney shot forward, McCabe's head snapping back, the old man grabbing the doorpost with both hands. Foliage whipped past. The tires hammered on the muddy, rock-strewn road. The vehicle bounced so vigorously that the rosary and garland of sampaguita flowers hanging off the rear-view mirror over the plastic altar on the dashboard with its image of suffering Christ jumped and swayed. A holding bolt on one of half a dozen automobile side-view mirrors above the windshield popped out, the mirror swinging down, held up by a single bolt.

The driver's small hands closed around McCabe's neck, fingertips digging into his larynx. McCabe stopped the jeepney and jerked the hand brake. He pushed his thumbs under the hands and tore them off his throat. He clamped the driver in a headlock and pulled him over the seat. The driver, strangely limp, let McCabe drag him out of the jeepney, across the road and into a colonnade of lianas, rising like twisted wire cables to interlacing networks in the trees. "I'm driving," he snarled, his face so close to the driver's he could smell his Palikero pomade. "Understand? Keep off me!" He started back to the jeepney, the driver walking right behind him. McCabe spun around. "Didn't you hear?" He started again, the driver shadowing him. McCabe grabbed his shoulders and shook them. "You're not listening. You'll jump me again, won't you?" The driver smiled bashfully and scratched the back of his ear.

"Snatch it easy," said the old man.

"What?"

The old man had gotten out and was blocking McCabe's path to the jeepney. He wore Billabong bucket hat, sunglasses, clean white shirt and black, freshly pressed slacks. "Cat like you busting his cork gonna get us all wasted."

"Who the hell are you?"

"Your worst nightmare if you don't cut the shit. Dig it, I spent thirty years as a U.S. Navy mess steward and eighteen years beating skins in Harlem. So, I know what's what with you ofays. You're bring downs. You think the world's your private clam bake. You wanna drive? Okay, drive. I'll cop him to the scene. But screw your head on right. Nixing out the driver is the wrong riff."

The jive didn't much surprise McCabe. He figured the old man was just another of the many Filipinos he met on the island with a whacky involvement with the United States. He said, "So you're more American than Flip. Here's my play."

"You a hep cat too?"

"Dig it." McCabe said. "I'm looking for our battalion chaplain. The chaplain's name is O'Toole. He jumped ship and is running around this island somewhere. I don't know where the hell he is. Our ships are sailing today—tomorrow at the latest. I hitched a ride on one of the few choppers coming to the island. In a few hours, there won't be any more arriving. The Marines will be outta here completely. I hired this jeepney to take me to town. That's where I'll start to look. But the guy drives like he's leading a funeral procession. I gotta move fast and find O'Toole quick and get him back to our ship right away."

"Earning my Navy chops, I never copped a chaplain jumping."

"I guess we're both searching for each other."

"Solid. The searcher and the searchee the same cat. I collar that. Stick with me."

The old man took his glasses off and spoke to the driver in Tagalog. McCabe wondered if Tagalog incorporated jive. The driver nodded and got in the back of the jeepney. The old man put his glasses back on and said, "Frantic."

"What'd you say to him?"

"Pakikisama."

"Paki ... what?"

"Pakikisama. It's how Filipinos run. Pakikisama ... be kind. Be helpful. It's what we are. It's what we have to be. It's in our juice, like cock fighting and scoffing up adobo. The driver digs that. He's no clucker. I just reminded him. How's your stretcher?"

"My what?"

"Your neck. He put a hurting to it."

"Forget that."

"The driver's cool. But he won't let you drive. I'll drive. Now don't get your balls in an uproar. I'll cop some speed."

The old man put such speed in the wheels McCabe gripped the doorpost. Shortly, they came upon a man changing his motorcycle flat. The old man stopped, got out, and in pakikisama fashion, held the bike steady while the man tightened the lug nuts.

"Goddamnit, old man, let's go," said McCabe.

"I know this cat," said the old man. "We've been jive for years. He earns bread running corpses on his Honda from jungle folk to town morgues. He digs the work. He says carting corpses helps the families of the fogged and also feeds his old lady and pips."

The old man, the driver and the corpse-hauler conversed in Tagalog. Impatiently hitting his fist against his palm, McCabe recognized the words "priest," "chaplain," "Marines" in the otherwise incomprehensible language.

The old man turned to McCabe. "Cat tells me he rapped with your priest when he came by in a jeepney a short while ago searching for you. Sent him to the bridge to find you. Says there's bad shit at the bridge. Figured you went there cause Marines go where bad shit is. Bad shit at that bridge will cop him extra work."

Highballing on the river road, the old man driving, McCabe beside him, there came through the vegetation ahead in the direction of the bridge the shouts of a mob. The old man stopped the jeepney. "This ain't cool," he said.

"Keep going!"

The old man took off his glasses and stared at McCabe. His face without the dark glasses was flat and squinty-eyed, a typical local. He had a glass eye. "The hell you say. This is a bad-ass deal." The old man replaced his glasses, becoming a hipster again, backed off the road then pulled forward and stopped. The jeepney headed back the way they came.

"Badbye."

"You can't leave me here."

"The driver says you owe him a Lincoln. MPC is cool."

"Wait a minute. You said you'd help."

"There's help. I'll help you find your chaplain. Then there's help. That's the help where I get myself fogged in the process. The first help, yes. The second help, nix that! Those shouts mean bad shit." He called in Tagalog to the driver who jumped out the back, came around and got behind the wheel. McCabe saw he had a clubbed foot clad in a leather, Hinkel boot.

"Boot him a Lincoln, lieutenant. A nickel note. A five spot."

"But what if the chaplain isn't here?"

"Grab another jeepney." The old man looked at McCabe through the dark lenses.

"I guess you want scratch too."

"Freebee on my part. Pakikisama."

"Pakikisama, my ass," said McCabe, handing over the pink-and-blue, Indian-in-full-headdress, ten-dollar MPC note. The old man handed it to the driver who looked at it and said a few words.

"The driver says he can't cough up change."

"Keep the change."

The driver holding the note with his thumb against his palm raised his hand to his brow. "He's saluting your pakikisama," the old man said. "He says he hopes you find the cat you're looking for."

"Tell him thanks for his hopes. But hopes ain't wheels."

McCabe saw his club foot was the gas foot. The jeepney went off slowly, funeral procession speed.

McCabe double-timed toward the shouting.

Behind him was a rumbling of a jeepney. Over his shoulder, McCabe saw the jeepney with the old man. It had gone off but was coming back. Its chrome Christ statue, arms outstretched, atop the Mercedes-Benz logo on the extended radiator housing flashed as the vehicle passed through beams of sunlight shooting out of the foliage. It rolled up to him and stopped. The old man said, "Okay, this is crazy. We were splitting. But we changed our minds. That dime note you laid out signifies you're a righteous cat. You got your boots on. So, we're not down with you yet. We're keeping pakikisama on the grill. Get this this racket: We'll truck on down to the bridge and scope the scene. See if it's cool for you to show your mug. Stay here. If you want to keep your frame in one piece, go nowhere. Be back in a few ticks."

McCabe waited on the side of the road, listening to the shouts of the crowd swelling and fading, swelling, and fading. At intervals, jeeps loaded with Filipinos went past, heading for the bridge. After three jeeps had gone by, a five-foot, orange-and-black snake started across the road. McCabe picked up a rock. "Forget it," he said. "Live." He threw the rock away. A few minutes later, a jeep racing past ran over the snake, splashing its insides across the red dirt. Another jeep came by. It stopped and backed up. A Filipino in mud-spattered, short-sleeved denim shirt and jeans said, "Are you nuts? You crazy American. I'm taking you the hell out of here. Don't you know what's happening?"

"Sister Lucia! What the hell?"

"Likewise, I'm sure."

"What're you doing here?"

"Tracking you down. It's a bad habit I can't shake."

"Well, I'm glad to see you!"

"Save it. What are you doing running around loose?"

"Unfinished business."

"Yesterday, I thought I'd seen the last of you."

"I'm heading for the bridge." McCabe looked at the snake, writhing in its death agony.

"Think again. Be heading away, Marine. Away and fast."

"How'd you know I was here?"

"The Lord works in the strange ways. A few miles back, I was helping a road crew. Don't laugh, it's God's work. You flew past in a jeepney. I couldn't believe it. I saw you were back! And headed for the worst possible place, the bridge. I got my jeep and chased you. Don't you know what's happening at the bridge?"

"No. What?"

"You don't want to know. Now get in."

McCabe stepped over the writhing remains of the snake and started toward the bridge.

Sister Lucia removed a shovel from the back where road work tools were neatly arranged. She eased the shovel blade under the serpent. While it continued to writhe, she laid it gently down in the weeds on the side of the road. She put the shovel back and hurried in front of McCabe and blocked his way. She was shorter and more fragile than he remembered. She seemed as if she had come to him from the distant past—though it was only a few hours since he had brought Baum's body on the jeep's hood protected from the engine heat by several borrowed blankets, to the church. At the time, Lucia was hoeing in a garden. She was the first person to spot the corpse. Her reaction showed how deeply Baum was loved. Now, standing in his way on the river road, this smaller-than-he-remembered nun said, "Jim Brown."

"What?"

"The only way to deal with Jim Brown is to bring him down before he gets started. Shoot the gap. Hit him before he takes a step. If he takes three steps, it's good luck and goodbye. That's how I'm dealing with you. You're not taking one step toward the bridge."

"I don't know what's happening at the bridge. I don't care. I'm looking for our chaplain."

"Your chaplain?"

"Father O'Toole. Sister, I'm in a situation that'll take a lot of your prayers to make right. Listen, one of our corporals was AWOL. You know him. His name is Phord. I went looking for him and found him near town. You gave us a ride to the chopper yesterday."

"Saw you both off the island. Good luck and goodbye and live in Christ's bosom even if it is a life in war!"

"Here's where the prayers come in: A noncom, Gunny Lawler, thought I was in town. He didn't see you drive us to the chopper. He was palletizing loads at the far end of the airstrip and didn't see us fly off. Later, he met up with O'Toole and told him I was in town. Hey, the Father's a crazy bastard."

"All you Marines are crazy bastards. Excuse my Greek."

"He's Navy. But he's crazier than most. When Lawler tells him I'm in town, the Father figures I'm AWOL. Not knowing I'm on ship, crazy O'Toole gets a ride back to the airstrip and goes looking for me. Now I'm looking for him."

"This is three card monte on a cardboard box on the street. Now you see it, now you don't."

"Except the mark knows what the dealer doesn't."

"Aren't you AWOL now?"

"We're going to war. So what? All I care about now is finding O'Toole. If he's at the bridge, so be it."

"You go to the bridge, and there's a good chance you'll get back to ship with a tag on your toe."

She clasped McCabe's hand in black-splotched gloves that smelled of asphalt. Then she took off the gloves and threw them in the jeep and took his hand again and looked at him, her eyes hard and soft at the same time.

"Listen to me: The girl, Mariko. She's lost control. The best way I can help her is by staying away. And if you know what's good for you, you'll stay away from it too."

"Knowing what's good for me has never been in my best interests."

"Knowing you that figures. Yesterday, I told you a mob at the bridge tried to beat up your corporal. Beat up, if he was lucky. Murder, if they had their way. She jumped in and allowed me to hustle him away. After I dropped you off at the airstrip, I went to the bridge. What I saw I didn't want to see. With Father Baum, I was all in. But not now. Not after what I saw yesterday.

"What did you see?"

"Mariko in a knife fight with the man who instigated the mob."

"What about pakikisama?"

"So, you've been studying the culture?"

"Through the bottoms of San Miguel bottles."

"She's a she-devil. She knows how to use a knife, and she'll use it. The guy she fought saw what he was up against. He turned tail. Knife fighting is not what Father Baum was about. Deal me out. "

Sister's Lucia's assertion about Baum convinced McCabe she did not know the truth. He wondered how she would react when and if she discovered it. He remembered just before he got on the chopper to leave the island, Lucia giving him Ajax's dog tags she found in the dead priest's pocket. She didn't know Baum had taken them from his corpse to plant them on a dead-or-alive Shimada.

McCabe guessed why the murder had taken place. He figured Phord taking Mariko away from the social in Ajax's vehicle compelled the lieutenant colonel to get a ride back to camp with Father Baum.

McCabe figured the idea of murdering Ajax came upon Baum instantly in a rush of malevolent inspiration. The Hitler youth, the military training, the months of savage desert combat, the years of prisoner-of-war afflictions had honed his nerves to act on violent instincts. His existential struggle with Shimada put tremendous pressure on those nerves. He must have thought he had accidently come upon a one-off opportunity to defeat Shimada by bringing on the Marines. It was madness, but it was logical and compelling to the person Baum was.

When Sister Lucia gave him the dog tags, McCabe was tempted to tell her what happened and why and how he suspected it happened. But inspired by his friend O'Toole's talent for keeping his mouth shut in circumstances that wrongly might have called for shooting it off, he said nothing. He gave the dog tags to ONI investigators and told them his conjectures. Now, as he interacted with Sister Lucia and remembered the dog tags, he thought, *the truth will out eventually, but not through me.*

"So what, Sister? Finding the chaplain is all I'm interested in."

The crowd noise grew loud again. "That crowd isn't having tea and crumpets. If your chaplain's there, God help him."

"All the more reason I've got to get him." McCabe began running. Sister Lucia got behind the wheel, hit the gas, and cut him off. She pointed to the seat. Her pretty mouth curled in an ugly way. McCabe hopped in. "Thanks for seeing it my way, Sister."

"Go to hell. Excuse my ... forget it."

"You have an expert's badge in tough love, Sister." Her eyes were still weeping for Baum.

He was thinking that if the truth does come out, she might take refuge in Just War: the saving of the Mangyan people's way of life and the preserving their ancient forests. Not a justification but a mitigation.

Sister Lucia stopped in a clearing where a mob of some half a hundred locals were milling at the end of the bridge. Beside the bridge, a short-logging truck was tipped over on its side, it empty trailer on the bank, its cab partially submerged. Water splashed over the exposed gear box, drive shaft and differential. The stench of diesel fuel mixed with a dead animal odor filled the air.

The shouting of the mob reminded McCabe of when he was a boy playing in Tompkins Square Park and a gang of a couple dozen youths came toward him wielding switchblades. Back then, thinking they were coming for him, he felt his throat close and sphincter loosen. They weren't after him. They went around him. They were after some member of a rival gang behind him who happened to be caught alone on their turf. Now, seeing and hearing the mob at the bridge, he felt that same choking fear.

"O'Toole!" he shouted and stood up in the jeep. Through a megaphone of his hands: "O'TOOLE!" People close by turned their faces toward him.

Sister Lucia said. "This no place for the likes of you."

"The big bastard can't be missed in this crowd."

"See him?"

"Damnit, no!"

He saw the old man and the jeepney. Some of the mob were rocking the vehicle. The old man and the driver were inside holding onto the door posts. Sister Lucia ran over. McCabe started to follow her. She shouted at him and made *back-off-you-idiot* motions with her big hands. She shouted at the people doing the rocking. They backed away. The old man got out and grabbed her hands and kissed them fervently.

The sister came back to McCabe and said: "Whew! That was close. I'm neighbors with the men rocking the jeepney. They're good Catholics. They listened to me. But a lot of these people are strangers. Come from Manila to start a revolt against Marcos. I can't guarantee they'll hear me out."

The jeepney did an about-face and took off toward the river road, the driver speeding now, the old man's brown face, behind his glasses, changed to a cauliflower color.

Sister Lucia went on: "That jive-talking old man just told me he heard that Mariko's dead. Murder's in the air. The violent faction's taken over. The old man's so scared he stopped talking jive in the middle of our conversation and started babbling in Tagalog."

"Sister, let's have one last look-see by the river." McCabe pointed at where the mob thinned out by the bank.

A ball of flame, capped by black smoke, erupted from the cab. The spilt fuel had been set alight. McCabe scratched an itch on his nose caused by the quick heat on his face. The mob cheered.

"That's it." Sister Lucia turned the jeep around. "I'm outta here."

"I'm not finished looking."

"Nonviolence is a joke here. It could've worked for Father Baum. He was a priest. He had some training in it. He had clout with the people. But she'll never get it off the ground. All her training's been on her back."

McCabe coughed hard in the smoke. "O'T-*uuuuul*..." He coughed again. He made his way through the mob down to the bank. The river was rat-gray and running high. A wild boar's carcass, swollen and emitting a bad odor, was snagged in roots at the bank. It bobbed in backwash, firelight flickering on curved tusks.

McCabe started toward the overturned cab. Beside the cab on the bank, a girl in khaki shirt and pants, her hair in a French braid was kneeling, stroking the head of someone sprawled in weeds. Her arm was wrapped in a bandage.

"You're Mariko?" he said. She nodded. Her Eurasian face was haggard.

"I heard you were dead."

"Not yet. It's him." She gestured with her chin at the ground. "He didn't have to do this. The mob tipped the truck into the water. This one rushed in from out of nowhere. What was he doing here? I thought the Marines had cleared out. The poor man didn't know how to swim. The current got him. He thrashed about but went under. Me and a couple of others pulled him out. I thought he'd quit. He didn't. He went back into the water. He was scared in that water, I could tell. But he went in. He got under the cab in the current. Pushing with his legs, he kept the cab from going all the way in. The driver had time to get out. Then the bank gave way and the cab rolled over on him. He disappeared under the current. By the time we got him out, it was too late."

A breeze thinned the smoke blowing over what was lying there in water-logged, Navy utilities. The chaplain's cross on the collar glittered in thin mud. McCabe saw the swelling on the upturned face had diminished. Both his eyes were visible now, staring eyes. "Mercy," he said and knelt and pressed his lips to the wet cheeks.

As the girl caressed the corpse's forehead, she said, "If he wasn't so big and strong, he'd be alive now. And for what? To save a stranger's life? What a waste."

McCabe was on his feet, straddling the body. "Don't touch him," he said. He pushed Mariko. She lurched backwards, stopping her fall with her hands in mud, a bandage flap loosening. McCabe swung his head from side to side as people gathered around him. "Nobody touches him. Back off! Back off!"

Death Before War is the first novel in a quartet. The second novel, ***Jan***, is completed and deals with Phord back from Viet Nam fighting heroin drug addiction in an alcoholic's home in the desert where the LSD-crazed woman who runs the home treats the men by having sex with them. The third novel, ***No-rank Man***, also completed, deals with McCabe back from the war getting involved in the Summer of Love in New York's Lower East Side as hippie life descends from love and idealism into madness, criminality, and murder. *www.brentfilsonbooks.com*

Brent Filson
www.brentfilsonleads.com

Brent Filson comes from a Marine Corps family. His uncle was a Marine artillery corporal. His son, Brent Jr., earned a purple heart as a Marine weapons platoon commander in Iraq. His son, Rush, was awarded a bronze star for combat in Afghanistan and rose from Marine platoon commander, company commander, battalion commander to acting regimental commander. His two nephews are Marine combat veterans. Brent himself was a Marine infantry platoon and company commander, serving in the Far East. As a civilian, Brent became an award-winning leadership authority helping thousands of leaders of all ranks and functions worldwide boost their effectiveness. Working with some of the top companies in the world, he has developed motivational leadership strategies, processes, and skill sets, and created and instituted leadership educational and training programs. He is the author of more than 25 books and hundreds of articles on leadership. He is also the author of children's books and young adult novels.

Also by Brent Filson
www.brentfilsonbooks.com

Fiction

Death Before War
Phord's Way
Jan
No-Merit Man
The Puma
Smoke Jumpers
Pier 92
Disaster Quarterback
Space Scooters
Pirate Kite (with Magalis)
The Ghost of the Dutchman (with Magalis)
Yagua Days (with Magalis)

Nonfiction

The Leadership Talk: The Greatest Leadership Tool
101 Ways to Give Great Leadership Talks
Results!Results!Results!
Authority is a Poor Excuse for Leadership
Defining Moment: Motivating People to Act
Executive Speeches: 51 CEOs Tell You How to do Yours
Case & Son
That Magical Berkshires October
A Monster in Your Closet (Understanding Phobias)
Famous Experiments of History and How to Repeat Them
Exploring with Lasers
Superconductors and Other New Science Breakthroughs
Another Bridge

Plays

On a Cambodian Highway
The Great High Wind

www.ingramcontent.com/pod-product-compliance
Lightning Source LLC
LaVergne TN
LVHW040046080526
838202LV00045B/3514